REIGN

THE CURE CHRONICLES, BOOK FIVE

K. A. RILEY

For everyone who messaged me about you-know-who.

SUMMARY

After narrowly escaping New York City with her life, Ashen finds her way home to the Arc with the help of an old friend.

But after a long absence, Ash isn't sure what she's about to find. The Bishop's deception and cruelty have turned her world upside down, leaving her reeling as a wedge is driven between her and Finn, forcing them to live separate lives.

Worse still, when she arrives, she is faced with the challenge of proving to the Arc's leaders that she's telling the truth about all that has happened since she left home.

As she fights an impossible uphill battle, she must confront betrayal, lies, and heartbreaking loss that will either lead to her vindication or her ultimate downfall.

With enemies vanquished, alliances solidified, and old friendships renewed, the end seems near for Ash in her final battle against tyranny...

Or is it?

Reign is the fifth and final book in The Cure Chronicles Series.

PROLOGUE

I KNOW what it is to fall.

Or so I've always told myself.

I was six years old when my father taught me to ride a bicycle. My first time out, I crashed hard, landing on the pavement and skinning my elbows and knees.

I suffered my share of face-plants racing around the playground at school, playing tag with other children.

I fell one time when I sprinted so fast in a foot race that my upper body surged forward and ended up landing nose-first in the dirt.

Until this very moment, I thought I understood the unrelenting force that is gravity.

But now, as my body tumbles through space, uncontrolled and helpless, I realize how little I knew.

Time is passing in a strange, impossible slow-motion, though I know how fast I must be careening toward the earth. I'm all too aware that the only thing that can possibly stop me is the ground far below. It will be a sudden end, and in all likelihood, I will feel no pain. Yet I'm calm, relaxed.

Almost indifferent.

How am I so at peace with death? Shouldn't I be scared?

The answer that floats into my mind is blissfully simple:

Rys promised me I'd be okay.

"I will not let you die if you leap," he told me. "But you need to do it. Right now."

Whether he was lying to make my choice easier, I can't say. But I'm choosing, in this moment when my life flashes before my eyes, to believe he was speaking the truth.

Clouds surround me, billowing uselessly as if to remind me just how tall the Behemoth is—how insanely high up I was when I leapt from its roof.

I know the clouds will not catch me. I know I will most likely die within a matter of seconds.

I chose to leap. I chose to escape the Duchess and her fiery arsenal of sadistic weaponry.

I jumped so she wouldn't have the satisfaction of killing me herself.

It's a dubious victory…but it's a victory, all the same.

Letting out a final breath, I close my eyes and wait for the end to come.

ENDING

My entire body jerks to a sudden stop, my chest and stomach colliding with something rock-hard.

This is it.

This is the end.

Only...

I'm not dead.

With a shock of full-body whiplash, I feel my torso collapse in on itself before jerking upwards. It's as if a gigantic fist has caught me in its clutches and is yanking me skyward.

I can't begin to understand how this is possible...but whatever has just grabbed me managed to do so without tearing me in half.

It's only after a few seconds that I allow myself to breathe and acknowledge that somehow, I really *have* survived.

I press a hand to my chest only to find my palm confronted by ice-cold steel. I feel my way downward. It's around my waist too, as well as my legs. I twist around, trying to look up and see what it is that's trapped me, but it's holding me so tightly that I can barely move.

Summoning all my remaining courage, I pull my eyes down to the Manhattan street that still lies far below me. As distant as it is, it's almost unfathomable how close my life came to a swift, horrifying conclusion.

Then again, playing tag with death seems to be my eternal, cycling fate.

Just as I'm becoming convinced I'm undergoing some strange transition into the afterlife, a single syllable spins on the wind, as if made of the air itself.

"Ash."

"I...I..." I sputter, convinced the voice is a contrivance of my addled mind.

"I've got you," it says. "You're okay now. Look to your right and you'll see."

With some effort, I pull my head sideways to see myself reflected in the exterior of the Behemoth, the immense structure that has been my strange and horrific home for the last several weeks.

I can now see that there's a monstrous metal contraption gripping me, its daunting, gleaming talons similar to those of an eagle.

Above me, hovering in the air, is an enormous silver bird that looks like a larger version of Atticus, Rys's extraordinary owl drone who has watched over me for months. Its wings beat slowly at the air, keeping it airborne. Its head is large and round, with a curved, menacing beak of onyx metal. As I watch, its belly cracks open and the claws that hold me begin to draw me upward into a dark chasm.

At the last moment before the drone pulls me inside, its reflection disappears entirely from view, as if to tell me I've conjured its existence from the depths of my imagination.

It's cloaked, I think. The same technology Finn used on the

4

uniform I'm now wearing. The same tech Rys uses to conceal Atticus from threatening eyes.

My genius friend has built himself an invisible drone.

As the mechanical arm pulls me into the dark space, my head reels, still half convinced that none of this is really happening. This surreal mayhem has to be a strange, wild dream in the last split-seconds before my heart finally stops beating.

My mind flashes with rapid-fire images, wretched memories of the events that led me to this moment: Finn, leaving in an Air-Wing with his brother and the Replik—the girl who looks identical to me, whose voice is mine, whose very eyes are carbon copies of my own.

As that image fades, it's replaced by a handsome, devilish face that I've grown to loathe.

The man known as the Bishop.

A man I disliked at first, before I made the mistake of trusting him. Over time and through a mountain of evidence he provided, I grew to believe he was capable of benevolence beneath his showy, cruel exterior. I suppose I was hoping all along to convince myself that not every leader in the world is a monster.

But I was wrong.

After what he did to me—and to Finn—I despise him with all the raging violence of a thousand warring berserkers.

I am determined that if I ever see him again, I will find the strength to tear him limb from limb. I will destroy him, even if I die in the process. He violated me, body and mind. He stole my identity from me—the most precious possession I had in this world—and replicated it, leaving the real me to die at the hands of the Duchess.

I may not be dead, but given that my entire life has been gifted to someone else, I may as well be.

A swell of nausea overtakes me as I think about the Bishop's sly eyes, his soothing, addictive voice. The sickening, overwhelming charm of him. The constant assurances that he longed to make the world a better place when in fact, his motivations were all rooted in selfishness and greed.

But perhaps cruelest of all was the hope that he inspired in me. Hope for a better future. Hope that he was as good a man as he claimed, and that with me by his side, he would grow even more benevolent over time. Hope that the world would benefit from all he was doing—what we were doing *together*.

He represented a dream I scarcely dared allow myself. And then he reveled in my pain as he snatched that dream away from me and left me to die a painful death. A punishment, I suppose, for being fool enough to trust him.

"Ash!" a voice calls from behind me, jarring me back to reality as a set of strong hands pulls me free of the steel talons and helps me into a sitting position. "Are you in there?"

"Rys," I say without turning around. I sink into the sensation of his hands on my shoulders. I need to feel them for a moment, to assure myself that I am indeed alive and that he's real.

"It's me."

A sudden recollection hits me. Words spoken from Rys's mouth, only a few minutes ago. "You...you told me you were hiding out in Sector Three, in the Mire. How can you possibly be here? How..."

"I lied," he says. "Mostly. I *was* there, until yesterday, but... let's just say Atticus was worried about you, which made *me* worried."

He lets me go after a few seconds and eases around to stand in front of me, looking into my eyes.

"Where are we?" I ask. "What is this thing?"

"We're in a manned drone. I call it the Eagle, for obvious reasons. I've been working on it for ages."

I shake my head, still too stunned to say anything meaningful. Tears stream down my cheeks, but I let out a laugh, covering my mouth to keep from losing it entirely.

Seeing my old friend's face in this moment is one of the greatest reliefs of my life. I can feel his sorrow, his sympathy. I am aware of the kindness blanketing me protectively. He knows what I've been through. He knows what's happened. He *saw* it.

He saw the Duchess in all her fiery glory as she sought to end me.

He saw the man who stole my life from me.

And he saw the other version of me, my odious twin. The entity the Bishop created, the quasi-human who has the same mannerisms, the same smile, the same laugh as me. The artificial yet oh-so-real girl who is currently on her way to the Arc to convince Illian to put his faith in the Bishop. The one who kissed Finn as if he belonged entirely to her.

I shake my head violently, tears now tumbling down my cheeks. "Thank you" is all I manage to say. "I don't know how you did it...but thank you for catching me, Rys."

"Of course I caught you. I wasn't about to lose you, Ash."

Just as I begin to feel safe and comforted, a loud, percussive *thud* startles me, sending my adrenaline into overdrive.

Something—or *someone*—has just collided hard with the aircraft's roof.

2

BEGINNING

I LEFT the Duchess on the Behemoth's roof. Angry, vengeful, out for blood.

With a jolt of horror, I wonder if there's any chance she leapt after me. But strong as she is, I can't imagine her surviving a drop from such a height.

"What the hell *was* that?" I ask, my breath tight in my chest as I pull my eyes to Rys's.

"It's all right," he assures me. "It's just Atticus. He's finding his way inside the drone through the roof."

"Oh, thank God," I breathe, wondering if the Duchess will die among the clouds. Maybe starvation will take her. Or possibly even hypothermia, if she doesn't manage to use her fire-summoning power to keep herself warm.

After all she's put me through over the months, I should be pleased to think of her demise. I should revel in her suffering and torment as her life drains from her body. I should delight in her languishing alone, so far from anyone she cares about.

But there is still a little humanity left in me. I can't help but think of Merit and Finn, of the mother they're losing without even knowing it.

My heart even hurts a little for her husband, the Duke. He may not be a good man, but I'm not convinced he's wholly evil, either. At most, he's weak and compliant, like so many others who have failed to rise up against tyranny.

"Ash," Rys says as Atticus appears behind him, squeezing his way through a narrow opening in the metal roof of the drone before it seals up behind him.

"Hmm," I reply, unable to come up with any actual words.

"We need to get the neuro-implant out of you—the one the Bishop gave you. If he can track you, he'll send someone after us. We have a long flight ahead, and this drone may be virtually invisible, but a decent fighter pilot could take it down more easily than I'd like to admit."

"Right," I say, reaching back to feel the small rectangular lump on the back of my head where a man named Trace tattooed me during my time in Brooklyn. At the time, I had been told he was simply marking me with some sort of Aristocratic symbol—a supplement to a disguise that would help me infiltrate the Bishop's inner circle. Little did I know he was injecting a sophisticated, invasive piece of bio-technology under my flesh. "Yeah, fine. Do what you need to."

Rys nods once, then turns to Atticus, who half flaps, half leaps over and lands next to me, the small compartment in his belly opening up. Out comes what looks like a narrow metal arm, and I try not to wince as it reaches around to the back of my head. A few seconds later, I feel a sharp pinch, then Rys says, "Done."

His eyes glowing bright blue, Atticus pulls the blood-covered implant in front of my eyes as if delighted to show it to me, and, shoving it into his silver beak, crushes it in a series of hard bites into little more than a pile of dust.

"The Bishop will know it's been tampered with," I warn. "He'll be able to see what's just happened. I'm pretty sure he was recording every move I made."

"Maybe," Rys says. "Or maybe he was getting a live feed. But while he's in transit in an Air-Wing, it won't be easy for him to watch you—especially if he's with Finn. Besides, from what I know of the guy, he's arrogant enough to assume you're dead by now. Whatever the case, we need to head home to the Mire before this crap-show gets even more out of control."

"Home," I repeat. A word that should feel like a warm hug feels toxic on my lips instead.

The house where I grew up is destroyed. According to what the Bishop told me before he left me to die, the power to the Arc is down...so it's entirely possible that we won't even be able to find our way inside without a struggle.

Worst of all, the boy I love is with someone else—someone who is so much like me that even *I* was confused when I looked into her eyes. For all I know, Finn could be as happy with her as he ever was with me.

As the weight of reality saps my strength, I nearly break down. To think how much the Bishop has taken from me, from so many others. In New York, he stole thousands of people away from their homes with the promise of better lives.

Adi's sister, Stella. Shar's young son. And countless thousands of others.

All so he could find a way to prolong his own life, create a species of pseudo-clones...and, of course, turn a tidy profit so his unnaturally long existence remains as luxurious as humanly possible.

"What are we going to do when we get back to the Mire?" I ask, my voice trembling. "What if we can't get into the Arc?"

"That's not even a question worth asking," Rys replies. "We'll find a way." He lays a hand on my shoulder, a gesture that's just intimate enough to remind me of the depth of his friendship. "You managed to find your way into the Behemoth against all odds, right? The Arc is a piece of cake compared to that beast." With that, he nods toward the hulking building that's still so close.

I want to feel reassured by his words, but somehow, they fall flat.

"Okay. Let's say we get in. Then what?" I moan. "I just tell everyone the version of Ashen who is there now is an imposter? How can I even prove that? She's more me than *I* am. She has Finn. She has my DNA. She even has the Surge." I'm still bitter that the Bishop stole that weapon away from me, a powerful gift Finn granted me some time ago. In giving it to my Replik, he made her stronger than I am and ensured that I would never have a chance of standing up to her.

"And you have me," Rys says. "And we have an army of hidden drones the Bishop doesn't know about."

"The bastard knows everything. I hate to tell you, but I'm sure he's fully aware of your birds."

"No way," Rys says with a shake of his head. "If he knew about my birds, he would have found a way to get to them. A man like that doesn't tolerate invasive technology—particularly the sort of tech that can watch and potentially incriminate him. Ask yourself this—if the Bishop knew about Atticus, why didn't he send his Scorps after him after all the time Atticus spent in New York?"

I'm about to offer up a hasty answer, but instead, I pause to contemplate the question. I suppose he may have a point. It seems unlikely that the Bishop would be oblivious to Atticus's existence...but I can't see a single reason he'd allow the owl to continue flying around New York, his keen eyes on everything the Bishop controls. I would at least have expected our enemy to send the Scorps to take Atticus into some sort of technological custody, so his researchers could dissect and replicate him.

Could it be that we've managed to hide this *one* tactical advantage from the enemy?

I suppose it's possible. The Bishop's specialty is getting inside the minds of *people*. Machines, not so much. Rys's arsenal of flying threats may be our greatest chance at a fair fight—if it should come to that.

"I genuinely hope you're right," I finally say.

"Trust me. I'm at least a *little bit* right. No one is omniscient. So while your Bishop may have eyes on a lot of things, he can't see everything at once. He's not God."

He's not God.

The nausea returns with Rys's last words. After seeing what I saw—the massive silo inside the Behemoth that was filled with humans, each floating inside a separate pod, their bodies frozen in some sort of paralytic, gelatinous liquid—it almost seems like the Bishop *is* some kind of malevolent deity. A cruel, vindictive, selfish god who sees humankind as nothing more than a means to an end.

"He may not be God," I echo. "But there was a time when I thought he was a saint. I was convinced he was a good man who could work miracles. I saw the evidence with my own eyes, Rys. Sick children, cured of disease..."

My voice cracks and I stop speaking, a tear streaking down my cheek.

"Ash?" Rys says.

"I have too much faith in people." I shake my head and let out a bitter half-laugh. "There was even a time, before I turned seventeen, when I believed in the Cure. We both did—remember? You and I both looked forward to stepping into the Arc for the first time, because we were led to believe there were some generous souls on the inside who would save us and our remaining family members from the illness that had killed so many of our parents."

When he doesn't reply, I pull my gaze up to meet Rys's.

With a nod, he says, "I remember."

"When I saw the Bishop curing children in the Behemoth, I really thought he was different from the Directorate. That all our disappointment and disillusionment would finally fade, because here was this man who came through on what he promised." I clench my hands, renewed anger building inside me. "I had no idea it all came at the vile cost of so many human lives, that the miracles were for sale to the highest bidder."

The awful truth was that those who weren't wealthy and powerful were seen by the Bishop as little more than genetic goldmines. His stores of humans were nothing more than crops, harvested to keep the ruling class young and healthy. Just as the residents of the Bastille—the unfortunate modern name for the town of Breckenridge—had cultivated an entire generation of young women to use as incubators for Wealthies' babies, the Bishop was finding new and malicious ways to use the bodies of "lesser" humans.

And right now, the bastard is on his way to the Arc,

intending to inflict that same grim fate on people I care deeply about. People I know and trust will suffer or even die.

No doubt the Bishop intends to take samples from the millions living in the Arc and use them for his benefit, to imprison many of them in grotesque pods like those in the Behemoth, to steal their organic material...or worse.

The Bishop has found a cure for old age, but it comes at a great cost. The price is humanity itself, and all I want is to stop him before he does even more damage.

"It's so ironic, isn't it?" I ask with a cynical snicker.

"What is?" Rys asks.

"The promise of a better life is the most powerful weapon people like the Directorate and the Bishop have. They assault us with that promise over and over again, and I'm not sure we ever learn. We trust and we hope, we listen as they bombard us with lies."

"Not for long, Ash. If we can get rid of the Bishop, something tells me we can get to a state of sustained peace. At least, I hope we can. Evil has always come in cycles, and there's no guarantee that we can push it back forever. But we're due for some good in the world."

All I want—all I've *ever* wanted—is to live in peace, if only for a few years. To have a chance at a "normal" life, if there even is such a thing as normal anymore. I want to feel the wind on my face, to breathe in fresh air. To walk through the woods without fear that soldiers with high-powered rifles will kill me merely for daring to exist in territory claimed by their overlords.

"Let's get out of here," Rys says, moving away from me to take the Eagle's controls in hand. "We'll head west. The good news is the Bishop, for all his charms, won't have been in the Arc long enough to fully sink his talons into Illian and the rest of the Consortium. Illian is a smart guy. He's not the sort to fall for anyone's lies—and he knows us well."

"*I* fell for the lies," I retort. "So did Finn. And don't forget—the Bishop has a Replik who looks and sounds exactly like me along for the ride."

"That's not enough to fool Illian."

"Maybe not. But there's something else, Rys."

He turns to face me, his lips sinking into a grimace. "Why do I get the feeling I don't want to hear this?"

Wincing, I reply, "Kurt is sick. I don't know how, but the Bishop made him ill—through a micro-drone, or a poisoner spy, or something. He's using it as leverage, a means to make an ally of Illian by magically 'healing' the person who's most important to him. It's all about manipulation. He knows where the jugular is on every person in the world—where their pressure points are. And he goes for the most brutal pain he can inflict to get them to comply. The guy is the cruelest genius the world has ever seen."

"Illian would do anything for Kurt," Rys replies. "Damn it."

"Exactly."

"Well, for now, let's just worry about getting home." Impatient, Rys turns back to the controls. "Why don't you get some rest? You must be exhausted."

I open my mouth to respond, but find that I have little to say. He's right—I'm too tired to think. I didn't exactly get any rest last night, and to say I'm bone weary gives my bones far too much credit.

Without another word, I step over to a short, padded bench seat and curl up in fetal position, my knees tucked virtually under my chin.

"Ash," Rys says when I'm settled in.

"Mmm?"

"Don't worry. We'll be okay. You and I always are, right?"

I nod and murmur a few syllables of vague agreement.

The last thought I have before I drift off is that I've somehow gone from having one mortal enemy to having three.

The Duchess.

The Bishop.

A girl who looks just like me.

But somehow, through it all, I've managed to keep my best friend.

3

VOYAGE

WHEN I STIR AWAKE, Rys tells me we're somewhere over Illinois.

"What? Already?" I ask, rubbing the sleep from my eyes.

"Already. This thing isn't as speedy as an Air-Wing, but we're making good time. Not to mention you've been passed out for ages."

My stomach knots itself into a tight ball as I push myself up to a sitting position, haunted by thoughts of all that's happened and all that is yet to come.

"You doing okay?" he asks over his shoulder as he pilots the eagle drone.

"As okay as I can be. But I'm not looking forward to what's coming. I know I should be excited. I mean, Kel is in the Arc. And…"

Rys fills in the blank. "Finn, too."

I nod.

I should be thrilled about the prospect of seeing him, but the truth is, I'm filled with dread. What if he doesn't believe me? What if he takes my Replik's word over mine?

One of the most treacherous, deceitful things the Bishop did while we were in New York was to keep Finn and me in the dark about the Repliks. We didn't know that Finn's research into cellular regeneration—which was allegedly going to help cure rare diseases—was largely being used to create copies of existing humans. "New and improved" versions, as the Bishop so kindly put it.

Finn was confined to a lab where he helped usher in new medical breakthroughs using biological samples from living humans, thinking those humans had volunteered in the venture. After all, many in New York had headed to the Behemoth voluntarily, just as Rys and I had walked into the Arc with hopes and dreams of our own.

As far as any of us knew, the Bishop was working scientific miracles that would make the world a better place for all.

If Finn had known about the Bishop's vile projects—about the number of people imprisoned in the Behemoth—he would have done everything in his power to put an end to them.

I think of my doppelgänger again. *The other Ashen.* The girl who has my face, my skin, my hair, even my scent. I've spoken to her, heard her voice, seen her smile. I've watched her kiss Finn...and seen him kiss her back. The final, most brutal weapon in the Bishop's arsenal.

The rage building up inside me makes me want to scream, and it seems Rys can sense it, because he turns to look over his shoulder and says, "We'll fix this, Ash. We'll get the bastard. I promise you."

I shake my head. I'm too angry to cry, but I will the tears to push themselves out. It might relieve a little of the venom building up inside me like a toxin that's been poisoning me slowly and painfully.

"The bastards always win," I say, almost under my breath.

"We always think we'll beat them—that good will win. But power is the only winner we ever see. The leaders who come and go try to convince us they're working for us, but we all know they're lining their pockets, making their own lives better while we lose everything and everyone we've ever loved. The Bishop is so power-hungry that he's basically made himself immortal, for God's sake."

"Sorry, but I have to disagree with you there."

"What? You're going to try and tell me he's not interested in power?"

"No—he's definitely in love with power. And wealth. And all the other things that turn people evil. But you got one thing wrong, Ash."

"Please," I say, crossing my arms over my chest. "Enlighten me."

"I believe what Rystan is trying to say," a strange voice replies, "is that no one is immortal."

That voice...wasn't Rys's. But there's no one else in the drone with us.

Except...

Nervously, I swing my head around to see Atticus looking at me, his eyes glowing a deep emerald shade. They're normally blue or red. Blue when he's in his regular state, and red when he's on high alert or in combat mode.

I've never seen them green.

"What the...?" I gasp. "Since when do you talk?"

Rys lets out a quiet chuckle.

"Seriously, did Atticus just say something?" I ask, my palms sweating. After everything I've been through, I wouldn't be surprised if my mind had finally lost all resilience and descended into the depths of some kind of wild madness. "Like, in his own voice?"

"He..." Rys begins, hesitating for a moment. "That is, he and I have been experimenting a little. I brought a specially programmed microchip with me from home. I've been developing it for ages. I inserted it into him while you were asleep. I guess it's working."

"I guess so." I stare into the owl's strange eyes, which seem more alert, more *alive* than ever before. "What exactly does it do? I'm trying to decide if I should be freaked out or happy that he's looking at me like that."

"The chip enhanced him," Rys says. "He's always been intelligent. Capable of problem-solving on the fly, of emotions, even. But this new tech gives him something approaching a human consciousness. The capacity for rational thought, as well as abstract thought."

"He's an owl. And not even a real one. He's a *robot* owl. No offense, Atticus."

"Maybe he is," Rys says. "But he's a super-*smart* robot owl. I'm just upping his skill level."

"What about your other birds? Your army of drones?" I ask. "Are they getting super powers, too?"

I mean it as a joke. But to my surprise, Rys responds seriously. "A few of them. I haven't had much time to work on them, and Atticus is...well..." He turns and looks at the owl, a smile on his lips. "I suppose it's okay to say he's my favorite of all of them."

Atticus lets out a low hoot that almost sounds like a purr of affection, but says nothing more.

"I'm not surprised. He's pretty special. I suppose I'm worried that he's going to change on me." I reach out and stroke my fingers over Atticus's head, amused by my own affection for him. "You've helped me so much," I say, a lump beginning to form in my throat. "You don't even know. You've saved my life more than once. Thank you. And thank *you*, Rys."

"All in a day's work," he tells me. But his jovial tone alters when he adds, "I'll never stop trying to make up for what I did to you, Ash. I promise you that."

"I know," I tell him, all too aware of the sudden quiet tension building inside the drone.

Rys's part in my mother's death will always be a sort of invisible wall between us, preventing a true resurgence of the friendship we once had. But I don't blame him for what happened, not anymore. My mother's death wasn't his doing. He may have led the Directorate to the painting in her room, but I know now that he never intended for any harm to come to her.

My mother died for one reason: because the Duchess, cruel and callous as she was, reveled in the deaths of any and all Dregs.

May that bitch rot in Hell, I say under my breath. *I hope she really is dead.*

It's a few hours before Rys announces that he can see the mountains in the distance. I peer out the window, eyeing the peaks on the horizon, the sun high in the sky.

A sense of dread assaults me. It's the first time I've ever found myself moving toward Finn and yet terrified of what I might find. The thought that I might have to persuade him that I am not an intruder in his life is enough to make me sick to my stomach.

He is everything to me.

Yet I may soon discover that I am nothing to him but a shadow of my other self.

I dread the notion that he believes the other Ashen to be real, that by now, he's allowed himself to sink into her arms, to cherish the feeling of her lips on his.

I hate her for doing this to me. She may be stronger than I am—she may, in fact, be entirely like me in every conceivable way.

But that's not enough to keep me from wanting her dead.

"What am I going to do, Rys?" I ask miserably. "How will I convince them?"

"I told you before," he says. "I knew there was something off about the other Ash. Finn will figure it out, trust me. And when he does, he'll murder the Bishop himself."

"I'm not sure I want him to. For one thing, the Bishop is powerful in ways we don't even know about yet. Finn could get hurt, or worse."

"And for another thing?"

I almost crack a smile when I say, "I want to do it myself."

Rys lets out a chuckle. "I can't say I blame you. But you're no murderer, Ash. You never have been. Look—let's start by seeing if I can land this gigantic bird back inside the Arc, okay?"

I nod, though I'm far from hopeful. I know the Bishop well enough by now to know the guy will do whatever it takes to keep us—and probably the rest of the world—out. If he figures out that Rys has helped me escape the Behemoth, he'll be waiting, and he'll be only too happy for a second chance to destroy me.

4

HOME

WHEN THE ARC finally comes into view in the distance, my heart migrates into my throat.

Gleaming in the sunlight, it looks almost beautiful. Thanks to a clever holographic foundation, the enormous structure appears to hover several stories above the ground, surrounded by the grim remnants of the Mire.

I can't tell from outside the Arc whether the electricity is working, let alone if the Bishop has begun to work his brainwashing magic on our allies in the Consortium.

All the same, a newly churning fear has begun to rage in my stomach as I watch Rys attempt to access the Arc's information network.

"The Arc's backup electrical systems are online," he tells me. "Which means not everything is working yet. I suspect the Bishop deliberately set it up this way so he'd be able to take control while the technicians scramble to get the systems running. He'll be looking for the Arc's eyes right about now."

"Eyes?"

"The Arc's surveillance systems. My guess is that he's already convinced Illian to let him take a look—which would mean he's watching the entrances, as well as everything else."

"How? He can't possibly have an eye on everything at once, at least not yet. He has Finn and the others to worry about, for one thing. You said yourself that no one is truly omniscient."

"True. But as much as I hate the Bishop from everything I've heard about him, I have to admit he's an impressive guy. I don't know how he's doing it, but according to my feed here, *someone* is tracking every camera in the Arc simultaneously. Your evil buddy must be capable of accumulating a crap-ton of data and assessing it at a pretty intense rate."

I nod, recalling how the Bishop announced proudly at the Hanging in Brooklyn that he "can see everything." The man's god-like status is hard to dispute, infuriating though it may be.

As we soar toward the Mire, Rys attempts to signal one of his contacts in the Arc to warn him of our pending arrival.

"There's no response," he tells me after a few seconds. "Comms are completely down—probably by design."

"Can you override the system or something?" I ask. "Open the pod bay doors remotely or whatever, so we can fly in?"

He shakes his head. "Unfortunately, no. We'll have to break in. You know, the old-fashioned way."

I swallow hard before daring to ask, "What if we can't just break in this time, Rys?"

"Ash. Come on. You know me."

My voice goes hard when I say, "No. Humor me. What if we cannot gain entry into the Arc, Rys? What will we do?"

He tenses, and I can tell he's doing his best to offer up an honest answer. "We'll have to wait this thing out. At some point, the Bishop will let his guard down."

"No, he won't," I say, my heart in pieces. "He doesn't let his guard down."

Rys heaves a sigh. "How about if we focus on what we can do instead of worst-case scenarios? Can't we at least try to be positive?"

I want to be positive. I really do. But maybe it's not in my nature. Or maybe months of cruelty and sorrow have led me to a place where I no longer remember what it is to feel hope.

The thought sits heavy inside me. I know the Bishop—I know how powerful he is, though I've only just begun to scratch the surface of his strength. The man took control of the Directorate in Manhattan. He took possession of the largest Arcology in the world.

He also took possession of thousands upon thousands of human beings without the world outside the Behemoth knowing about it.

For one man to manage all that is unfathomable.

When my face contorts into a pained expression, Rys adds, "It's okay. The Bishop has his methods, I have mine—and I have the added advantage of knowing the Arc like the back of my hand." With that, he examines his right hand and says, "Huh. I never noticed that mole before."

With a roll of my eyes, I mutter, "My sense of humor died on the Behemoth's rooftop, Rys."

"Sorry. Okay, look—once we're close enough, I'll get us inside. Have I ever failed you?"

I scowl at him. "Is that a serious question?"

"Not entirely," he replies with a shrug. "But mostly. All I want is to reunite you with Kel and that too-good-looking dude of yours. I promise, if I can make it happen, I will."

I breathe a sigh of frustration, eager to see what he has in mind. If anyone can help me, it's Rys. But it's entirely possible that even *he* won't be able to work the miracle needed to get me inside.

In an effort to retain the tiniest sliver of sanity, I summon a shard of hope inside my mind, reminding myself Finn is only a few miles away.

The sooner I can see him, the better.

As much as I want to put my arms around him after all I've endured in the last twenty-four hours, the simple truth is that I desperately need to talk to him. To warn him and Illian about the Bishop's true motives in invading the Arc, and about how the Bishop orchestrated Kurt's mysterious illness and the power failure.

Every minute the Bishop spends with Finn and Illian is a minute when the bastard may sink his encroaching psychological claws deeper into their minds.

"I'm going to put us down near our old stomping grounds," Rys tells me over his shoulder. "I'll conceal the Eagle in the woods near the old drainage pipe. I don't want to risk being spotted by anyone—not even our friends."

I nod and wait as he steers the drone toward a bit of dense forest not too far from Sector Eight, the neighborhood where Rys and I grew up together. He manages to bring us down in a small clearing near the stream where we used to retrieve fresh water. A place that was once dear to me but now inspires nothing but rage and fear in my heart.

When we've landed and the Eagle has powered down, Rys grabs a small pack and slings it over his shoulder. He cracks the drone's roof open and we climb out with Atticus flapping overhead, his keen eyes on the lookout for any threat.

"This should be easy," Rys tells me. "The Bishop and Finn can't have been inside the Arc for more than a few hours by now. Which means all we have to do is find our way to Illian and fill him in. Once he knows what we know, this whole nightmare will end."

He sounds so confident that I almost allow my shoulders to relax. It's even tempting to smile. Almost.

Staring straight ahead as we begin to make our way downhill, I tell myself he *must* be right.

But if he is, why do I have this hideous feeling that everything is about to go very wrong?

A chill penetrates straight through my clothing as we make our way down toward the drainage pipe Rys and I have walked through so many times over the years—our escape route from Sector Eight into the surrounding foothills.

For the first time, it hits me just how much time has passed since the day I was first brought to the Arc by two Chaperons. It's been months now, and a bitter winter has already begun to rear its hostile head.

The chilly air smells fresh and clean in the woods, undisturbed as it is by the toxic presence of civilization. But as we descend toward the Mire, the atmosphere turns thick, a hint of charcoal and ash attacking my senses. A grim, harrowing reminder of the burnt-out graveyard we're about to step into.

As dread begins to overtake my mind, Rys stops me with a hand on my arm, pulling his chin up to the sky.

"Atticus has detected something," he tells me, his tone hushed.

"In Sector Eight?"

"No. But not far off." He pushes his sleeve up, sliding a hand over his arm to pull up a holographic image that looks like an aerial view of the circle that is the Mire, divided into the Sectors the Directorate forced us into years ago.

"What's wrong?" I ask when Rys's brow wrinkles.

"Activity in Sectors Six and Seven," he tells me, nodding toward the projection. "Looks like construction."

"That's weird. Isn't it?" I look more closely, to see yellow bulldozers and other vehicles moving slowly over rough terrain while people in hard hats meander between them.

"A little. If the Arc's power is still down, I would have expected everyone to be locked inside, or seeking shelter until they receive their next set of orders. The last thing I'd expect is to see crews working diligently while the Arc is so unstable."

He stares at the projection a little longer before pointing to it once again. "Look here," he says as he gestures to the shifting image. "In Sector Seven, they've actually begun tearing down the perimeter wall. There's a huge gap where they've taken the concrete away."

I see what he means. The wall is half broken down, a gaping hole carved into its side as if someone's taken a wrecking ball to it then swept away the detritus.

"That has to be Illian's doing," I reply. "He always said he'd open up the Mire and reunite the Sectors. This is good news, right?"

"Hopefully, yes." Rys pulls his sleeve down again and says, "I think we should head over there. The construction workers are Illian's employees—they're probably mostly former Dregs, like us. They'll be able to tell us what's going on."

"I'm not sure we should go anywhere near them," I reply softly, though I can't exactly explain my hesitation. "What if…"

"The Bishop has only been in the Arc for a few hours, at most," Rys assures me, reading my darkest thoughts. "Even if he's gotten to Illian already, the workers probably don't know who he is, if that's what you're worried about."

It is exactly what I'm worried about, I think. But he's right. There's no way the Bishop has his hooks in these Dregs. Not yet, at least.

With a sigh and a nod, I agree to head to Sector Seven. Which means that instead of proceeding into the drainage pipe that's brought us so often to our home turf, we hike around the perimeter wall until we locate the gaping hole we saw in the projection.

Crumbled concrete surrounds us on all sides, broken down like it's been pummeled by a giant's fist. It's a sight that shouldn't be nearly as beautiful as it is, and as I stare at it, I feel my eyes prickle with sharp tears.

However afraid I might be, I can't deny that the shattered wall is a symbol of victory, of freedom. A beautiful reminder that my people are no longer prisoners of the oppressive regime that once devastated us.

All thanks to the Consortium, an organization founded long ago by my father and his allies.

"Thank you, Illian," I say under my breath as I step forward, wiping the tears away. "You're a good man."

I can only hope Illian is strong enough to resist the Bishop's tactics.

Atticus flies overhead, circling the area protectively, his eyes on the ground.

"I'm going to activate his stealth mode," Rys tells me. "There's no need to draw eyes to him."

"Agreed."

We hike into Sector Seven, relieved to see the construction crew hard at work bulldozing the remains of a few buildings to clear space for new ones. So far, at least, the Mire feels like a place of progress and hope. A clean slate where new lives will soon begin.

"Looks great!" Rys calls out, his voice jovial as he strides toward a small group of men in reflective red vests and helmets of various colors. "Illian's got you working hard, huh?"

One of the men turns to him, a puzzled look on his face. He must be wondering how we got here, given that every other person in the area is decked out in safety gear and clearly came from the Arc.

He doesn't appear hostile, at least.

"Where the heck did you...?" he begins to ask with a smile, eyeing the break in the wall. But when his eyes lock on me, they go wide. "Holy crap. You're..."

"Yeah, yeah, she's the Crimson Dreg," Rys says with a mock roll of his eyes.

I tighten at the nickname bestowed on me by the Arc's rebel forces back when we were working with the Santa Fe faction of the Consortium. "Crimson Dreg" always sounded a little too much like the pseudonym of a thief of some sort— one who roamed about at night, stealing from unsuspecting people as they slept.

I never wanted the sort of notoriety that came with such a title.

"Ashen Spencer," the man replies as if he's confirming the theory. "Well, I'll be damned."

"I thought the power was out in the Arc," I reply, ignoring the strange, unwelcome moment of adulation. "Is it up and running again?"

The young man nods. "As of a few hours ago. We thought we were under siege, honestly. The whole place was starting to panic—no power means no Conveyors, no food, no anything. But the backup power sources flared to life and everything just kind of went back to normal."

"Weird," I say, trying to behave as if I have no clue how such a thing could be possible. "Do you know why it went out in the first place?"

I could simply tell him, of course. I could inform him that there's an infiltrator inside the Arc—a man who doesn't belong there. A man who intends to take the place over, who plans to hurt people like us.

But instead, I wait to hear what he'll have to say.

The man, who can't be more than twenty, shrugs. "No idea. I just do what I'm told. You know how it is—we follow orders from above. Anyhow, we're working on getting the walls down so we can get the Mire back to its former glory."

"Did you live here?"

"Proud resident of Sector Four," he says, puffing out his chest. "It wasn't hit as hard as Six, Seven, or Eight. But I'll tell you, I can't wait to get home and start living the life I was always promised."

"I hear you," I say with a smile, feeling a little more at ease. "I feel the same way."

Just then, a flash of light explodes somewhere high above us. At first, I'm convinced a streak of lightning has just sliced its way across the sky. But when I pull my chin up, I'm horrified to see a large holo-display that seems to be projected on the low-lying cloud cover, aimed squarely at the group of construction workers on the ground.

"Message from the boss," one of the other workers says.

"You mean Illian?" I ask.

The man we were talking to nods, and another one calls out, "Everyone, shut it!"

The crew goes silent and we all pull our eyes to the sky. I

find myself pressing close to Rys, though I'm not sure why I'm feeling so apprehensive.

It's Illian's face that appears above us, his familiar, kind eyes staring into the lens of some unseen camera.

It should be a reassuring sight. But instead, I feel a potent jolt of fear.

5

ENEMIES

"As you know by now, the power in the Arc was cut off for a time," Illian announces, his tone grave. "Backup generators were also off-line. The situation was dire, and all we could determine at first was that it wasn't system error that caused it—it was an external force from an enemy far away."

Rys and I exchange a look.

External force, I mouth. We both know exactly who did this, and why.

"Does he know?" I whisper. "Do you think—"

Rys shakes his head. "Not sure."

But when Illian continues, my heart sinks.

"Thanks to a tip from a new ally, we have come to the conclusion that the power failure was the work of the man we know as the *King*—a man who used to rule the Arc alongside the most powerful members of the Directorate. He fled some time ago to New York, as many of you are aware, and we have determined that he seeks vengeance on the Consortium for driving him from this place."

"No!" I gasp under my breath. Turning to Rys, I whisper, "If he thinks it was the King...that means..."

"The Bishop has already pulled him to his side," Rys says with a nod. "Yeah. I know. This is bad."

The truth is, I don't entirely know what happened to the King and Queen, who used to reside on the Arc's top level. They pandered to the Bishop when they arrived in New York, bringing him gifts and knowledge in exchange for safe passage into the Behemoth. As far as I know, they live in one of its many floating residences, safe from the threat of Dregs like us.

I doubt if they'll ever be heard from again in the outside world.

"Rest assured," Illian continues, "that all is well now, and we are working to ensure such a failure of our electrical systems never occurs again. The good news is that we have a powerful new friend—one who can keep the King from interfering in our affairs. A man who has just arrived from New York City, along with two of our most valuable Consortium members."

The men of the construction crew look around at one another, seemingly confused.

"Who's this 'powerful new friend?'" one of the men asks.

"Our new ally is a man known as the Bishop," Illian announces as if in response to the question. "You've seen Ashen Spencer speak highly of him in the many videos she sent us from New York—of the breakthroughs his team was responsible for. They have worked medical miracles together, saving countless lives..." Illian pauses, clears his throat, then proceeds. "Including the life of my partner, Kurt, who was touch-and-go with a rare illness until just a few hours ago, when the Bishop arrived and managed to save his life."

I can see the love in his eyes for Kurt, the pain and fear he must have felt when he thought he might lose him.

But instead of warmth and sympathy, a deep, roiling rage begins to stir inside me. Kurt was ill because of the Bishop. It's all smoke and mirrors. The Bishop found Illian's greatest weakness and exposed it like a raw nerve. He knew full well that the threat of losing Kurt would break Illian down into something malleable, the easiest of marks.

"The Bishop has traveled to the Arc to be with us for a time," Illian continues. "And he has brought Ashen Spencer and Finn Davenport home to us. They are now resting comfortably after their long journey."

"Resting comfortably in a place where they can't see this video, I'll bet," Rys mutters.

"Why do you say that?" I ask.

"Because our friend Illian is about to say something Finn wouldn't like."

I'm confused by his meaning for a moment, but I eye the crowd around us, realizing all too quickly what's about to happen.

The young man who was speaking to us earlier turns to me and raises an eyebrow as if he's seeing things. After all, I'm supposed to be "resting comfortably" with Finn, not standing in the rubble of Sector Seven with Rys.

"I don't like where this is going," I say under my breath.

"Me neither," he replies. "Not at all."

"I'm afraid I have some bad news to impart to you all—news that is quite distressing." As Illian's booming voice continues, his tone and expression are solemn. "The Bishop has informed me that there is an imposter seeking entry into the Arc. A young woman who resembles Ashen Spencer in almost every conceivable way. Do not be fooled. She is an enemy in disguise—a sophisticated one, mind you, but a disguise all the same. A Holo-veil, meant to replicate the real Ashen's appearance. The young woman—or rather, the creatures who *seems* like a young woman—is considered armed and very dangerous," Illian continues. "She may look human, but take my word for it—she is not. She intends to hurt me, and she will kill anyone who gets in her way. Make no mistake—she will take you down if you try to keep her from the Arc."

As Illian continues to issue a list of the threats I pose to every single person in or out of the Arc, two of the construction workers, who have been muttering to each other while glancing over their shoulders at me, start making their way toward me, their faces twisted into menacing sneers.

"You," one of them says. "He's talking about you—*whoever* you are."

"He's not! I'm the real Ashen Spencer. He's talking about a...a clone," I stammer, struggling to find the words to explain it. But every word out of my mouth sounds exactly like what I would say if I were the so-called infiltrator.

"That's Rystan Decker," one of the men says, nodding to Rys. "I recognize him. He's on our side."

His companion shakes his head. "The boss said Ashen is with Finn Davenport, not Rystan."

"The boss is wrong," Rys retorts. "She's not lying. The Bishop is a psycho—*he's* the liar. He's conned Illian, and now, he's luring you all into a trap! Do you seriously think this face is a disguise?" With that, he gestures to me, and for a second, the men pull their eyes to me as if they're trying to work out whether or not Rys could be telling the truth.

"The Bishop restored our power. He's saved countless lives," the worker says, regurgitating the words like they've already been drilled into his head. "We all know Illian wouldn't lie to us. He's a good leader. A good man. And if you're a good man, Rystan, you'll let us have this imposter."

I'm staring at the men, wondering why they're so quick to believe Illian. Yes, he's a good man; it's true. But there has to be more to this. Why would they turn on me so quickly?

"When did the power come back on?" I ask.

"What?" one of the men asks.

"The power. When did it come back online?"

"A few hours ago, just before we left to come work out here. Why does it matter?"

I turn to Rys, who furrows his brow trying to figure out my point. "What are you thinking?" he asks.

"The Bishop did something to me," I whisper. "While I was in my residence in the Behemoth. There was something in the air—some drug that made me compliant. Happy. Eager to please. It made me...I don't know, worship him. I think he's done the same to Illian, and probably to these men, too, though I don't know how."

"Impossible," Rys says. "How could he have gotten to them?"

As we exchange hushed words, the men edge closer to us both, and Rys and I tighten, feeling the angry tension building in the air around us.

"I don't know," I say, my eyes darting around as I realize we're nearly surrounded. "They're not thinking rationally, though. Look at these guys. A minute ago, they were behaving normally. They were friendly. Now they look like they want to murder me. That's not normal."

Rys takes one look at the construction crew now standing a few feet away in a sort of makeshift military formation. In their hands are shovels, drills, and any other tools they were able to grab, and they're holding them tight across their chests like weapons.

Rys instinctively positions himself between me and the line of threatening men. I know now that he sees it—the look in their eyes of people who want to kill, to tear me apart like rabid wolves. Their ability to think critically or rationally has deserted them. There's no part of these men that feels even remotely compelled to give me the benefit of the doubt.

"What would it take to prove to you that this is Ashen?" Rys asks the men, forcing his voice into an authoritative timbre.

"Give her to us," one of the men says with a vicious twist of his lips. "Let us...examine her."

A terrifying smile works its way over his lips and he steps forward, a hammer in one hand as he holds the other out, gesturing to Rys to hand me over.

"I don't think I can do that," Rys replies. "She's my friend, and—no disrespect intended—you guys look like you might tear her arms off."

The man lets out a feral snarl, but doesn't move any closer.

"Rys," I mutter out of the corner of my mouth. "I'm still wearing my uniform...I can..."

He nods his understanding.

"Quick," he replies. "Hide. Now."

ESCAPE

IN A FLURRY OF MOTION, I pull my silver stealth-uniform's veil over my head and half-jog backwards, pressing my fingers into my palms to activate the suit's invisibility mode and conceal myself from the men's eyes.

I watch warily as I back away, terrified they're going to turn their rage on Rys. But instead, they scramble toward the place where I was just standing. They look terrifyingly like a pack of wild beasts, snarling and growling as I leap away from them, dodging this way and that in an attempt to pull myself out of their reach.

By now, Illian's announcement has come to an end, the projection vanished into thin air as though he knows the hunt has begun.

When he's realized his life isn't in immediate danger, Rys spins around, searching for me. When he doesn't see me, he leaps away from the men and sprints toward a large, doorless truck with enormous tires. Climbing into the driver's seat, he waits.

It only takes me a second to understand that he's expecting me to leap into the passenger's seat, so I dart over and do so. The climb is a struggle, but eventually I throw myself in next to him and huff out, "I'm here."

I lean forward to look past Rys at the crowd of still-searching men. By now, one of them has noticed Rys's takeover of the truck. The man points, shouts something to the others, and like a flock of perfectly synchronized raptors, they turn in unison and begin to run in our direction.

Rys lifts his arm to his face and whispers a few sharp words. Then, like a silver missile, Atticus comes swooping out of the sky at the men, his talons slicing at the one who seems to be leading the charge. The man shrieks in pain, tumbling to his knees, blood dripping down his cheek from his scalp.

The others are instantly terrified into crouched, whimpering submission as the silver owl's talons threaten to shred them from above.

"I need to get you out of here," Rys says, pressing a few buttons on the truck's dashboard. The vehicle shoots forward, surging its way over piles of loose dirt and rubble. As Atticus's unrelenting assault continues, Rys steers the vehicle through the gap in the wall, taking us around the Mire in the direction of Sector One.

I twist around to see Atticus continuing to dive-bomb our would-be attackers as we hurtle over the rubble and follow a makeshift dirt track around the perimeter of the Mire.

"He's already gotten his claws into them," I moan, seeing the damage he's inflicted. "I know he had to, but...they're Dregs, like us. They've already turned against me, and the Bishop hasn't even been here for more than a few hours."

"They didn't turn against you," Rys says. "They turned

against someone they thought was an intruder. Even so, you're right—the Bishop most definitely has them in his grip. But we'll fix this."

"How can we possibly do that?" I cry. "They won't even let us inside, let alone anywhere near Illian."

"I don't know yet," he replies. "But the truth will get us to Illian, and it will win. It has to."

"Even Illian is convinced I'm an imposter!" I snap. "How can you possibly claim truth will win against someone as powerful and deceptive as the Bishop? You know men like him don't care about truth, and neither do their followers."

Again, Rys says, "I don't know."

And this time, he seems defeated.

A thought occurs to me then. "Finn might have seen the broadcast. If he did, he'll know about the Replik. He'll know there's a second version of me. Maybe it will be enough to cast doubt in his mind..."

But Rys shakes his head. "There was a symbol in the lower right corner of that video—a sort of watermark. I know it from my time working for the Directorate. It means the footage was aired only outside the Arc. It was a deliberate effort to warn anyone on the outside to avoid letting us in."

"It doesn't matter," I huff, pulling myself out of stealth. "Once the construction workers and everyone else is back inside, rumors will spread. Word will get out; it always does. Finn will definitely hear about it."

"You're assuming those guys will be allowed back inside," Rys says, a heavy sadness in his voice, and it only takes me a second to understand what he's saying.

"You...you think the Bishop will have them killed?"

"Killed, or more likely, they'll be questioned, then become

the first of the Arc's residents taken for his experiments. Don't forget why the Bishop traveled out west. He's looking for a batch of new subjects to experiment on after depleting New York's population." He turns my way and looks me in the eye. "I'm really sorry, Ash, but even if Finn finds out about the Replik, you and I both know the Bishop will do whatever it takes to convince him that the Ash who's with him is the real one. If he has to drug him, hold a gun to his head, whatever, he'll do it. He needs Finn on his side as a trusted ally of Illian —not to mention that he needs Finn's brain if he plans to continue his disgusting experiments. Honestly, I'm almost impressed he's managed to keep the truth about the Repliks from Finn."

"The Bishop has a way of making people see what they want to see," I reply with a wince. "He shows you a world that looks beautiful and full of hope, when all around you, terrible things are happening. He pulled the wool over my eyes for a long time, Rys. Finn is working for the Bishop—probably even replicating biological samples. But if he knew about the Repliks, he would have told me."

"There are plenty of medical reasons to replicate biological samples," Rys says thoughtfully, nodding in agreement. "To grow organs and tissue and all sorts of things. It's possible that Finn knows that much—just not how far the Bishop has taken it. Look—I recognized the difference between the Replik and you, but then again, I'm not drugged up on some Bishop-style cocktail. Finn has had his head messed with for months by that turd of a sub-human. We can't possibly know what he's thinking."

My breath is tight in my chest when I reply, "All the more reason I need to get to him as soon as I can."

We hurtle along the round perimeter wall, and I turn to make sure no one is following us.

"I don't see any pursuers. But I don't see Atticus, either," I tell Rys, my voice tight. "Is he okay?"

"He's fine. When he's done distracting those poor fools, he'll join us again."

"They're not fools," I reply with a scowl. "They're people like us who believe Illian is a good leader. It's not their fault they've been corrupted, any more than it was my fault I thought the Bishop was a good guy."

"You're right," Rys admits sheepishly. "I guess the key is to take back the Bishop's power, then. We need to show the world he's the imposter. You and I need to tear his mask off, Ash. It's the only way."

"That's the thing. He's not *wearing* a mask. Whether we like it or not, he's real. Except…"

"Except what?"

I clench my jaw. "There's more to him than any of us knows. He's powerful in ways we haven't even seen yet. If he's already got his talons in Illian, we've got a hell of an uphill battle ahead of us."

"We'll show Illian the truth. We just need to get to him. We can't head to Sector Eight—they'll expect us to seek refuge there. We'll go to the Financial District instead, and take the tunnel into the Hub."

I recall with a horrified lurch in my gut what that tunnel represented the first time I used it. It was the first time I managed to escape the Arc—when I was fleeing for my life after the Duchess and the rest of her Directorate companions forced me to fight the King's son.

The good news, I suppose, is that the Duchess and the Directorate no longer run the Arc.

The bad news is that the people I considered my closest allies have now turned against me.

It's not long before Atticus comes in to land on the truck's roof and Rys tells me the men have ceased their pursuit.

I should feel reassured.

But I don't.

7

THE TUNNEL

IT'S several minutes and far too many breathless over-the-shoulder checks before we arrive at Sector One.

Its wall, like that of Sector Seven, is largely broken down, and Rys is able to navigate the truck over the rubble and straight to the entrance of the tunnel that will lead us to the Hub, the central point underneath the Arc where the trains from the various Sectors used to drop off their infrequent passengers.

"Can we drive in?" I ask, but Rys shakes his head.

"No, unfortunately," he tells me. "The tunnel hasn't been cleaned up yet. The Financial District isn't exactly Illian's top priority in the Mire, as you can imagine. This is the place where all the mayhem started all those years ago. It was mostly occupied by Wealthies trying to figure out how to get even richer. Rumor has it that the Directorate started out in the banking tower over there." With that, he nods to a dilapidated glass skyscraper that was once stunning, but now looks like it's about to succumb to the innumerable vines scaling its exterior.

"Glad to hear Illian has his priorities mostly straight," I tell Rys.

He pulls the vehicle to a stop at the tunnel's entrance. We climb out and turn toward the dark passageway with Atticus flying overhead, his keen eyes watching for any threats. I find myself wondering as I stare into the tunnel's depths if there will ever come a time in my life when I don't feel like a prey animal being hunted by creatures who want to kill me for their own sport.

Just when I'm about to take my first step, a sudden blast of noise startles me into a crouch next to a pile of discarded building materials. Rys, too, squats down next to me, a protective arm around my shoulders. We twist around together, acknowledging tacitly that the sound came from somewhere high in the air above us. The thundering, deafening roar grows louder, echoing through the entire sky.

I pull my chin up to stare at the clouds, only to see four aircraft moving like missiles across the broad blue expanse of the sky. They disappear as quickly as they came, and I can only assume, given their velocity, that they had no intention of stopping in the Mire.

"What *were* those?" I ask, trembling.

"Not sure," Rys says. "They looked a little like old fighter jets. But..."

"But what?"

He simply shakes his head. "I couldn't say, honestly. They could belong to the Consortium. Illian has allies all over the place. They might be headed to the west coast. I've heard rumors about conflict out there. Rebels against Wealthies. The usual song and dance."

"Sure," I reply, trying to convince myself that's the case, that they were simply making their way through our territory as they shot toward their destination. I want to believe they had nothing to do with the Bishop, with what's happening in this place.

It was just a coincidence, I tell myself, but my nagging brain is quick to remind me that in my life, there's rarely such a thing as a coincidence. In all likelihood, the jets were scrambled to pursue Rys and me.

You're too late, I tell them with a silent sneer.

Rys rises to his feet, reaching a hand out for my own.

To my surprise, I let out a quiet laugh as he pulls me up to stand next to him.

"What's funny?" he asks.

"I just had the strangest déja vu," I reply. "Do you remember when we were kids and went to the Fall Fair? There was a haunted house there."

"If you mean the plywood shack that was supposed to *look* like a haunted house, yeah, I remember. There were people dressed in rubber masks leaping out at us from every dark corner."

"I knew they weren't really threatening, but something about them terrified me. Maybe it was the fact that they were concealing their true faces—that I had no way of reading them properly. For all I knew, they were cruel, heartless adults looking to prey on us. Anyhow, I remember screaming when one of them jumped out at us. And I remember you laughing at me."

Rys immediately looks sheepish, as if an apology is lingering on the tip of his tongue.

Still holding his hand, I add, "You took my hand when you realized how scared I really was. Do you remember what you said?"

He thinks for a few seconds, then nods.

Then together, we recite the words like a vow:

"It's okay, Ash. If they come for you, I'll protect you."

Rys looks away. "I meant it," he says. "I haven't always come through, but I meant it."

"I'd forgotten," I tell him, a sudden, painful sorrow filling my chest. "Until this moment, when I took your hand. But I remember how it made me feel to know you were looking out for me. That I wasn't alone. It meant the world, Rys."

"I've still got your back," he says, awkwardly kicking at a stray piece of concrete.

"I know you do."

I don't know what we're about to face—what we'll find inside the fortress that is the Arc, if we can even make it inside. I don't know if our allies will see me as anything other than a stranger, an enemy.

I can only hope when the time comes, Rys and I will protect each other.

Rys pulls his hand away as if the sensation stings him mildly, and a new memory slips its way into my mind, one from when we had first turned seventeen. A flash of another time Rys took my hand, as we returned to the Mire from the foothills outside the wall.

I suppose I've always known his feelings for me were more than mere friendship. But I also know that as much as I care for him, I will never feel the sort of love for him that I do for Finn.

"Rys," I say softly.

Neither of us has taken a step. Neither of us knows quite what to do.

"Yeah."

I chew on my lip before saying, "You're one of the best friends I've ever had, if not the best. I will think of it all my life—of the many times you've saved me. I hope you know..."

He cuts me off with a gesture of his hand. "Yeah," he says with a sad smile. "I know. And it should be enough for me, shouldn't it?"

"I can't tell you how to feel. I can only tell you how important you are to me, and hope you understand what that means."

He looks into the distant darkness, lets out a sigh, and says, "Look—I'm not stupid. I know you love Davenport, and I get it. The guy is annoyingly perfect. Hell, it's all I can do not to fall in love with him myself. It just...hurts a bit sometimes, you know? When you and I were kids, I thought maybe we'd end up together someday. But I was never brave enough to take a chance with you. I was always scared you'd push me away."

I nod.

I don't entirely know what to say—Rys's feelings have been obvious for a long time, though we've never really talked about them. The thing is, he's like a brother to me. A brother who has occasionally inspired my wrath, but a brother all the same.

And it's possible he'll never fully understand that I love him almost unconditionally.

"We should go," he says, breaking an awkward silence.

I turn to begin the trudge through the tunnel. "True. This will take hours."

Hours that we don't have. Hours when the other Ash will be convincing Finn that she's me. Manipulating him into doing whatever she or the Bishop wants. Hours when...

No. I won't think about it. None of it matters. That Ash is not real; she's nothing more than some organic matter laid over a skeleton. All I need is to convince Illian that I'm the real one.

The problem is, I'm the same as her. I'm organic matter stretched over a skeleton, too. We're all just flesh, sinew, and bones.

How do I convince him she's a liar?

"I'm sending Atticus ahead to assess the Arc's functionality," Rys says as we scramble over large chunks of detritus. He pulls up something on his right forearm—similar to the band I've seen him use to control his drones. But this one is black, and when he streaks a finger over its surface, it lights up with a series of fine lines that look almost like a language.

"Atticus," he says, "I need you to get close enough to figure out how many of the service elevators are guarded."

We hike for some time, taking care not to break our ankles on the uneven terrain, and Rys occasionally takes off the small pack he's carried since we left the Eagle to offer me a protein snack or swig of water. We walk largely in silence, though I occasionally catch him looking at me out of the corner of his eye.

"Finn loves you like crazy, you know," he says after an hour or so. "Things will sort themselves out."

"I'm not worried," I lie.

"Hell, *I* would be," he says with a chuckle. "In case you've never noticed, Ash, you're—*she's*—beautiful. You have a beautiful clone, and he's with her right now. That has to sting a little."

"She's not me," I snap, though I know those words, like everything else, are a lie. The Bishop injected me with a neuro-implant that read my brain for weeks. He stole my memories, my emotions. My joy, my pain, my anger, everything. He replicated me in every conceivable way.

The other Ash quite literally *is* me. She probably even loves Finn, in her own twisted way.

"She's an infiltrator," Rys says. "But don't worry—we'll figure out how to get rid of her."

I notice immediately that he didn't say "kill." It's for the best, I suppose. I'm not sure I could murder another version of myself—*even if it is the Frankenstein's monster version.*

"You make it sound so simple," I moan.

"It is. Provided we can get inside, I mean. So let's shut up and get moving."

We walk, scrambling over the concrete and steel fragments until we come to a steel utility door embedded in the tunnel's wall. Once again, Rys lifts his arm to his face and speaks to Atticus.

"Any luck?" he asks.

I don't hear a response, but it seems Rys does, because he nods and turns to me as a click sounds and the door opens outward.

"Wait—we're not going to the Hub?" I ask.

"We can't risk running into Consortium guards," Rys explains. "So we'll have to figure out another way. In the meantime, you should activate your uniform's cloaking ability again."

I'm about to do as he suggests, but a thought occurs to me.

"You know what? I don't think I should be cloaked. I *want* the Consortium Guards to see me."

Rys looks puzzled, and as he pulls the door shut behind us, he crosses his arms and leans back against it. "I'm all ears," he says. "Explain."

"I need to speak to Illian. He's my friend, my ally. He knows me. I've spent hours—no, *weeks*—with him. And I'm pretty sure a Consortium Guard would bring me straight to him."

"Ash—you heard Illian's announcement. He's convinced he's seen the real Ash already, and thinks you're the infiltrator. He's told the entire Consortium Guard that you're a danger to them. We could be killed by someone who isn't sensible enough to figure the truth out before he pulls the trigger."

"I'm willing to take that chance," I tell him with more resolve than I feel. "It's the only way to get to Finn. We can't expect to sneak our way around the Arc and magically extract him. We need to expose the truth about the Bishop, about what's been done to so many innocent people in New York, all of it."

Rys narrows his eyes at me, exhales, then uncrosses his arms as if surrendering to my lunacy.

"Fine," he says. "But for the record, I think this is a terrible idea."

"Duly noted."

8

ARRIVAL

Rys and I proceed down a long corridor until we come to one of the large Utility Conveyors designed to transport furniture and other large goods into the Arc.

To my surprise, no guards are on duty outside its doors.

"Okay, this feels...weird," I say under my breath. "I thought they were watching all possible entrances. They must know I'm with you—which means they know we'll try to get in a back way."

"*Weird* is an understatement," Rys agrees. "I'm liking this less and less. There's a one-hundred percent chance they want to find us, and they also know the most likely way into the Arc is this corridor. But..."

"It's like they don't care," I reply, completing his thought.

Rys nods. "Exactly. But hey—since there's no welcome party, let's head up to Consortium Headquarters and see what we can find. Maybe we'll get lucky."

"I wouldn't count on it."

My heartbeat throbs in my ears as we step inside the

Conveyor. We're so close to Illian, to Finn, to the Bishop. So close to ending this nightmare before it gets out of hand.

If I can just look into Finn's eyes, I'm confident that he'll see the truth, even if I don't say a word. The Bishop may have worked some sort of dastardly brainwashing on us both. But I know the whole, dismal truth, and soon, Finn will, too.

"The Consortium Headquarters are located on Level 297," Rys tells me as he programs the Conveyor to take us directly to our destination, and the doors seal shut.

"Where's Atticus?"

Rys slips a finger over the band on his left arm. "He's still monitoring the Arc's systems. He's okay."

Still, Rys seems to have grown agitated, clenching and unclenching his hands as we begin our ascent, and at first, I don't understand why.

It's only when the Conveyor grinds to an abrupt, alarming halt a minute later that I move instinctively closer to him.

"What's happening?"

"I think we've come to the end of our little journey," he tells me. "Unfortunately."

"What does that—"

I don't have time to finish the question before the doors sweep open and we're greeted by four men in Consortium garb, each pointing a terrifying-looking weapon directly at our faces.

A nauseating sense of déjà vu assaults my gut. The men are supposed to be allies. They're *supposed* to protect Dregs like Rys and me from the tyrants who used to run the Arc—the same tyrants who murdered our parents and stole us from our homes.

I'm still wearing my silver uniform. I could overpower the

guards. I could take each of them down in turn—probably before any of them got a shot off.

But in doing so, I would put Rys's life at risk and prove Illian's point.

I am dangerous.

"We would like to speak with Illian," I say, thinking fast as I focus on the guard closest to us, whose hands are shaking as if he's terrified I'm about to explode in some sort of atomic blast.

He turns to look at the others, who appear flummoxed.

"You expected a fight," I say, pressing my palms into the air to show them I'm unarmed. "I'm not dangerous. I'm not who —or what—Illian thinks I am. But I need to speak to him, because he and the entire population of the Arc are in grave danger. I need you to believe me. Please."

One of the men—who looks like he can't be older than nineteen—steps toward me, but I can see that he, too, is shaking. "Why would we believe you over our leader?"

"Maybe you shouldn't," I say with a shrug. "But why don't you leave it up to your leader to decide who's telling the truth?"

"Fine," he says, his tone a little more confident now. "We'll take you to him. But if you try anything, you will be shot. Understood?"

"Understood," I reply. "My friend here should be allowed to leave," I tell the men, pointing to Rys. "He hasn't done anything other than bring me to the Arc."

The guard shakes his head. "Sorry. No. You're both coming with us."

"It's okay, Ash," Rys says. "I can help clarify who you are. Let me."

I nod and turn around to face the wall, an act of submission to show the men I mean them no harm. When Rys follows suit, one of the men secures our wrists behind our backs with some kind of steel cuffs, and the four of them cram us back into the Conveyor before issuing a command that it take us to Level 290.

Rys and I exchange a look of shock and wait as the Conveyor shoots us upward.

"Isn't that where…" Rys begins, and I nod.

"Where the Davenports used to live. The Duke, Duchess, Finn, Merit."

Sure enough, when we leave the Conveyor, the guards guide us to the Davenports' residence, where we find Illian seated in the elegant living area.

I gasp audibly when I see him, legs crossed, on the couch where I've seen the Duchess so many times.

He's flanked by security guards, who tighten as we enter the room. Illian rises to his feet, but doesn't smile. There's not so much as a flicker of recognition in his eyes, though I'm sure I spot a split-second expression of surprise.

Of course, I think. *You didn't expect me to look so much like me, did you?*

"Leave us," Illian tells the four escorts when he sees that our hands are still bound behind our backs. "It's all right. She can't hurt me."

The young men look more than a little relieved when they pivot and head back the way we came.

Illian gestures to the couch, and Rys and I seat ourselves, the two security guards positioning themselves across from us. They're older than the other guards and more experienced looking, though I don't recognize either of them.

"Where's the Bishop?" I ask, my tone more abrupt than I intend.

Illian seats himself in the Duke's former armchair, his spine straight, and looks me in the eye. "I will answer that one question, because as I understand it, you are implanted with Ashen Spencer's memories. Therefore, I can't say I blame you for thinking it's acceptable to take a casual tone with me. Ashen and I are friends. Colleagues. She is a valuable ally."

"You haven't answered the question," Rys says, and Illian shoots him an irritated look.

"The Bishop is occupied at the moment, helping Kurt to heal from a sudden illness, if you must know." He inhales a deep breath, collecting himself, then says, "Rystan, you left the Arc without informing me. You brought back this..." He gestures toward me with a hint of disgust on his features. "This...Replik. Do you know what sort of danger you have put us all in?"

"Yes, I do," Rys says. "None whatsoever, because this is Ashen Spencer. The Bishop is messing with your mind. Don't you see—"

Illian raises a hand and snaps, "Stop!"

Leaping to his feet, he nods to the security guards. "You know what to do with both of them," he grunts in a voice that doesn't entirely seem to belong to the man I thought I knew.

"Illian!" I half-cry. "You *know* me! What are you doing?"

He shakes his head, his expression morphing instantly from anger to sadness. "I know you think we know each other," he tells me. "But we've never met. Ashen is with Finn, happy and safe. I have spoken with her. I know her. And I know what the Bishop has done for us all."

There it is, I think as one of the guards yanks me to my feet. *There's the true answer.*

Illian doesn't seem like himself, because he's *not* himself. He's been charmed, drugged, whatever. His mind is not his own. The Bishop has stolen it, just as he stole mine and those of so many others. He is the world's finest manipulator, and we've already lost Illian to him.

"What are you going to do with us?" I ask as the guard begins to march me toward what used to be the Davenports' front door.

"I'm going to give you a chance," Illian says, his voice reasoned and calm, even kind. "If you're lucky."

"A chance at what?"

But he doesn't answer me.

I turn to look over my shoulder and shout, "Illian!" just as the guard shoves me out the door and into the corridor.

"Don't, Ash," says Rys, who's behind me. "He's a lost cause."

"No, he's not. He's just preoccupied with Kurt. Once he understands what's going on…"

But even as I say the words, I know the folly in them. Expecting Illian to recover from the Bishop's spell is like expecting someone to forget how to breathe. The Bishop is part of him now, a new, pleasant reality. And in his mind, deeply embedded, is the notion that the Ashen he saw with Finn was the only true one. When he looks at me, he sees little more than an android, a creation crafted by a genius able to replicate human DNA. I'm a laboratory experiment, and the Bishop is the Doctor Frankenstein who made me.

As the guards drag us onto the Conveyor to take us to the Hold, I begin to wonder if Illian is right.

Maybe I'm *not* Ashen Spencer, after all.

Maybe I've simply been implanted with a sophisticated series of memories—some real, some fabricated.

For all I know, I was never trapped on the Behemoth's

rooftop with the Duchess. For all I know, she could be living comfortably in her residence right now.

"Rys," I say as we shoot downward in the Conveyor, my stomach tying itself in knots. "Tell me I haven't lost my mind."

"I want to," he replies. "But I'm beginning to think I've lost my own."

9

HOLD

WHEN WE REACH the prison known as the Hold, I find myself hoping Illian has instructed the guards to put Rys and me in a cell together—or, better still, to free Rys entirely.

But to my horror, the first guard shoves him into a small, sparse chamber to the right side of the cold, sterile corridor, and Rys spins around just in time to call my name before the door slams in his face.

My cell, on the other hand, is at the end of the corridor, isolated and chilly.

The guard shoves me inside and slams the door shut without so much as a word. I sink to the floor, dazed and horrified by the surrealism of all that's happened since Finn and I left for New York City. The Bishop's hold on all of us. His lies, his manipulation. His creation of an entire new version of me and of who knows how many other people.

I invested so much hope in Illian, in our bond, our history. I had faith that, like Rys, he would see me for what I really am.

But it seems the Bishop delved quickly and deeply into his vulnerable mind, and the worst part of it is, I can't even bring myself to be angry with Illian. He has been forced into an addiction I know all too well. He's been through the wringer, confronted with the near-loss of the person he loves most. His mind is not his own right now, and as far as he's concerned, the one person who can keep his life from crashing and burning is the Bishop.

Meanwhile, my hatred for the Bishop grows more intense by the second. I'm filled with a deep, vicious longing to get my hands around his neck, to throttle him until his eyes bulge out and he gasps his last breath.

I know, though, that such a moment is unlikely ever to come. I've never witnessed the Bishop's full range of powers, but I can imagine all too well how destructive he could potentially be. His ability to charm and manipulate is dangerous enough, but Finn has warned me that underlying it all is an arsenal of brutal internal weaponry that could take down Illian, me, and anyone else foolish enough to get in his way.

These are the thoughts that race through my mind for the next several hours as I alternate between pacing my cold cell, sitting on the stained cot, and wondering if anyone will ever bring me something to eat, or if they really think I'm some hybrid robot creature who doesn't need sustenance.

I don't know how much time has passed when the door opens and Illian comes striding in, two guards following him to stand protectively behind him.

Illian keeps his distance, telling me to take a seat on the cot. I do as he commands, crossing my arms over my chest in protest.

"I feel," he tells me, standing his ground several feet away, "that I owe you a bit of an explanation. I was abrupt with you earlier, and for that I apologize."

"It's all right," I tell him through a tightening jaw. I'm not entirely sure I mean it. "You were worried about Kurt. How is he doing?"

Illian almost smiles when he replies, "He's better. Thank you. Your friend the Bishop has worked a miracle."

I half-snarl, "He is the farthest thing from a friend."

"He saved Kurt's life."

"He is the reason Kurt was ill in the first place!"

Illian lets out a strange, soft chuckle. "Ashen," he says, "Or whatever I should call you—I wish you could hear yourself. How ridiculous you sound. The Bishop was hundreds of miles away when Kurt fell ill, with no access whatsoever to the Arc. He cannot possibly have been responsible for Kurt's sickness."

"You underestimate him," I say. "You don't know what he's capable of. He has access to the King's resources—to everything he controlled in the Arc. That man can do anything he wants."

"The King can't control our systems anymore," Illian tells me with a sharp look of warning.

"Of course he can. You said yourself that you thought he was responsible for the power failure. The irony is that you weren't far off, Illian. The King probably *did* have a hand in it —just not in the way you think."

Illian shakes his head. "I only mentioned the King because the Bishop expressed a concern about him. The truth is, the power outage was most likely caused by a simple glitch in the system. So please—stop hurling your ridiculous conspiracy theories at me. I am not so easily swayed."

"But—"

Illian shakes his head and holds up his hand, cutting me

off. "Look, I know you *think* you know the truth, so I'll explain a few things. While the real Ashen and Finn were in New York, we worked to encrypt every possible bit of access to our systems so they wouldn't be vulnerable to those on the outside. You know—*Ashen* knows, I mean—how much the Directorate wanted to do us harm, so we worked hard to shield ourselves."

"It doesn't matter. Whatever protective measures you had in place, the Bishop bypassed them. He got to Kurt, to the electrical grid. And he can get to you and every other person in here."

Once again, Illian lets out a laugh, and I begin to wonder if he's enjoying this.

"What's so damned funny?" I ask.

"The Ashen I know would be happy to hear Kurt is doing well. She would trust me. She *does* trust me, in fact. You're giving yourself away as the intruder you are, with all this hostility and anger."

"The Ashen you know would do anything to protect you and the rest of the Arc," I snap. "If you can't see that, all I can say is the Bishop really has taken over your mind."

A flash of rage passes quickly over Illian's face, but he settles, like some force inside him has warned him against losing his patience with me.

"There is another reason I know you're not Ashen Spencer," he says.

"Enlighten me."

"The Ashen I know would have fought tooth and nail if someone tried to separate her from Finn. Yet you didn't. You showed up here, uninvited and hostile. That is entirely contradictory to Ashen's character."

"I showed up here with Rys," I say. "After the Bishop

63

imprisoned me with a psychotic woman who wanted to burn me alive."

"So you say," Illian replies. "But there's something else. Something the Bishop told me, and unfortunately, it can't be disputed."

I narrow my eyes skeptically when I ask, "What exactly are you talking about?"

"The Bishop told me Repliks are identical to us in almost every way. The one major difference is that they don't inherit nanotech from their human counterparts." He takes a step toward me, a sincere look in his eye when he asks, "Can you honestly tell me I'll find nanotech in your system like that which gives Ashen the Surge?"

"What kind of a question—" I begin, but I stop talking almost as soon as I've begun.

I know exactly what he's asking, and why.

The Bishop stole the nanotech from me when I was in the Behemoth. He had me drugged, and his people infiltrated my body and took the Surge—the one power that might be enough to fight him—from me. He implanted the tech in the Replik, giving her the physical advantage...but also making her more *real* in Illian's eyes than I am.

I push myself back against the wall, burying my face in my hands. My shoulders shake with laughter.

"That bastard thinks of everything," I say quietly, my voice quivering with unhinged amusement. "What he's done to me. What he's done to us all...it's genius, really. I'll give him that."

"I know how hard this must be for you," Illian tells me, his voice softening a little. "You think you're the real Ashen, the one who grew up in Sector Eight. But it's only because of the memories he implanted in you. I'm sure it feels very real, and I do feel for you—I really do. I honestly wish there could simply be two Ashen Spencers. I'm very fond of her, you know—which means I could probably grow fond of you, too."

"I know you're fond of her," I tell him, pulling my chin up. "Because I *am* her. And if the Bishop hadn't gotten into your mind, you would see it as clearly as your hand in front of your face. You are my friend, Illian. And you're in danger."

He nods, his head cocked to the side, patronizingly accepting that I believe it all to be true.

"The Bishop is going to hurt our people," I add, my voice rising in anger and frustration. "He's going to use them for his own vile purposes—and trust me, the consequences will be even worse than what the Directorate did to us all. The sooner you understand that, the better."

"You're wrong," a deep voice responds from the doorway beyond Illian and the two guards. "He is going to turn the Arc into the paradise it was always meant to be."

Bile rises in my throat, and I slam my eyes shut against the soothing lilt of that awful, addictive, and all too familiar voice.

HIM

I LEAP off the cot and retreat into the cell's shadows, pressing my back to the cold concrete of the wall, my breath coming hard as the Bishop steps into the cell.

He looks just as he always has. Impeccably dressed, strands of dark, shiny hair falling in gentle waves around his shoulders. As I stare, I'm assaulted by the horrible realization that I still find him exquisite to look at, his sculpted jaw and weapons-grade cheekbones disturbingly alluring.

His eyes, which look almost black in the cell's meager light, manage to be inviting and menacing at once, and his lips are curved into a smile that would seem intoxicating on almost anyone else...but on his cruel face, it feels like a poisonous mist slowly seeping into the air.

"Hello, Ashen," he says as he steps closer. When Illian turns to him, a confused look in his eyes, the Bishop adds, "Goodness, we must find a more suitable moniker for you, Replik. I know 'Ashen' feels natural to you—it's how I designed you. How I orchestrated that intricate synthetic mind of yours."

"The only thing you did to my mind is steal it," I say almost under my breath, shooting a look Illian's way. "He took my memories. My emotions, my experiences, everything, and implanted them in that...thing."

The Bishop lets out a low, menacing laugh before he replies, "Illian already knows how I created you. I warned him, you know. About how you would try to access the Arc after having convinced Rystan that you're the girl he grew up with. Poor, sad, puppy-dog-eyed Rystan. He would do anything for Ashen—even convince himself she's real when she's clearly not. It's not his fault or yours, of course. I suppose I did too good a job. Your implanted memories tell you without a shadow of a doubt that you are, in fact, Ashen Spencer. That your experience on the roof of the Behemoth was that of a human girl against a woman. Do you know, I left you with the Duchess for your own sake?"

I stare daggers at the Bishop, my blood boiling inside my veins. "Oh?" I ask. "And how, exactly, did you think that leaving me defenseless while she burned me to death was 'for my own sake?'"

"I didn't leave you defenseless," he laughs. "You had that uniform. And a blade."

A blade I wish I still had.

The Bishop sighs. "I knew it would be best to let your time come to an end, Replik. Anything else seemed like a cruelty. Look what's happened to you—you came all the way here, only to find yourself in a prison cell. Now what are we going to do with you?"

"You're going to tell Illian the truth," I reply, my tone full of bile. "You're going to do the right thing, for once in your twisted life, and..."

"Truth," the Bishop replies. "Illian knows the truth. I suspect your friend Rystan does, too, bless him."

"You're right. He does. He knows I'm Ashen Spencer."

"Does he? And how is that, exactly?"

"He just *does*," I snap, frustrated by the fact that I have no better explanation to offer him or Illian.

"I see. So, if we put you and the other Ashen in a room together, you're telling me Rystan would absolutely, without a doubt, be able to pick the correct version of you?"

"I…" I begin. "Yes. Of course he would." Turning to Illian, I add, "Do it, please. Put that monstrosity and me together, and let Rys speak to us. Or better still, let Finn see us both. Finn doesn't even know about the Repliks. It's not fair to let him think the Ashen he's with is the real one when he has no idea what's happening."

"Finn knows all about the Replik program," the Bishop retorts. "As disappointing as it sounds, he knows full well that they exist. Don't forget, he helped develop them."

I shake my head violently and the words fall from my mouth as my heart sinks like a stone. "But in the Behemoth, you told me he—"

"I know what I told you. Come, now. You really think I could have kept such a secret from a young man as clever as Finn?"

"He may have helped," I reply. "But he didn't know what he was working on. Finn and I talked. He never told me, and he would have—he wouldn't keep a secret like that from me."

"He didn't keep it from you," Illian interjects. "That's what we keep trying to tell you. You are not Ashen. You weren't with him all that time, even if your memory banks tell you you were." He steps closer, laying a hand on my shoulder. "I'm sorry. I can see how hard this is for you to understand."

"Hard?" I spit. "Hard is trying to open a jar that's stuck. This is cruelty. It's the Bishop's game, messing with my mind. Gaslighting me when he knows the truth. Misleading you. All for his own vile pleasure."

Illian doesn't have a reply for this, but he steps back as if he's slightly worried I'm going to strike him.

"Does Finn know about her?" I ask. "My Replik? Does he know he's with one of your creations?"

The Bishop doesn't reply at first. He simply smiles that awful, charming grin of his, and pushes his hair back. "He knows the Replik remained behind, on the roof of the Behemoth. As far as he knows, his mother finished her off."

"No. He can't think that," I say, turning to Illian. "If he did, he would fight to get me back. He would know…"

"I offered Finn proof that he is, in fact, with the genuine version of you," the Bishop says. "The case is closed."

"What proof?" I nearly shout. "You have no proof!"

The Bishop's smile intensifies, and it's all I can do not to hurl myself forward and tear the grin off his face.

"It was proof enough for Finn," he says simply.

I step toward the Bishop, who doesn't flinch or so much as raise a hand. "You're a filthy liar, and I will kill you before this is over," I snarl through clenched teeth.

"Enough!" Illian snaps, more irritated than I've seen him in a long time. "I already told you, I've seen Finn with Ashen. I have spoken to them at length, and I assure you, there is no question in my mind that they are the two people I've spent so much time with."

"There's something you need to know," I stammer, desperate to get through to him. "The Bishop told me Repliks have a skeleton made of a synthetic material. You could simply take a sample and tell from that, Illian. Or take a sample of my bone marrow, or whatever…It would prove conclusively which one of us is lying."

Illian seems to contemplate this for a moment, but to my surprise, he shakes his head. "I'm sorry, Ashen. That won't work."

He stops speaking, seemingly torn up about something.

It's not until the Bishop speaks that I begin to understand his reluctance.

"You see," the Bishop says, "the first thing I told Illian upon my arrival was about you and the others we created in the Behemoth. I even offered to let his own medical team run a series of tests on the real Ashen—and, well…he can fill you in himself."

He turns expectantly to Illian, who says, "They compared her samples to every piece of DNA we have in our possession relating to Ashen Spencer. There is no doubt in my mind that the young woman with Finn is her—the Ashen I know."

"Illian!" I shout, stepping toward him. The two guards move forward in warning, and I freeze in place. "Look—it's me, damn it! You found Finn and me by the water that day, in the woods. We were together on the trip to Santa Fe. We watched people die together—Peric's parents…"

He puts a hand up. "Do you really think I didn't put the other Ashen to the test?" he asks. "It's the first thing I did. She told me the same things. Details about how Kurt and I met, about Kel, about her life in the Mire."

"Let Rys see us both," I plead. "Let him speak to us. Please. He'll tell you which of us is real. He's known me longer than anyone."

Illian shoots the Bishop a look, and the Bishop nods. "Fine," he says. "I see no harm in it. It would put the matter to rest, after all."

Illian nods, and I see something then, something behind his eyes that horrifies me. A look I know all too well.

There's more to this than simple skepticism. More than a lack of faith in who I am.

This is the spell the Bishop weaves—the dark sort of toxic, chemical magic he uses to charm and placate those who ultimately end up serving him. For whatever reason, Illian has fallen victim to his charms. It doesn't matter if he sees samples of my bone marrow or anything else; he will believe the Bishop until the day he dies...or the day someone breaks him free of this ghastly spell.

"It hurt, didn't it, Illian?" I ask. "When Kurt was ill. The thought of losing someone you loved so much was painful —wasn't it?"

A dose of fury infiltrates Illian's features. "Of course it was!" he snarls, looking sideways at the Bishop as if accusing him of designing me to be cruel. "What kind of sadistic question is that?"

"I'm trying to explain to you how much it would hurt me to lose Finn," I tell him, trying to keep my own voice even. "It would hurt Finn to know the girl by his side is an infiltrator. Can't you see that? Can't you see what's happening here? The Bishop is manipulating you—using the other Ashen to get to you. He's going to destroy this place and turn it into a surreal hellscape, just like he did to the Behemoth. I've been trying to explain to you that he's not your friend. He's not a friend to any of us."

"You're wrong," Illian says with a wince, struggling against something internal, something inside him that's trying to fight its way out. "There is no intruder with Finn. He's very happy and at peace."

"Get Rys," I say quietly. "Get the other Ashen. Put us together. I promise, he will tell you which of us is real."

"Fine," Illian replies with a sigh and turns toward the cell door. "I'll speak to Rystan. I'm tired of this game."

The Bishop remains behind, staring at me even as the guards follow Illian out into the corridor.

"What have you done to him?" I ask through gritted teeth. "That's not the man I know."

"Oh, he most certainly is," the Bishop says with a derisive laugh. "Has it not occurred to you that perhaps you're simply not as desirable a companion as the new, improved version of yourself? Given the need to make a choice, it's clear that Illian has chosen her, as has Finn. You have been supplanted, Ashen, and it's killing you."

"Neither of them would ever choose her over me," I say. "They're two of the most loyal people I've ever met in my life."

The Bishop raises an eyebrow, which is enough to prompt me to step forward, my hand lashing out to slap him across the face.

But he catches my wrist, twisting me around, my arm wrenched painfully behind my back.

"Careful now, Ashen," he whispers into my ear. "You wouldn't want to have to rely on me to mend your broken bones, would you?"

Summoning all the strength the silver uniform grants me, I twist free and spin around to glare at him. The look of surprise in his eyes tells me he's underestimated the garment's capabilities.

"Impressive," he says. "Truly. I must remember to commend Finn on his expertise." With that, he turns to leave. "I'll see you soon. Once we've retrieved the other Ashen, that is."

"Wait!" I call out before he can open the door. "You knew Rys and I would come west. How?"

He turns back to me, raising his chin. "I didn't know, in fact. I suspected the Duchess would burn you to death in quick order. I am impressed that you showed up, however."

"You're saying you didn't see what happened?" My brows meet. "No—of course you didn't. You couldn't watch me when you were in the Air-Wing, because Finn might have learned the truth. Isn't that right?"

For the briefest instant, he looks vulnerable, as if he isn't entirely sure how to answer the question.

But as quickly as the expression came, his face sets in a look of arrogance and he simply says, "I see everything, Ashen. I *know* everything. I don't need to watch you at every moment to know what you're up to."

"I don't think that's true," I say quietly, a smile slipping its way over my lips. "And you know what? I think the almighty Bishop is *afraid* of what will happen if Finn learns I'm alive. Tell me—why is that, exactly?"

"I am afraid of nothing, Ashen. And in case you're curious, I could strike you down where you stand with ease. You are not so powerful as you think—and I am stronger than any entity you have ever encountered. Do not test me."

I have no doubt that he's right on all fronts, but his arrogance is enough to enrage me.

"So do it," I challenge. "Kill me. Right now."

A look of anger passes over his eyes, but it vanishes almost instantly. "It is in my interests to keep you alive—for various reasons. You see, you are going to help me, as is your Finn. And the most delicious part is that neither of you will have any idea it's happening."

My voice trembles as I ask, "What does that mean?"

"I'd love to tell you you'll find out soon enough, but the truth is, you will be none the wiser when it happens. Don't worry, Ashen. It will be painless. Mostly."

With that, he leaves the cell, shutting and locking the door behind him.

TEST

OVER AN HOUR PASSES before I hear thudding footsteps approach in the corridor outside my cell. After a brief struggle with the lock, a man in a Consortium uniform opens the door and steps inside.

He's young, thin, and looks vaguely apologetic when he says, "I was told to bring you with me. We're…going to see your friend Rystan."

I nod, rising from the cot to join him. Part of me is tempted to steal the weapon at his side, which looks like some sort of club, and knock him out, then escape the Hold. But I have no idea what the Bishop might do to Rys if I don't show up for this rendezvous, and besides, the last thing I want is to prove to Illian that I am the dangerous, unpredictable creature the Bishop claimed I was.

Leaving the cell behind, the guard and I walk down the hall until we come to a Conveyor. He tells me to step inside and I do so, pushing myself into the far corner with my hands behind my back in an attempt to reassure him.

"That's one of those stealth uniforms, isn't it?" the young man asks. "I'm surprised they let you keep it on."

"I guess they didn't have anything else to offer me," I tell him.

He slips his fingers over the Conveyor's control panel, which has been redesigned since I was last in the Arc. I try to decipher what he's doing, to figure out what the new symbols mean, but he's too quick.

"Well," he says, turning to face me, his hand on his club, "I guess I'll just have to hope you don't kill me."

His lips are twitching as he speaks, almost as though he's amused to find himself in a position of power over the dangerous intruder-girl.

If you only knew who I really am, I think, glaring at him. *I could take you down before you took another breath. The only reason I don't is that I'm the real Ashen. I'm your ally, Dreg.*

As I study him, I notice something attached to his chest—a small, silver pin in the shape of a tree.

I recognize it. The symbol they called the "Tree of Life" in the Behemoth—the symbol of the Bishop's worshipers, medical staff, and minions.

"Where did you get that?" I snap, pointing at the pin.

The guard appears frightened for a moment, but the expression quickly passes and instantly, a look of ire flashes over his features.

"Why the hell would I answer your questions?" he asks, taking a step toward me and extracting the club.

"Try it," I snarl quietly, standing my ground. "Just try to hit me. See how well it ends for you."

He freezes mid-stride and backs away, feeling the tension in the air.

Smart man, I think.

"One of them gave it to me," he mutters, pointing to the pin.

"One of who?"

"The Acolytes. The ones who came with the Bishop."

"Acolytes…" I repeat. "You mean followers? I didn't think anyone came with the Bishop."

The guard shrugs, and as I stare at him, I recall the fast-moving planes Rys and I saw as we made our way toward the Arc from Sector One. Were they transporting the Bishop's people? How many are there in the Arc now?

I conceal a shudder at the thought, smile, and ask, "What does the tree mean?"

I know full well what it means. Subservience. Brainwashing.

But I want to hear it from him.

He opens his mouth, looking like he's going to offer up a confident reply. But instead, he pauses as if the answer has suddenly eluded him, shrugs again, and says, "The Bishop is a great man, as the *real* Ashen Spencer would tell you. It's his symbol. It just shows that I support him."

Next to the pin on his chest is a circle crossed by two swords—the symbol of the Consortium. There's something jarring and nauseating about seeing it next to the Bishop's pin. *The bastard is mocking me for the thousandth time.*

"Are others wearing the same pin?" I ask, my voice faltering.

The guard nods. "They brought thousands. They gave them out to anyone who wanted them."

"I see."

So, I think, *as easily as that, he slipped into the Arc and won over its vulnerable population.*

Perhaps Illian, as good a man as he is, isn't strong or

dynamic enough to maintain a leadership role. Maybe it takes a silver-tongued viper like the Bishop or the Duchess to convince so many they're worth following.

It has been the way of the world since the beginning, after all. We humans are addicted to drama, to excitement. We get a rush watching someone who seems larger than the rest of us, whether they be good, evil, or somewhere in between.

And there's no question that the Bishop is larger than life and a force to be reckoned with.

I remain silent for the rest of the Conveyor ride as we rise several more levels, stopping at a large chamber that I recognize. Its walls and floor are sleek, black onyx. The room is empty aside from a long table flanked by a series of chairs.

I shudder as I look around, realizing I'm back to where I was when I first entered the Arc. I'm about to be dissected by people in positions of power, just as I was then.

People who don't see value in me beyond whatever it is I have to offer them.

"One rule," the guard tells me. "Don't speak unless spoken to. Understood?"

I nod. *Fine. I'm not allowed to speak.*

But you didn't say anything about screaming.

Facing me, Illian sits some distance away at the long table. The Bishop, dressed from head to toe in white, stands behind him, and when I walk in, he nods to a guard at the far end of the room, who opens a door that seems to be embedded deep in the wall itself.

The other Ashen strides in, wearing a silver uniform identical to the one I have on.

I know without asking that it, too, is Finn's creation. He gave it to her, thinking she was me. He armed her, thinking he was protecting *me*.

The thought of it makes me feel so sick that I almost double over with pain.

I watch, hopeful, waiting to see if Finn comes through the same door. But the guard seals it shut after my Replik enters.

Of course. There's no way the Bishop would allow Finn near me. It would betray his lie and spoil whatever nefarious plans he has for me.

I stare at the Replik, examining her from head to toe, asking myself what it is about her—about this *monstrosity*—that could possibly have convinced Finn she's the real me?

My question is quickly answered. Her eyes look like mine, and her dark hair matches mine exactly. She chews on her lips in the same nervous way that I do. She even has the same scar on her chin that I acquired as a child—on a day that I remember so well it may as well have taken place last week.

My mind begins to dance a dangerous, flowing dance of confusion and self-inflicted gaslighting. For a moment, I doubt myself. I wonder for the second time—if she has all my memories and I do as well—how do I know which version of Ashen I am?

Snap out of it, I tell myself. *You were on the roof of the Behemoth with the Duchess. She wasn't. Hold onto that memory. It's the only thing that separates you.*

After a few seconds, Rys walks in through another door. His hands are cuffed, his expression one of irritation.

He looks at me and seems to breathe a sigh of relief.

But almost immediately, his eyes lock on the other Ash, and he looks suddenly grief-stricken.

Oh, God.

He doesn't know which is which.

FURY

"Where is Finn?" I call out to my Replik, who turns to stare at me, a quizzical expression in her eyes. "What have you done with him?"

I know the question is a risk. I'm not supposed to speak unless spoken to, after all. But I'm trying to drop a not-so-subtle hint to Rys that I'm the one who was in the Hold... which means I'm the real Ash.

But she's more intelligent than I expected. Which, I suppose, is a foolish thought, given that she and I basically share a brain.

"I was going to ask you the same thing," she snaps back immediately. "I haven't seen him since I watched you leave with him in that Air-Wing."

"You thieving bitch!" I snarl, so angry that my cheeks go instantly fever-hot. "You know perfectly well you're the one who left with him!" I take a long stride toward her, but the moment I move, a guard inserts himself into the space between us.

"Now, now, ladies," the Bishop says in an almost mocking

tone. "There will be no back and forth between you, or your friend Rystan will suffer for it. Do you understand?"

I grit my teeth and scowl. I want to break all the rules and to shout to Rys I flew in the eagle drone with him and Atticus —that alone is proof that I'm the real Ash, after all.

But I can't do it. Not if the Bishop plans to hurt Rys for my insubordination. So I shut my mouth and wait as my insides knot themselves into nervous spasms of pain.

The Bishop turns to Rys and gestures him toward the Replik and me. "Feel free to look closely at both of them. Ask them anything you like. I promise not to interfere—unless they break the rules."

Rys does as he's suggested, but his steps are hesitant, almost timid, as he walks into the space between myself and my twin. He turns first to the Replik, then to me.

"Do you both know who I am?" he asks.

"Rys," we say in unison. I glare at my twin, irked as always by her audacity.

Turning to the Replik, he asks, "Where did we meet?"

My mind assures me she won't know the answer. She wasn't there. She didn't even exist on the day he's asking about.

But then I remember that as far as her mind is concerned, she was there. She lived the experience in just as real a manner as I did.

"On the playground on Bailey Street," she says. "We were playing on the swings. We were four years old at the time." She smiles when she adds, "I remember the striped shirt you had on."

"Do you remember what happened after the swings?" Rys asks.

My Replik lets out a quiet laugh and points to her chin.

"This happened," she says with a roll of her eyes. "We climbed the oak tree at the far end of the park and I fell. Had to get two stitches. I bled everywhere, and my mother was so angry with me."

Once again, I feel like I'm being robbed of my own existence. How dare this girl—this awful creation—speak of my mother, of my experiences? How dare she steal them as if they're physical objects to possess?

Rys turns my way, his face and voice stoic. "What was my favorite toy when I was little?"

"Your red fire truck," I tell him. "It broke when you were eight and you cried for days."

He asks the Replik another question. "What color did we paint my room when we were fourteen?"

"Neon green," she replies with a laugh. "I hated it, and so did you. You repainted it blue after about four days, as I recall."

He nods solemnly then turns and takes a step toward me.

"How did your father die?" he asks.

The question takes me aback.

"What?" I stammer.

"Your father. How did he die?"

I hurl a rage-filled look at the Bishop for putting us through this. Not only Rys and me, but my irritating doppelgänger, too. I may abhor her, but presumably she feels the same emotions I do. The same sense of loss when she thinks about my father and all that he meant to me.

To us.

"The Blight," I say, struggling to keep my voice steady. "The illness he helped create."

"That's right," Rys says softly. "And I'm sorry."

Striding over to my doppelgänger, he asks, "How did your mother die?"

The other Ashen's voice cracks as mine so nearly did. It breaks completely when she begins to recount the tale of my mother's death. A death that may not have occurred if not for Rys's revelation that there was a painting in her bedroom—one that could offer the Directorate a clue to the Consortium's hiding spot.

For a moment, I almost pity the Replik for her sorrow—until I remember the entirety of her emotional payload is stolen from my very soul.

The questions Rys is asking are direct, even cruel.

But I know why he's asking them.

He wants to figure out which of us seems more human. More emotional. He wants to see a deep truth in our eyes as he studies us.

The other Ashen tightens her jaw for a moment, her lip quivering, but seems to steady herself when she says, "It wasn't your fault, Rys. I want you to know that."

Ask me something else, I think. *Something about what happened when you came to get me—when I jumped off that roof. She may not know about it. The Bishop may not have told her.*

But Rys doesn't ask about it. He simply turns to Illian and the Bishop and shakes his head.

"I'm sorry," he says. "I can't tell which is which." He sounds genuinely tormented—which isn't exactly an emotion I associate with Rys.

My stomach rolls over on itself, and my self-control shatters.

"Rys!" I cry out. "Of course you know! Tell them!"

"Let me ask some more questions," he pleads.

"Of course," the Bishop says. "Ask as many as you'd like. Take your time. This is of the utmost importance."

Rys nods his thanks, turns my way, and steps over to me. Lowering his chin and staring me in the eyes, he asks, "Do you know how much I care about you?"

My mouth drops open and I stare at him, trying to figure out what he means by asking this question. How is my response going to offer up further evidence of my true identity?

"You know I do," I tell him.

My eyes go wide and I tighten, puzzled. Is he trying to figure out whether or not I have a heart? What *is* this?

"You know I would do anything to keep you alive."

I nod and whisper, "Rys—you *know* this is me, right?"

He nods so slightly that I'm certain I'm the only one who can see it.

"So what are you doing?" I glance over toward the long table. "Tell Illian. End this madness."

For a few seconds, I'm convinced he's about to do just that. But instead of replying, he ignores me, walks over to the other Ash, and asks at full volume, "If the Bishop commanded it, would you be capable of killing me with the Surge right now?"

She nods, smiling. "I could," she says. "But I won't, of course. You're my friend."

"No. Of course you wouldn't hurt me." Rys backs away, crosses his arms, and throws me a final, unreadable glance.

He turns to Illian then, gesturing to the Replik, and announces, "*This* is Ashen Spencer," he says. "The real one."

"Are you sure?" Illian asks, rising to his feet. From the look on his face, he's far from certain.

"I'm sure," Rys says with a nod.

Letting out a shout, I step forward, but a pair of strong hands grabs my arms and holds me back.

"Don't say a word," the voice commands from behind me.

"Thank you, Rystan," Illian says. He looks over at the Bishop and asks, "What should we do with them?"

"Put them in a cell together," the Bishop replies confidently. "Let them enjoy each other's company for a little. Rystan has an inquisitive and clever mind. Perhaps he would like to find out what makes a Replik tick while he's in custody."

The Bishop knows I'm no Replik, so the suggestion is shocking. Why the hell would he want us together? If he wants to punish us, shouldn't he keep us isolated from one another?

But when I look over at Rys, my blood boiling, it hits me.

My oldest friend has just betrayed me yet again. He's just ensured that Finn and I will remain separated. Finn will end up with the other Ash, and I will most likely die in the Hold.

The Bishop is doing this for sport, hoping we'll murder each other, just as he hoped the Duchess and I would do on the Behemoth's roof.

Unfortunately, he might be right.

I've rarely been as pissed off at anyone as I am at Rys right now. He knew what he was doing. He knew the consequences. And he did it anyhow. But why?

LOST

I TRUDGE ALONG QUIETLY AS the guards drag me back to my cell, throwing Rys in alongside me.

When the door has locked and we find ourselves alone, I turn to face him.

I'm still in my silver uniform. I could pummel him into oblivion if I wanted to.

And the truth is, I sort of want to.

"What the hell, Rys?" I ask, my voice a thinly-veiled snarl. "You knew all along which of us was the Replik."

"Yeah, I knew," he says, pointing to his chin with his index finger. "Because of this."

"This?" I ask, squinting to see what he's gesturing at.

"Your scar," he says. "I hadn't noticed before—but it's gone."

"No, it's not. I saw it when I was looking at her."

"No. I mean it's gone from *your* chin."

I reach up and feel the place where there's been a slight indentation in my flesh for many years now. But I can't feel it. "What the..." I stammer.

"He did it to you at some point. He must have."

My stomach heaves as the realization hits. "It's how he convinced Illian. How he could convince Finn, too, if he needed to," I say. "Finn would look for the scar."

Rys nods. "The Bishop probably makes sure there's one subtle, identifying feature that distinguishes each Replik from its human counterpart."

"But you knew! I don't understand why you didn't tell them the truth," I moan. "I could have gone back to Finn—you could have freed me. Illian would have—"

But Rys is shaking his head. "I'm so sorry, Ash. But no. I couldn't have freed you."

"What do you mean? Illian was counting on you to tell him the truth. Now he thinks I'm nothing more than a weird carbon copy of Ashen Spencer."

Rys holds up a hand. "Just let me speak!" he snaps. "I wanted nothing more than to protect you, Ash. Do you really think I wouldn't free you if I could, let alone free myself?"

I don't have to think about what he's asking. I know he's right. There's no conceivable reason why he'd ensure we both stay locked in the Hold.

"Okay, then. Explain yourself. Please."

He lets out a grim sigh before saying, "The Bishop came to me before they brought me into that room. He told me to 'do the right thing.' I knew what he meant, and I wasn't going to obey him, of course. The guy is a lunatic. But he told me if I didn't, that he would have a Consortium assassin kill you before the day was over."

"Consortium assassin? Is that even a thing?"

"It is now, apparently," Rys says. "Look—I told you I'll do anything to keep you alive. You're my family, Ash. You're all I have in this world, other than my mechanical menagerie of birds. I wasn't willing to let you go. If the Bishop wants to play his game a little longer, that's the price I have to pay for keeping you alive, I guess."

I lean my back against the wall and slowly slip to the ground, the cold stone jarring yet soothing through my back.

"Thank you," I say. "I mean, I knew you wouldn't deliberately betray me, but…" Pressing my face into my hands, I moan, "What are we going to do, Rys?"

He slips over and sits next to me, putting an arm around my shoulders and pulling me close. I yank my chin up and look at him, only to see he's eyeing the cell's corners.

"You think he's watching us," I whisper.

He nods, and under his breath, replies, "I'm sure of it. It's probably why we're in here together, instead of in isolation cells." He leans closer and whispers, "I'm going to find a way to get us out of here. Atticus knows where we are. The guards took my arm wrap away, but I'm still connected to him remotely."

He backs off and says, "I don't know," his voice clear and loud for the sake of anyone who might hear it. "I think we're screwed. We both know you can't escape from the Hold."

I nod. "Yeah. I know that all too well," I say before leaning in and whispering, "How soon…"

He understands my meaning. "Soon," he says under his breath. "But we need to be patient. They'll be watching us closely for a few days."

Days. That's too long. Too much time spent waiting as the other Ashen sinks her claws into Finn and the Bishop manipulates Illian into further submission.

But I don't say it. I have no control over this situation. No hope of forcing Illian to release us. He believes what he believes, and like so many others, he's being controlled by a man who is insanely powerful.

The best I can hope for is that somehow Rys uses his impressive mind—and his impressive army of flyers—to get us out of this mess.

The next few days pass agonizingly slowly.

Rys is unable to connect with Atticus, whether because of the Hold's thick walls or some other force at work. So we bide our time and wait, trying not to simultaneously lose our minds and souls as the minutes tick by.

A guard brings us what looks like cold, gelatinous gruel in the mornings and the evenings. I've always been fed simple food in the Hold, but at least it's usually been relatively decent. Sandwiches. Rice. Stew.

I'm convinced this new twist is some contrivance of the Bishop's. He wants us to feel pathetic, to remain hungry, irritable, tired.

Rys and I each have a wool blanket and a narrow cot, and we arrange the cots to sleep next to each other at night, not so much for companionship as for warmth.

We share a toilet that sits in one of the cell's corners. Rys kindly turns away when I need to use it, and I return the favor. Showers, of course, are an impossibility, and no one lets us out for exercise. I'm convinced part of the Bishop's plan is to torture us into despising one another, and I find myself growing grumpy with Rys on occasion, mostly out of a lack of nourishment and sleep.

We speak often, but only about topics that won't incriminate us. Our childhoods, our homes, our parents. Kel. We seldom mention Finn, except in whispered conversations.

"At least they're not bringing us to the Arenum to make a spectacle of our deaths," I say at one point with a snicker. "I guess they'll just let us slowly starve to death. Or kill each other."

"Or die of body odor," Rys says with a lift of his arm to sniff his pit, which induces a violent gag on his part.

"If we ever get to shower again, it'll probably be the best feeling in the history of the world," I reply, grateful to be able to laugh.

Three full nights pass before we hear a scratching sound on the fourth night. It sounds at first like a rodent clawing at the wall, and my mind travels back to the first time I was put in the Hold, when I met my neighbor, a mysterious man who ended up helping me.

The man turned out to be an old acquaintance of my father's—and I'm not sure I can bring myself to hope for such good fortune this time around.

"What is that?" I whisper, grabbing Rys by the arm.

He shushes me, waits a few seconds, then puts his hand over my own. He doesn't speak, which only causes me to tighten more.

"Rys?" I say under my breath.

Turning to him, I see the whites of his eyes glowing bright. I'm not used to seeing Rys looking panicked, and when he does, it's with good reason.

He shakes his head and says, "I don't know. But I have a bad feeling..."

It's enough to prompt me to push myself to my feet and press my back to the wall.

Maybe it's just someone coming to feed us. Or speak to us. Maybe it's time for that coveted shower at long last.

But when the door opens and I see the Bishop's face, I know nothing good will come of this moment.

Neither of us speaks as two men in Consortium gear enter the cell, following the Bishop, who gestures toward us with his hand.

I brace myself, waiting to be grabbed. I'll fight if I need to. I'm still wearing Finn's uniform. Maybe it will give me enough strength to overpower the men, to fight them off long enough for Rys to escape.

But the men don't stride over to us. Instead, they simply hold their right hands out before them, clenched into fists. At the Bishop's command, they open their hands and two small insects that look like wasps buzz through the air toward Rys and me.

The last thing I remember is calling Rys's name and reaching for him, then hearing his voice say, "It'll be okay, Ash. It'll be okay."

14

DREAMS

I DREAM INCESSANTLY NOW. Vivid images, swimming through my mind. Of water—the ocean, lapping at my feet. Of mountains, cool breezes, the wind tangling my hair into knots. I dream of my brother Kel, of Finn's smile.

Of a home somewhere far from here, looking out at the vast expanse of an ocean.

The dreams are pleasant, like lilting, soft music. Visual lullabies that calm me and keep my mind away from torment. Each time I venture toward a recollection of the Bishop or the Directorate—each time I contemplate the unending war we're fighting—I'm pulled away from those thoughts into something like a mental panacea.

Occasionally, it strikes me that I've been asleep for a long time, that my dreams have gone on for an eternity, stringing one into the next like phrases of beautiful music.

But I'm unbothered by the thought. *It's all fine,* I tell myself. Just like Rys said. *It'll be okay.*

When I hear his voice calling my name, I'm convinced it's part of yet another dream.

"Ash. Ash!"

I'm drowning suddenly, inhaling liquid into my lungs. I feel a wave wash over me, feel my arms flailing, my hands seeking something to hold onto.

My vision is blurry as if I'm under water, and as much as I try to focus on something, I can't at first. All I see is bright light all around me.

"Ash. Breathe."

Rys's voice comes again, and this time his hands are holding my wrists. I pull them away to wipe my eyes, then I see his face. His hair is plastered to his forehead, soaking wet. He's shirtless, wearing only a pair of boxer shorts that seem glued to his thighs.

I pull my chin down to see that I, too, am verging on naked. But more shocking than that, I'm half-curled up in a puddle of some kind of gelatinous liquid, my legs dangling above a white floor.

I try to speak, but I can only make a sort of gurgling sound until Rys shakes his head. "I said breathe," he repeats, and I inhale deeply, the liquid burning my chest before I exhale and manage to clear it somewhat.

"Where..." I finally sputter.

"They had us in suspension, floating in what used to be Sensory Deprivation Tanks," Rys replies. The strangest words I've ever heard, and yet, horrifyingly, they make perfect sense to me.

"Used to be?" I reply, turning to look around.

"Yup," Rys says bitterly. "They were used by the Wealthies when the Directorate was in charge around here. For relaxation and decompressing. But I guess with this place full of former Dregs who have never heard of sensory deprivation, let alone the idea of relaxing, the Bishop convinced Illian to let him repurpose them."

"Do you think Illian has any idea that we were imprisoned in them?"

I look down at the tank I just stepped out of. It looks like a bath tub, except for the fact that it has a clear, hinged lid that gives it the air of a transparent coffin. Peering around the chamber, I see many more, lined up like hospital beds, each containing a floating, unconscious resident of the Arc.

In the Behemoth, there was an enormous silo filled with the grotesque containment systems, egg-like and clear, each containing a person curled up in fetal position.

Here, there are only a few hundred, which seems almost like a blessing—and yet, it's a horror.

Only a few hundred stolen lives.

"I honestly don't know," Rys replies, his tone laced with a sort of melancholy. I know without asking that he's as reluctant as I am to believe Illian would let anyone do such a thing to either of us.

Then again, he thinks I'm a creation of the Bishop's, and that Rys is a traitor.

"How did you—I mean we—get out?" I ask.

Rys looks back over his shoulder, and I follow his gaze. In a high corner of the room, Atticus appears, turning his head around to stare into my eyes. "It took him a while to find us, then some time to access this place," Rys tells me. "I'm sorry. I didn't know…"

"Know?"

Rys bows his head, shaking it slowly. "I didn't know this would happen."

"How long have we been trapped?" I ask nervously.

Rys glances at Atticus, who replies for him. "Five months, seventeen days and three hours, approximately," he replies.

I stare at him, dumbfounded. If Rys had said those words, I'd insist he was joking. Five months? Five months of my life, spent curled up helplessly, while the world continued its course? While Finn continued to live, with a false version of me by his side?

I'm…almost eighteen, if that's the case.

"I know," Rys says. "Bit of a shock."

"Bit?" I snap. "This is a disaster! Who knows what's happened while we were—what? Asleep? Comatose?"

"Yeah, I know. Look—if we're going to figure that out, we need to get out of here, Ash. There's no doubt in my mind the Bishop's got an eye on this space, and if he sees that we've gotten out…"

I glance around before saying, "What about all of them?" as I gesture to the other pods. "They're prisoners in here."

"We can't free them, not right now. Atticus only brought enough adrenaline for two of us."

I look down to see that there are two needles on the ground. Rys must have used one to wake me from my long slumber. No wonder I shot awake with such a strange jolt.

"Let's get out of here, then we'll work out what to do next. But first, we need to get ourselves somewhere safe."

I nod, reluctant to leave but fully aware that if we stay here a minute longer, we will probably find ourselves face to face with the Bishop once more.

15

A NEW HOME

AGAINST THE GRIM chamber's far wall is a set of hooks, and on each hook is a white lab coat with the Consortium's crest on its left breast pocket.

Rys and I each grab one and put them on, all too aware of what a poor job they will do to disguise us. Still, we'll be a little less conspicuous in them than we would in our soggy undergarments.

When Rys tries to open the door, it refuses to budge.

"Atticus!" he calls. "Quickly, now."

The owl swoops down and reaches for a silver panel on the wall. The small hatch in his belly opens and a sort of metal appendage emerges, its rounded end slipping over the panel's surface like a fingertip. After a few seconds, the door forces itself open.

We rush out into the corridor with Atticus behind us and make a mad dash for the nearest Conveyor.

"I'm surprised there are no guards," I say breathlessly as we run, my legs feeling like limp spaghetti noodles beneath me, barely able to support my weight.

"No point in employing guards to look after comatose humans," Rys says bitterly. "The only reason we managed to get out is my wonder-bird here."

"True."

When we're on the Conveyor, Atticus issues a silent command and we begin moving almost instantly.

"Where are we going?" I ask, but Rys shakes his head and pretends to zip his lips shut.

We emerge a few minutes later in a familiar area full of crowds of happy-looking pedestrians and teeming with scents from all over the world.

The Escapa Level. The holiday zone where the Arc's residents come to escape their lives to vacation in what look impressively similar to various tourist hotspots from around the globe. I understand instantly why Rys wanted us to come here.

It's the easiest place to hide in plain sight.

It's also the level where we're most likely to swipe clothing and food without anyone noticing.

"The Bishop will find out before long that we've escaped," Rys says, leaning in toward me as I walk. "But we probably have a few minutes, at least. After five months it's unlikely he's watching us twenty-four hours a day."

With a quick release of breath, I tell myself he's right. If it's been that long, the Bishop's focus has probably long since shifted. Hell, maybe he's even gone back to New York City by now.

I look over my shoulder, searching for Atticus, who has gone into stealth mode. "Where are we going to go?" I ask in a hiss.

"I have a place in mind," Rys replies. "Trust me, okay?"

I nod, glancing around, relieved to see that the place at

least looks relatively normal. People are milling about just as they always did, looking blissful and calm.

Good to know not everyone inside the Arc has been relegated to coma pods.

My mind moves quickly to Finn. To what he's been doing for the last several months—months he's spent with the *other* Ashen.

A searing jolt of envy hits me then, mixed with potent anger. I have been violated and robbed of my time with Finn.

But the violation committed against him might be even more egregious. He has been led to believe the woman by his side is me, when she's anything but. She is nothing but a shadow of who I am. A carbon copy, programmed to please the Bishop, to fool Finn, to lie and to cheat.

"We'll find your guy as soon as we can," Rys tells me, reading my body language as we walk. "For now, though, just follow my lead. There's no way in hell I'm letting us end up back in the Hold."

He reaches out as we walk by a stand displaying cotton clothing and grabs a shirt from a hanger, shoving it under his lab coat.

I follow suit, taking hold of a long yellow tunic and swiping it as the shopkeeper turns their attention to a customer.

We continue to steal clothing until each of us is in possession of one full outfit, then slip behind one of the booths to pull some of the garments on.

"Atticus is monitoring for patrolling drones," Rys whispers. "But we need to be quick anyhow."

Within thirty seconds, we each look entirely different. All but our faces and hair.

"Any drone will recognize us immediately," I warn Rys,

who says, "I know. Which is why we need to proceed to phase two."

I'm tempted to ask about phase two, but choose instead to keep my mouth shut. All I want is to get out of here, to hide from inquisitive eyes and to start working out a plan to get to Finn.

Rys and I make our way toward another Conveyor—this one next to a large hotel. Warily, we look around, ensuring that no one is following us as we climb on board the Conveyor.

When we're inside, I breathe a sigh of relief before saying, "It's weird. Everything seems so normal."

The words have barely left my mouth when a loud alarm starts sounding at regular intervals. The Conveyor's walls flash blood-red and I instinctively huddle next to Rys, who puts an arm around me. All of a sudden, I feel weak, as if my legs are going to give way beneath me, and for the first time it hits me that I haven't used my muscles in months.

"It's all right," he says softly. "I expected this."

"They know where we are, don't they?" I ask.

He shakes his head. "I don't think so. This is an Arc-wide alarm. It's a call for help."

As if to confirm what he's saying, Illian's voice erupts over the central speakers of the Arc as we shoot downwards.

"Two prisoners have escaped," he says. "Please report any suspicious activity to the Consortium. You will be rewarded for it."

I pull away from Rys, confused. "He didn't say who we are," I say. "He didn't even describe us."

"No, he didn't. I wonder..."

"Wonder what?"

"If they're still somehow keeping you a secret from Finn. I wonder if there's a chance he doesn't know about you."

I suppose it's possible. But I despise the thought.

We continue to descend until the Conveyor finally halts and lets us out at Level Five.

Atticus and I follow Rys into a long corridor until we come to a white door at its end. Judging by the numbers on each door, they lead into various residences belonging to the Arc's denizens.

"I can only hope this place is still unoccupied," Rys tells me. "To be honest, it's sort of our only hope right now."

"Whose residence is it?"

Rys takes a deep breath then, instead of answering my question, says, "You still trust me, right?"

I nod. "Of course. You're about the only person on earth I trust right now. Well, you and Kel. And Finn."

Except I'm not even sure I can trust Finn anymore.

I think of Kel then, and wonder where my little brother even is. What has he been doing for the last several months? Has the Bishop gotten his hand—or his mind—on my only sibling?

If he has, I'll kill him so slowly he'll beg for his life to end.

When we step through the door into the residence, I look around, stunned. We're on one of the Arc's lowest floors, which would usually be an indicator of modesty. The lowest levels have always been occupied by those known as "Serfs." The working class, those who used to serve the Aristocrats.

But this place is enormous, with high ceilings and a vast assortment of elegant, expensive-looking furniture. It almost reminds me of the Davenports' former residence.

Rys shuts the door behind us and takes me by the shoulders as if to pull me out of my current mental fog.

"The alarm is still sounding out there," he says, "which means we need to lay low for a while."

"What is this place? Whose is it?" I ask, but Rys puts a finger to his lips as he skulks over to a panel on the wall. After inputting a series of codes, the wall seems to move...*only it's not the wall that's actually moving.*

I realize as I'm staring that small creatures have begun to emerge from its surface, slipping out of the plaster and drywall. Rodents the size of mice. Sparrows, pushing their way out of tiny holes and flapping around. Other creatures that look alarmingly like insects, rapidly making their way across the floor.

At first I look around for the nearest chair to leap onto, thinking we're at the center of a massive infestation. But I quickly realize the creatures aren't actually alive—they're all silver, all made of the same sort of metal as Atticus.

"These are all yours?" I stammer, leaning down to pick up what looks like a field mouse.

"They are," Rys says with a relieved breath. "I wanted to make sure they hadn't been discovered. Thing is, this residence wasn't mine originally, but I snatched it up in secret after the Consortium took over. It belonged to a man who used to abuse Dregs—you might remember him. His name was Piotr."

"Piotr!" I say, nearly dropping the mouse I'm still holding.

Piotr was the cruel Directorate member who trained me and my fellow seventeen-year-old classmates. A man who put us all through our paces when we first came to the Arc.

A man who forced my classmates to kill a boy called Luke as I watched, too stunned and too weak to stop them.

For what he did to us all, I will never forgive him.

Rys nods. "He's in the Hold, or possibly worse, by now.

Either way, I can promise you he won't be showing up here anytime soon—unless the Bishop convinces our friend Illian to release him."

"I wouldn't put it past him. But here's hoping it won't come to that." Looking around, I add, "What are we going to do, Rys? We're as trapped here as we were in our Sensory Deprivation Tanks."

"Not quite," he tells me. "Here, I have control over a mechanical army." Rys smiles mysteriously as he says the words and gestures to the walls, where creatures are still making their way around as if waking from a long hibernation.

I cross my arms. "What exactly are you planning?"

"I'm not entirely sure yet," he confesses. "But for now, let's sit tight and get our bearings. We need to find Finn and Kel, and figure out if there's any hope of getting to them without getting ourselves killed. We need a way to access them. A gathering, something public, ideally."

I'm about to reply when a voice begins speaking from the room next door to the kitchen where we're standing. I jump, terrified.

"We're not alone," I whisper.

"It's a broadcast," Rys says. "That's…"

"The Bishop's voice," I conclude, dashing into the living room to see what our enemy has to say. It can't possibly be a coincidence that only a few minutes after we managed to escape our captivity, the bastard is issuing a public address.

A screen flares to life in the center of the room, the Bishop's face larger than life and as annoyingly handsome as ever, his eyes narrowed in a look of determined rage.

Worst of all, he seems to be staring right into my eyes.

He can't see me, I tell myself. *He doesn't know I'm here. Rys would tell me if there was any risk.*

"Citizens of the Arc," the Bishop says, "I have a very important announcement to make. I apologize for its timing, directly on the heels of the alarm a few moments ago."

"Please believe me," the Bishop continues, "when I say I bring good tidings, and that we in the Arc have cause for celebration."

Something in his eyes, in his tone, fills me with an all too familiar dread. Whatever he has to say, it can't possibly be good. This man is cold-blooded and psychotic.

I shoot Rys a look. "I thought this would be about the alarm," I tell him. "About us."

Rys shrugs. "Me too."

"Why is the Bishop making this announcement, anyhow?" I ask. "And not Illian?"

The dread heightens as it hits me. Is the Bishop running this place now? Has he become some kind of horrid dictator here, just as he was in New York?

"There's going to be a wedding," he says gleefully, clapping his hands together in front of his chest.

My breath traps itself in my throat, and I freeze.

NEWS

By now, the sound of blaring alarms has faded to grim silence, but two syllables echo inside my mind like a hideous portent.

Wedding.

Are Illian and Kurt getting married?

Or is the Bishop about to wed the Replik version of his former girlfriend, Naeva? I wouldn't put it past him. The man loves a spectacle, after all—and he certainly enjoys being the center of attention.

But my questions are answered with a nauseating death blow when two faces materialize on the screen with the subtitle:

The Happy Bride and Groom To Be

When I see the faces, I sink to my knees in the middle of the living room.

One belongs to Finn.

The other…is mine.

Only it's not mine at all.

It's my Replik, complete with her chin scar. Correction: *my* chin scar. The one that she stole from me, just as she stole everything else.

"What the hell?" Rys asks, and it's only then that I realize he's come up next to me, crouching down to put a protective arm around my shoulders.

"The Bishop is doing this on purpose," I reply. "He knows we escaped, and he's doing this to torture me or to draw me out. It's the only explanation."

"Come on, Ash. It's pretty sudden, don't you think? We've only been conscious for an hour or so. Do you really think the Bishop could have orchestrated an engagement in the last few minutes?"

I inhale a strangled breath, my body tightening with the wretched truth behind what Rys is asking. He's right; there's no way Finn would agree to such an impulsive act.

This *must* have been discussed before today.

It just seems so…strange.

"Fine. Maybe the Bishop has had this up his sleeve for some time," I reply miserably. "And he's only revealing it now as a punishment for me. Either that, or…"

"Or what?"

"Or Finn has been replaced with a Replik."

Rys shoots me a dubious look.

"Ashen Spencer is a heroine for our times," the Bishop's voice announces jovially, interrupting our speculation. "And it is so very fitting that the Crimson Dreg will finally marry the young man of her dreams—the new Duke of Davenport."

I nearly choke on the air I'm breathing.

"*Duke?*" I sputter. "Finn has been named Duke? Are we living in some upside-down alternate universe? Finn would hate that title. He hates everything about the Aristocracy, about the insinuation of social ranking."

"Atticus!" Rys calls, and the owl immediately comes flapping in from the next room, landing with his talons hooking into the back of the nearby couch. "Explain this to us, please. How did Finn become a Duke?"

Atticus closes his bright eyes for a moment, seeming to process something before reopening them and staring first at Rys, then me.

"During the time you two spent incarcerated," he says in his slightly robotic voice, "The Arc was divided into an official hierarchy. It was the Bishop's idea, though Illian approved it and offered the Consortium's blessing. There were some protests from the residents of the Arc, but they were quickly shut down by Acolytes bearing the Tree symbol."

"Acolytes?" I ask. "The Bishop's followers? Are there a lot of them now?"

"Thousands," Atticus replies matter-of-factly. "Their numbers have grown over the months. They follow the Bishop, hang on his every word, do his bidding."

"Of course they do," I reply with a roll of my eyes. "The Bishop is a born cult leader."

"The Serfs," Atticus continues, "those who toil on the lower levels—have been relegated to menial tasks, just as they were in the days before the Consortium. Only those who serve the Bishop closely have been granted titles. Finn Davenport is one such person. Kurt and Illian, too, were given titles."

"What are they?"

"Kings," Atticus says. "They were named the two Kings of the Arc."

"Kings," I repeat, glancing at Rys, my brow sweating, heart

pounding. "It's happening all over again. Everything we fought against has reared its head."

He shakes his head. "No way. You know Finn can't possibly enjoy being called Duke. Not after all the craziness with his parents. Besides, it would mean his new wife would become the *Duchess*."

Oh, my God.

He's right.

The thought is enough to make me heave.

"We have to stop this wedding from taking place," I say. "There's no way he can marry her." Turning to Atticus, I ask, "Where will it be? And when?"

"In the Royal Grounds," he replies. "In a week's time, according to the Arc's Notification Center."

"A week," I repeat, turning to Rys. "We need to get to Finn. Now."

"Ash, hold your horses," Rys replies. "You know as well as I do that we can't just show up uninvited. The Bishop will be looking for you. You said it yourself—he *wants* to find you, and this whole spectacle is most likely a means to get you to show yourself."

"There has to be a way," I say, pacing the room. "Damn it. I'd give anything to have my silver uniform back. This would be a great time for stealth."

Rys goes silent for a moment, scratching his thick head of hair, then says, "There may be a way. It's risky, but it could work. Atticus and I will need a few hours to get the pieces in place. Just...give me a little time, okay?"

I nod, desperate enough not to ask any more questions. The only thing I care about in this moment is finding a way to tell Finn the girl he's marrying is a fraud.

I pace the residence at least five-hundred times while Rys locks himself in one of the bedrooms with Atticus, presumably to put a plan in motion. It's all I can do not to chew my nails until they bleed, and I have to intertwine my fingers on top of my head to resist the urge.

Finally, Rys emerges, rubbing his hands together.

"So tell me," I say. "What's your plan?"

He steps over to a long white cabinet and opens one of its doors. Inside is a series of small metal boxes, and Rys picks one up and hands it to me.

"Open it," he says.

It looks a little like a jewelry box, and I wonder for a moment if I'm about to find a necklace or something equally useless inside. As pretty as jewels are, they would do nothing to improve my current mood.

I crack the box open, pulling its lid up on its hinges to see what looks like a large insect inside. As I stare, its wings begin to flap, and I slam the box shut in horror.

"What…is that thing?" I ask, feeling the vibrations of the box between my fingers.

"A Cicada drone," he says. "Larger than a micro-drone, smaller than my birds."

"What does it do?"

"Well, for one thing, it flies," Rys laughs. "But I think the more pertinent question is 'how will it help us get to Finn?' And for that, I have an answer."

"You're telling me we can use this thing to get him a message?"

Rys grimaces. "In an ideal world, yes. But we both know the Bishop will be watching Finn like a hawk, expecting you and me to make a move. So instead of communicating directly, we're going to start with simple surveillance."

I trust Finn. I love him deeply.

But I have no idea what has happened in the last several months. No idea if he has turned to the Bishop's side entirely and embraced the other version of me.

All I know is that every moment he spends with the other Ashen is another moment when he slips farther away from me. A moment of manipulation, of gaslighting.

I know Finn. He's loyal. He's trusting—at least, he used to be.

If the Replik has spent the last several months spouting pro-Bishop propaganda, Finn may just be too blinded by his loyalty to see the truth.

"I'm all ears," I tell Rys, impatient to hear his plan.

"We can't speak directly to Finn. Not yet," he says. "It's too risky. The Bishop could be monitoring him through the same kind of neuro-tech he used on you—seeing what he sees, hearing what he hears. But according to Atticus, Finn is still working daily in his lab, and we can access him there. If I put the Cicada into stealth mode, he'll be able to follow Finn, too. We can watch him, see where he's living."

"I don't see how that will help," I say, nauseated by the idea of laying my eyes on Finn while he's with...*her*. "We need to talk to him. Tell him what's going on. It's not right to let him keep living like this. He needs to know the whole truth, and now."

Rys seems taken aback for a second, but he nods and says, "I'll try and think of a way to get him a message, then. But we won't be able to speak to him, even if we want to. The Cicada doesn't have that capability. The best I can do is deliver a coded message of some kind."

I agree that this seems like the best course of action, and Rys and I get to work.

He paints the Cicada with the same silver compound he used on Atticus to give him the ability to shift into stealth mode and tells me we need to give it an hour to dry.

An hour that feels like an eternity.

I wander around the residence, examining everything as I try to decipher what belonged to Piotr and what belongs to Rys.

It's not difficult.

There are glass-doored cabinets filled with weaponry from machine guns to knives to poison-filled vials. All are locked, but I have no doubt that Rys could easily find his way inside them.

Rys's possessions are more elegant than guns and blades. He has stashed a massive arsenal of creatures in this place, concealed in every nook and cranny. Inanimate birds, waiting to be brought to life, perched on shelves, in drawers, on the sills of the faux-windows lining the living room wall.

There are also outfits in a closet in the bedroom—Directorate uniforms, some large enough to fit Piotr, but others that I'm sure once belonged to Rys. Consortium uniforms, too.

I find myself wishing we had access to holo-veils for us both. If we dressed in Consortium gear and found our way to the upper floors, maybe we could get to Illian, to Kurt.

To Finn.

But it doesn't matter. The fact is, all we have are our faces, conspicuous as they are. No doubt Rys has publicly been deemed a traitor by now, and I have no real hope of convincing anyone in power that I'm the real Ashen.

My best hope lies with Finn.

When an hour has finally passed, I return to Rys, who is prepping the Cicada for its journey through a series of ducts and vents.

"I've given the little guy his instructions," Rys tells me. "We'll get him through the vents and do some Finn-watching."

Dread consumes me at the thought of spying on Finn. Not because I don't want to see him—I'm desperate, in fact. But because I need to find out the truth.

Maybe he's happy. Maybe he truly believes he's living his best possible life right now, and me walking back into it would only complicate things.

Maybe my focus should be on finding Kel, on freeing those the Bishop has taken prisoner.

On letting Finn go.

"Fine," I finally say. "Let's figure out what the hell is going on."

I watch intently as Rys brings the small creature over to a vent and pulls it away from the wall to let the insect inside.

"Come on," Rys tells me, taking me by the hand and dragging me to a small, dark office off the living room. It's a room I haven't seen before, and the second we enter, I feel both claustrophobic and vaguely terrified.

The room is full of screens—some holographic, others solid tech. I can only guess Piotr used to use them to watch Dregs. No doubt it was part of the Directorate's strategy for deciding which of us to murder.

Right now, at least, only one screen is turned on, and the image I see isn't a Dreg or any human. It's darkness, shifting slightly every few seconds. I can hear a faint, echoing buzz as I watch and realize what I'm seeing is the air duct from the Cicada's point of view.

It's several minutes before the Cicada starts making his way in an upward trajectory through mile after mile of the Arc's duct systems until he finally veers off and levels out.

My breath tightens when after a time, a flash of light blinds me briefly, and I realize the Cicada is approaching the end of his journey.

The robotic insect comes in for a landing, easing his way toward the vent casing covering the shaft.

I gasp when I see a person at work somewhere below him —a tall, dark-haired young man, bent over a table covered in what look like high-tech microscopes, computers, petri dishes and the like.

"Finn," I breathe, reaching for Rys as if to steady myself.

"Do you think it's really him?" Rys asks, his voice soft. "There's no chance we're looking at a Replik?"

I nod. Without even looking into his eyes, I know.

"That's the real Finn. Without a shadow of a doubt."

FINN

Finn is alone in the lab, which doesn't entirely surprise me.

He's always been secretive about his work, and now that he's experimenting on the Bishop's behalf, I'm sure he's been ordered once again to keep all his research from the eyes of others.

I can't help but wonder what he's working on. How much does he know? Surely by now, he's aware of the Replik program.

Is it even remotely possible the Bishop has kept it from him all this time?

Does he know about the people being held in Sensory Deprivation Tanks here in the Arc?

No. He can't. If he did, he would have put a stop to it...or died trying.

I want to reach out, to touch his image. To try and pass my emotions through space and find a way to reach into his mind. But I know it's impossible.

I watch as the Cicada pushes himself through the narrow slats in the vent and flies down toward Finn.

"You're sure the Cicada is cloaked?" I ask Rys, who nods.

"Undetectable and absolutely silent."

"So, what do we do now?"

"We watch."

I shut my mouth and narrow my eyes as the artificial insect lands on the table to Finn's left. I can see more clearly now. Finn is staring at a sample of some sort, his gaze intent. But he looks tired and distracted, possibly even a little agitated. As I watch, he stops what he's doing, puts his face in his hands, and lets out a loud groan.

When he pulls his hands from his face, he says, "How the hell am I going to pull this off?"

"Is he speaking to us?" I whisper as if afraid he'll hear me. "Does he know we're watching him?"

"No," Rys says, but he looks as puzzled as I feel. "I mean, there's no way he could know."

I want to answer Finn's questions; I even open my mouth to speak. But Finn turns away to pull another sample close, examining it intently.

It's like the words we heard were nothing but an after-shock, a reaction to a thought meandering its way through his mind.

We watch him work in silence for several minutes until finally, he turns out the lights and leaves the lab. The Cicada stays with him, following him out and onto the nearest Conveyor.

When the doors slide shut, another of the Bishop's broad-casts begins. A screen flares to life in front of Finn, who pulls his eyes to the perfectly sculpted face before him, an indecipherable half-smile on his lips.

Once again, the Bishop begins to speak about the upcoming wedding as if it's the greatest event in the history of the world. I realize after a moment it's the same broadcast we saw earlier.

"Can you focus the Cicada on Finn's face?" I ask, and Rys quickly obliges, flying the hidden creature almost close enough to count the hairs on Finn's head.

I watch his eyes, his lips. He's still smiling, and as the Cicada closes in, he says, "I can't wait to marry you, Ash."

The words are bittersweet and my heart aches as I hear them.

I would give anyone to be the one marrying you, Finn. But...do you really think the person you're marrying is me?

Rys puts a comforting hand on my shoulder as if he can sense my sadness, and we watch in silence as Finn heads to Level Seventy-Eight and down a hallway to a dingy-looking door.

With the Cicada following closely, he opens it to reveal a small, sparsely decorated apartment. Inside, there's little more than a couch, a chair, a small coffee table, and as the Cicada flits around the space, I spot a few items in the bedroom...including a single bed.

"It looks like a bachelor pad," Rys says. "The Duke of Davenport isn't exactly living in the lap of luxury, is he?"

"I'm confused. I assumed he lived with *her*. I thought..."

"Guess not," Rys shrugs.

Finn seats himself at the kitchen counter with a bowl of reheated soup and digs in, looking weary.

When a knock sounds at the residence's door a few minutes later, he gets up to face it, running a hand through his thick, dark hair.

"Come in," I hear him say as the Cicada swoops ahead of him to show us the door, which flies open. A second later, the

Bishop enters the residence with an elegantly dressed woman just behind him.

"Naeva?" I say quietly.

"Is that..." Rys begins to ask.

I nod. "I met her in New York—she was spying on him for our side. Everyone referred to her as his lover. But when he learned the truth about her, he disposed of her and replaced her with a Replik. I'm surprised he brought her here. She seemed like a liability."

"How do you mean?"

I shrug. "It was like...like her software wasn't quite right, if that makes sense. She didn't behave like a human should."

"The one we're looking at could be a second or third generation model," Rys says. "Keep an eye on her."

"Hello, Finn," the Bishop says, striding into the residence as if he owns it. "I'm so sorry to intrude."

"Not at all," Finn replies with a smile that feels more effusive than it should. "I'm very pleased to see you both."

"We came to see how you're feeling about the upcoming wedding. As you can imagine, we're both extremely pleased for you."

"Over the moon," the Naeva lookalike says. "We're just so happy for you and Ashen both."

I tighten as I watch and listen to the Replik. Rys could be right—she does seem more sophisticated than the one I knew in New York. More put-together, more...human.

I watch Finn's face intently, waiting for his reaction. Is he as excited about his coming wedding as his guests? "Thank you so much," he says. "Needless to say, I'm euphoric. So is Ash."

"Glad to hear it," the Bishop replies. "But I must say, I'm

surprised to find you still living in this wretched studio apartment, instead of by your fiancée's side."

I'm convinced for a moment that I feel a tension building between the two men. But Finn casts the Bishop a glowing smile and says, "Ash and I made an agreement a while back. No sleeping in the same bed until we're married. So for a few more nights, I'm staying here, and Ash is staying in the large residence with Kyra and the boys."

I shudder to think Kel and Merit are living with the Replik —but I suppose I'm grateful to know my old friend is close at hand in case anything happens.

"I'm sure Ashen loves that," Naeva says, clapping her hands together.

"She does. They all do."

"I find that a little hard to believe," I say under my breath, but I go silent in an attempt to listen.

"As for the guest list for the wedding," the Bishop says. "Have you given it any further thought?"

Finn nods. "Ash and I have agreed that we both want a large wedding. And your Followers, of course. Your Acolytes are loyal to our cause, and the wedding wouldn't be complete without them."

"He said 'our cause,'" I say, turning to Rys. "What do you think he means?"

Rys shakes his head. "I can't tell. But judging from his demeanor, I'd say Finn knows just about everything. Either he's fully on board, or the Bishop has some hold over him— some way to control him. I just don't know which it is yet."

"Well," the Bishop says, "we can't quite accommodate the entire Consortium, but we'll do our best. My followers are working as we speak to secure the Royal Grounds for the big event. You two will make a handsome couple, to be sure, and I know Ashen is overcome with bliss. She has dreamed of the coming ceremony for some time."

Finn doesn't react immediately, but a sort of delayed grin finds its way to his lips after a few seconds. "So have I," he finally says. "Marrying Ash is the greatest honor I can imagine."

The Bishop steps forward and lays his hands on Finn's shoulders. I recoil inadvertently as I observe the gesture. I'm all too familiar with the narcotic effect of his touch, a sort of mind-bending shot of pleasure and forced supplication at once.

"Thank you," Finn says, his smile growing with a squeeze of the Bishop's fingers. "It means a great deal to me—to *both* of us—to have your blessing and support."

"It means a great deal to me to be included in your ceremony," the Bishop replies, looking to Naeva. "To both of us."

"He's lying," I say slowly.

"The Bishop?" Rys replies. "Of course he is. I'm sure everything out of that bastard's mouth is a lie."

"No. I mean Finn. He's not happy about this wedding—he's dreading it, even. He would never want a big wedding with tons of people he doesn't know. It's not in his nature. For that matter, it's not in mine. Honestly, I'm kind of surprised the Replik would say *she* wants it."

"I suspect the only person who really wants it is the Bishop," Rys says. "He wants as many eyes on the event as possible. It's his great political tool to distract from all the crimes he's committing in the background."

I watch as Finn forces himself once again to look into the enemy's eyes. There's something wily in his stare—something knowing, almost mischievous, and I wonder if the Bishop can see it, too.

I hope, for Finn's sake, that he can't.

"Like I said, I'm looking forward to the big day," Finn says. "But I'm also a little apprehensive. This is a huge deal—I want to make sure I get everything right."

"It's natural to be nervous," the Bishop assures him. "It's a big commitment that you're making. But you understand why such a union is necessary, yes? Sometimes we must make sacrifices for the greater good."

"Marrying Ash," Finn says, hesitating before completing the sentence, "is no sacrifice. I love her. She's my soul mate. She's everything to me."

Suddenly, my heart sinks.

I'm confused.

Right now, Finn doesn't appear to be lying. In fact, he appears to be oozing with an almost overwhelming sincerity. His voice is filled with affection, with the sort of warmth I've been craving since the last moments he and I spent together in New York.

My heart falters in my chest as I swallow the ugly realization that maybe he really *does* believe the Replik is me.

"That said..." Finn adds, "I understand that our wedding— our bonding—is necessary to give the Arc's residents hope for a better future. Ash and I have fought long and hard to bring Dregs and Wealthies together, to equalize them in the eyes of society. Our marriage is symbolic. We both understand that, and we understand the importance of this event."

"Yes. You will bring the Arc's residents hope...and so much more," the Bishop says, stalking around the small apartment, slipping his fingers over the various surfaces as he moves through the space like a cat quietly stalking a mouse. Naeva remains in one place, her smile plastered to her face as if she might suffer a massive electric shock if she lets it fade for a single second.

"In the olden days," the Bishop continues, "as I'm sure you know, separate kingdoms were frequently united through marriage. A princess of one region wed to the prince of another, all to strengthen political bonds and unite noble families. You, a high Aristocrat, are marrying a Dreg. You and Ashen are the ultimate proof that our world has changed for the better. Proof that the old animosities have faded to nothing, and that no one need fear the new Order."

I shift from one foot to the other, suddenly agitated.

There is no new Order. The old animosities are alive and well, you jackass. The only reason they seem faded is that your kind keeps killing my kind and hiding the evidence.

But believe me, the animosity is there...and stronger than ever. And someday soon, you will see the wrath of those you've wronged.

Finn contemplates his reply and finally says, "It's not a Wealthy marrying a Dreg that will give the Arc's residents the peace they want. They want equality and respect, but they also want safety. We need to let them know they have nothing to fear. Not from your Acolytes or the Consortium."

"Of course," the Bishop replies. I can almost feel him trying to keep his voice in check. "I am here to ensure their safety. You know that. I am here to offer them equality, after years of oppression and servitude of the working classes. But there is another step necessary before our world can advance still more."

"Which is?"

The Bishop raises his chin and stares at Finn. "Trust," he says. "I need the people's trust. I need their faith. Their willingness to contribute to the great cause." He steps closer and, standing mere inches away, adds, "Believe it or not, young man, there are some in the Arc who do not approve of my methods. There are some in our population who are unwilling to be subject to my testing, in spite of all the good it can do. I am counting on you and Ashen to bring them around. Your wedding—the event of the decade—will unite the people. It will help you to create a sort of bond with them. You will be the Arc's sweethearts, and I intend to ask you to once again be spokespeople for me—after the wedding is over, of course. There is so much we can do, if we simply put our minds together. So much about humanity that we can still improve."

"You're talking about the Repliks," Finn says, point blank.

My heart starts pounding.

If I had any doubt whatsoever that he knew about the existence of the Bishop's clone-like creatures, it's gone now.

Rys and I shoot each other a look, eyebrows raised, but neither of us asks the question on both our minds.

Does Finn know that Ashen—the woman he's about to marry—is also a Replik?

The Bishop seems to tighten only for a second before he replies, "The Repliks are, of course, an integral aspect of the research I've been conducting for years. A means to create one life where another is fading."

"From what I've seen, they're incredible," Finn says enthusiastically. "Really. I wish you'd shared your data with me when we were still in the Behemoth. I could have helped you develop them. What we've been able to do in the last few months is astounding. I'm so excited about the program, I can't even tell you."

"What's he talking about?" I ask, looking around for Atticus. "How can Finn possibly be this excited about Repliks? Even if he was drugged out of his mind on one of the Bishop's special cocktails of 'worship me' chemicals, Finn would know Repliks are the product of an immoral mind."

Wouldn't he?

Atticus closes his eyes as if accessing information, then opens them and replies, "In recent months, the Bishop's team created Repliks of several elderly residents of the Arc—some of whom had only weeks to live. He managed to give them new life in their new bodies—at least, that's what a news article stated."

"So, Finn thinks they've found the cure for old age the Bishop promised," I say softly, and Rys nods.

"If you keep cycling through various new bodies and keep the same mind and memories, I suppose you could live forever—provided your consciousness is transferred into the new body."

"Except it's not," I reply bitterly. "I'm not living inside the new Ashen. She's just a copy of me. I don't feel what she feels, see what she sees. We're strangers to each other, really. The Bishop is lying about how Repliks work. The truth is, he's replacing sick and dying people with newer, separate versions of themselves even as he kills off the sick and the dying."

"Tell me," the Bishop says to Finn, "what are you enjoying most about the Replik program?"

Finn ponders the question for a moment before saying, "The enhancements. I have been able to take human subjects and recreate them almost down to the last molecule, while granting them abilities that their human counterparts never had. There are new, improved versions of so many of us just waiting to be activated. I can't wait to show you what I've been working on in the last week or so."

"Ah, yes. Your special secret project," the Bishop says. "How is it coming along?"

At this, I tighten and stare at Finn once again. What special project?

Finn, what are you up to?

"Extremely well," Finn says with what looks like a genuine smile. "I'm calling it 'Project Narcissus.'"

"Like the myth?" Naeva asks.

"The myth about the youth who falls in love with their own reflection," Finn replies. "It seemed like an apt title, given that Repliks are basically mirror images of ourselves."

"I must say, I'm intrigued," the Bishop says. "When will you reveal your results?"

"Shortly after the wedding. And I promise, you'll be the first to see what I've come up with."

"Wonderful." The Bishop claps his hands together. "Well, Naeva and I will leave you to it. Please do let me know what you and Ashen require for your upcoming nuptials. I assume that Kurt and Illian are taking a keen interest in the ceremony?"

"Very keen," Finn says. "Illian has promised to help me with security—just in case anyone shows up who's not meant to."

"Good. Please be sure that he does the same for the engagement party tomorrow, would you? Unwanted guests are repugnant parasites."

"Of course. I wouldn't want anyone to crash Ash's and my special event."

Looking pleased, the Bishop gives a final bow of his head, takes Naeva by the hand, and leaves, dragging her behind him.

"Engagement party," I repeat softly, turning to Rys. "Are you thinking what I'm thinking?"

"God, I hope not—because something tells me what you're thinking will get us both killed."

PLAN

"WE NEED to find a way into that party," I announce as soon as the Bishop has left.

Rys, who's normally game for anything regardless of how foolhardy, narrows his eyes at me and says, "You heard the Bishop. Security will be through the roof, Ash. Look—you and I just came out of a months'-long coma. Our brains are probably mush. Maybe right this second isn't the time to formulate a cunning strategy."

"It's the *perfect* time. Look, Finn's in charge of the whole thing, right? Maybe—"

"Maybe what?" Rys blurts out. "It's not like he's going to be lax about it. He's ecstatic about this wedding. You saw his face when he said he wants to marry you. *Her.* Whichever."

With a sly smile, I nod. "Yeah. I saw his face. Which is exactly how I know he's miserable."

Rys lowers his chin and looks at me like I've just told him he has three heads. "I don't know what you were watching, but the guy I saw…"

"The guy you saw was putting on a very convincing act.

That's all. I know him better than anyone. He's hiding something, Rys. Trust me."

"If he's acting, why would he go through with a whole damned wedding? Why agree to marry her?" Rys crosses his arms and throws me a stubborn glare. "I'm sorry, but it just doesn't add up."

"You've admitted yourself how smart Finn is. Don't you think he might have a plan in place?"

"He might. Or he might not. We also know the Bishop is extremely good at mind control. Maybe he's implanted Finn with a new neuro-chip or something to make him extra compliant, or worse. Look, there are endless possibilities, none of which necessarily involve Finn trying to get out of a wedding he seems genuinely euphoric about."

"Hey," I say with a sigh, pointing to the projection from the Cicada's stealth camera. "Finn is leaving the apartment. Can the drone follow him? Maybe whatever we see there will be enough to convince you."

"Fine," Rys grunts, and silently, we watch as Finn heads down the corridor toward the nearest Conveyor. The Cicada manages to slip in behind him just before the door whooshes closed.

He heads to Level Two-Ninety-Three, stopping at the ornate door of a residence that must once have been inhabited by an Aristocrat family like Finn's own.

The Cicada stays just behind Finn as he opens the door and slips through. Before I can see much of anything, I hear a high-pitched voice calling out.

"Finn! You're back!"

The Cicada spins around to reveal two happy faces darting toward Finn as he opens his arms and embraces them both. Tears well in my eyes when I see Kel and Merit—as I take in how much they've grown in the months since Finn and I left for New York.

"The Bishop made a liar of me," I say softly. "When we left, I told my brother I'd see him soon...and it's been so many months now."

"Not your fault," Rys says. "You didn't lie. You had no control over what happened."

"I hate him so much, Rys. I hate that bastard for what he did to all of us."

"I know."

My fury only grows when I see a young woman emerge from a door at the end of the hall and make her way toward the three of them, an enormous smile on her lips.

"There's my handsome fiancé," the Replik says, all but pushing Merit and Kel out of the way to get to Finn. It's obvious that she intends to kiss him on the lips, but instead of reciprocating, he takes her gingerly by the waist and presses his lips to her forehead.

He's done the same to me a thousand times. Yet something about his body language with her seems different, almost forced. Like he wants to get his lips away from her as quickly as possible.

Or maybe it's just wishful thinking on my part.

He lets her go, reaches for his brother and mine, and says, "Where's Kyra?"

"She's gone to visit a friend," the Replik replies. "She'll be back late tonight, she said."

"Ah. Well then, who's up for building a blanket fort?"

Both boys cheer as they go tearing back down the hall toward what looks like a bedroom in the distance, ignoring the other Ashen as they sprint away.

But just as they reach the bedroom door, Kel spins around, glares at the Replik, and says, "Boys only!"

Finn turns and shrugs his shoulders half-apologetically as if to say, "What can I do?" before disappearing into the room with the other two.

"Holy crap," Rys says as the Cicada follows Finn. "I'm starting to think you're onto something. Even Kel seems to know she's not you."

I nod, my emotions mixing together like oil and water. Kel would never have excluded me from any activity like a blanket fort in a million years.

On the one hand, I'm pleased that he seems hostile to the Replik.

On the other hand, if he knows—if he truly *knows* she's not me—he could very well be in grave danger.

"Don't worry," Rys tells me, reading my expression. "Kel's a young boy. There's no way the Bishop would go after him."

"Don't underestimate that asshat," I say. "If he thinks for a single second that Kel is smart enough to figure out what's going on…"

"Kel is clever. But he probably doesn't even know Repliks exist. There's no way Finn would have told him, so I really don't think…"

"Wait," I say, taking Rys by the arm and nodding toward the projection. "Listen."

Finn is talking to both boys, though his hands are on Kel's shoulders. The door behind him is closed, and he's speaking in a virtual whisper.

"You need to be nice to her," Finn says. "Just for a little longer."

"Why?" Kel asks, pouting. "She's being so…weird."

"We're planning a wedding," he replies. "She's got a lot on

her mind. It's natural that she'd seem strange. Just do me a personal favor and try to pretend, okay? It's important to me."

Kel looks down at his feet for a moment before nodding. "Okay, then. For you, Finn."

"Thanks, buddy."

Even after their brief chat, Finn doesn't open the bedroom door. Instead, he, Merit, and Kel spend the next half hour constructing an intricate fort of blankets and quilts before climbing in.

"After you and Ashen are married," Kel says when they're all lying inside, "where will you live?"

Finn doesn't reply right away. Instead, he drags a finger upward, tracing the stitched hem of one of the quilts before finally saying, "Near the ocean, with you two. Your sister loves the ocean. But before we can do that, we have to sort a few things out."

"Like what?"

"That," Finn says, "is a secret. But you two will know soon enough."

When they've spent some time in the fort, they head out to the kitchen, where Finn tells the other Ashen he's about to prepare some dinner.

"Ash," Kel says as he grabs some glasses out of the cupboard, "where do you want to live when you and Finn are married?"

Rys and I exchange a glance even as Finn shoots a warning look at Kel.

"Right here, of course," the Replik says. "In the Arc, near you and Merit."

"*Near* us?"

"Kel…" Finn says.

"What do you mean, *near* us?"

The Replik laughs, runs a hand through his hair, and says, "We wouldn't live *with* you, of course. That would be weird. So we'd give you a residence next door to ours, or somewhere close by. Wouldn't that be fun?"

Merit lets out a laugh. "You'd let two kids live on their own?"

At that, the Replik seems to freeze for a moment as if she's just had some sort of system error. She looks to Finn, seeking a proper response.

"Of course not," Finn says. "Kyra would live with you. You'd like that, right?"

Not surprisingly, the boys look dejected. Much as they love Kyra, it's obvious they'd hoped to stay close to Finn and "Ashen."

The Replik, on the other hand, looks euphoric.

"I don't get it," I tell Rys. "She's me. She was programmed to have all the same attachments, emotions, everything. Why would she be happy that Finn is basically rejecting our two brothers?"

"She's probably like everyone else in the world," Rys replies. "She adapts, develops, changes over time. She was programmed with your internal memories, emotions, and so on months ago but since then, she's been her own entity, morphing into something new. I suppose her new persona is the one we see before us."

"A selfish bitch?"

Rys can't help but let out a quiet snort. "It's not that hard to be selfish, Ash. A lot of people are extremely good at it."

"Yeah, well, I guess I never thought I'd be one of them."

"You're not. She's not you, remember? Which is why Kel doesn't like her and why Finn looks like he'd rather kiss a decaying carp than her lips."

I watch the projection some more and determine that he's absolutely right. She's clinging to Finn like a suckerfish and he's doing everything to subtly push her away.

Finally, as if relenting, he puts an arm around her. "Don't worry, boys," he says. "I promise, you two will be very happy after the wedding takes place."

"How can we be happy if..." Kel begins, but he stops speaking and, scowling, turns and walks away.

"Finn has a plan," I say quietly. "I don't know what it is. But he has a plan."

VOYEUR

THAT NIGHT, after they've had a bite to eat, the Replik walks Finn to the residence's door.

But before he has a chance to open it, she takes his hand and asks, "Are you sure you wouldn't like to sleep over tonight? There's plenty of room in my bed."

She ogles him flirtatiously as she speaks, which only fills me with a profound desire to stab her in the eye with a pencil.

"Not tonight," he says, his tone gentle, as though he knows he's letting her down. "There's something I need to do. But don't forget—our engagement party is tomorrow. I'll see you then."

Finn takes her by the waist, and once again, he kisses her forehead. The gesture again seems forced, rather than affectionate. Still, she smiles sweetly at him as if she's grateful for the small token of fondness.

In that moment, I feel the slightest twinge of pity for her.

You want him to love you so badly, but some part of you knows he never will. You can see it in his eyes, though you may not understand it.

"I can come with you!" she blurts out. "I can help with whatever it is you need to do…"

"You should stay and watch the boys until Kyra gets back," he tells her with a shake of his head. "We'll see each other soon enough."

"Yes, of course," she replies with a smile. "Sweet dreams, Finn."

"Sweet dreams…*Ash*," he says, putting a strange emphasis on my name, as if it tastes different to him than it used to.

Kel leaps into the hallway and grabs the other Ash to drag her into the bedroom he's sharing with Merit. "You can come in now that Finn's leaving," he says. "The *Only Boys* rule has been dropped."

Something in my brother's body language tells me he's being deliberately aggressive to put on a show of fondness, or maybe he's just trying to distract her.

Or maybe it's all wishful thinking on my part.

The Cicada follows Finn down the hall to the Conveyor. Instead of heading to the lab, he goes directly to his small apartment, throws himself onto the bed, his hands locked behind his head, and closes his eyes. He stays in that position for such a long time that I become convinced he's fallen asleep.

"While Finn's off in la-la-land," Rys finally says, "what say we check in on the Bishop?"

"How?"

Rys pulls a small box out of his pocket and opens it. Inside is another Cicada.

"You're not serious," I tell him. "If he catches us…"

"He won't," Rys says arrogantly. "Besides, aren't you just a little bit curious about what he's doing when he's not ruining your life?"

"A little," I confess.

Some part of me imagines that when the Bishop isn't wandering around Arcologies destroying others' lives, he's sitting in a dark room somewhere, staring at surveillance monitors. I'm genuinely curious to know if my theory is correct.

"Go ahead, then," I tell Rys. "But don't get us caught."

"Never."

He sends the Cicada through the vent and it's only a matter of a few minutes before it's found its way into a lavish residence occupied by the Bishop and Naeva, who are seated in the living room.

She's watching a movie projected on a large screen on the opposite wall, and the Bishop is sitting in a nearby armchair. His expression is intense, almost angry as he turns her way.

"Rub my shoulders," he commands.

Instantly, she picks up a small, transparent remote control, turns off the projection, and rises to her feet to position herself behind him. She begins to massage his shoulders as he commanded, her face expressionless.

"It's been a long day," he tells her. "Ashen and that Rystan boy are still missing, and the incompetent fools who work for me have no real leads. But I *will* find them."

"Of course you will," Naeva tells him, her voice silk-smooth. "You're a living god, my love."

"A living god. I love when you call me that." He reaches for her hand and takes it in his, kissing it before squeezing it.

At first, it appears that the gesture is nothing more than a sign of affection, but after a few seconds, she lets out a whimper of pain.

"You're squeezing...a little...too hard," she moans as his grip tightens.

"Am I?" he asks with a chuckle. "Are you telling me you can be hurt, my little clone?"

"You know I can be. I have nerve endings, just like you."

"Ah, but you heal quickly. I gave you that gift, remember?"

He releases her hand, rises to his feet, and turns to her. Now I can see her face. There's fear in it, and sadness. Her hand, which she pulls up to her cheek, looks oddly disjointed as if he's broken at least one of her fingers. As she stares at it, the finger contorts itself unnaturally, its joints shifting and clicking into place before it seems to settle into a normal position.

"Healing from pain doesn't mean the pain doesn't exist," she says quietly, her cheeks stained with tears.

"One day, we will abolish pain," he replies. "I will be praised for the breakthrough. For ending a sort of human suffering that has been with our kind since the beginning of time. But it will be a shame, don't you think? Pain reminds us that we're alive, after all. Doesn't it, my love?"

She nods, her eyes pink with tears that have yet to fall.

And for the first time, I know beyond a shadow of a doubt that Repliks can feel just as we can.

I wonder silently if the other Ashen will feel it when I kill her.

"Turn it off," I tell Rys. "I can't watch any more of this."

He does as I asked and turns my way.

"You were right earlier," he says. "We need to get into the engagement party. We need to get you to Finn. To put an end to this man, once and for all."

"I thought you said it would be impossible," I tell him.

"I don't care," Rys says. "Look—I'm rooting for you two, Ash. You need to get to him. You have to let him know you're...you. Something tells me the only way to bring the

Bishop down is to bring you and Finn back together, so whatever we need to do, let's do it."

I let out a quiet, bitter laugh. "Something tells *me* you already have a plan bouncing around inside that brain of yours."

"Sort of. But it's going to mean taking a few risks. Are you prepared to do that?"

I nod. "I'll do whatever it takes to get to Finn before he marries that…*creature*."

"Good. Just…give Atticus and me a bit of time, okay?"

I nod. "As long as I get into that party, you can take all the time you need."

Rys disappears into one of the bedrooms for a time, and I busy myself pacing the floor and trying to come up with a plan of my own.

If only I could get to Illian and Kurt and convince them of the truth. If only I could show them the Sensory Deprivation Tanks and the Bishop's victims confined inside each of them.

I have every faith that they'd believe me then, whether or not the Bishop has them both in some kind of drug-addled, submissive state.

By the time Rys re-emerges after about half an hour, I haven't managed to accomplish anything other than mangle the tips of my fingernails as I chew nervously on them.

"Good news," Rys tell me. "I've hacked into the Arc's main computer. It didn't take long to find a list of every person employed as a caterer for the Consortium."

"Okay," I reply, failing to see how this is exciting news. "What good does that do us? It's not like you and I can just pose as caterers—whoever's doing tomorrow night's hiring will know we don't belong."

Rys smiles cunningly. "That's not quite what I was intending," he says. "A couple of our old friends are employed by the company that's catering this particular affair, and I think you'll be pleased to find out one of them is Kyra."

My eyes widen, and for the first time in a long time, I feel a dash of excited hope.

"Kyra?" I stammer. "Really?"

"Really."

"What's the plan, then?"

"To get our hands on a black Consortium uniform for each of us…and to go from there. By tomorrow evening, I should have everything I need to get us into that damned party."

Something occurs to me then. "Does Kyra know about the Replik?"

Rys shrugs nonchalantly and throws me a smile. "No idea," he says. "But we'll find out soon enough."

SURPRISE

AT FIVE O'CLOCK THE following day, after I've spent hours pacing some more, fretting, and quietly telling myself not to allow despair to overtake my mind, Rys hands me the promised uniform and what he calls a "Scrambler," a small device that temporarily sends a shock of static to any nearby camera so it can't focus on my features.

Something tells me it still won't be enough to get us into the Engagement party.

When I begin to question him, he tells me to have a little faith.

"Come along, Ashen," he says when I've changed my clothes. "We're going somewhere special."

"Always with the surprises," I reply with a roll of my eyes. The truth is, I'm grateful for any distraction he can offer.

He brings me to Level Forty, to a small shop that sells household appliances.

Not exactly what I was expecting.

"What are we doing here?" I ask as we enter the shop. "Please don't tell me we're about to buy them a wedding gift."

"Far from it," Rys tells me. "Like I said, have a little faith."

With that, he guides me to the back of the store, waving briefly at the owner, who smiles and waves back just before Rys and I slip into a large storage room.

"You know him?" I whisper-hiss when we're inside.

"I do. He's an old friend—one who hasn't succumbed to the Bishop's charms. I trust him."

"Good. That makes one of us." Looking around, I note the row upon row of shelves covered in boxes of various sizes. "Are you ever going to tell me what we're doing here? I'm starting to get nervous."

"I'm expecting a visitor," Rys says. "Someone you'll be pleased to see."

My heart rate accelerates violently in my chest, but I tell myself it can't possibly be Finn. He's the groom—not to mention that he's being closely watched by the Bishop. There's no way he'd find his way down here mere hours before the party begins.

We spend another twenty or so minutes in the storage room before I hear someone finally enter through the front door of the shop. Whoever it is speaks briefly to the owner, then makes their way back to the room where we're standing.

"Here we go," Rys whispers, and on instinct, I back into the shadows, prepared for anything.

When the storage room door opens, I let out a gasp.

Kyra.

She looks the same as always—calm, collected, mature. But when I step forward and her eyes meet mine, a look of panic overtakes her face.

"Ash…" she sputters, pulling her eyes to Rys. "Both of you! What's happening? I'm about to head to the engagement party. I was just picking up an extra toaster. I…"

"Kyra..." I say, eyeing Rys sideways.

"What Ash is trying to tell you is that she's not herself," Rys interjects.

Kyra looks confused, but not frightened or apprehensive, at least. "What do you mean?" she asks.

"What he means is that the Ash who's been with Finn since we—*they*—got back from New York...isn't the real Ash," I tell her. "She's a sort of clone. An imposter. A creation of the Bishop's clever scientists. She exists only as a mouthpiece for the Bishop's evil."

"But..." Kyra begins to protest, but as soon as the words tumble out, she seems to lose her conviction. She presses her hands to her hips and stares at me. "All this time, we've been talking to a fake version of you?"

"That's exactly what we're telling you," Rys replies.

Kyra points to me, a strange chuckle rising up in her throat. "So much makes sense now. You—the other you, I mean—seemed so weird, come to think of it. You were constantly telling me how great the Bishop was, almost like you were infatuated with him. I was starting to think you were in love with the guy. And when we spoke, it was like you knew me, but you didn't, not really. I don't know how to explain it. We've had a few deep conversations over the months, but you've always seemed...I don't know..."

"Distant?" I ask, recalling watching the early version of Naeva's Replik in action. "A little out of it?"

"Sort of," she says. "More like you were just...happy all the time. Which isn't a very Ashen Spencer way to be. The Ash I know is constantly worrying about something. But I just sort of chalked it up to everything being good with you and Finn." She furrows her brow when she adds, "Come to think of it, I couldn't figure out why Finn was off sleeping in that dingy studio apartment. Now it's starting to make sense. So, he knows it's not you?"

"I'm not a hundred percent sure," I say, "but I *think* he knows."

"Look, Kyra," Rys interrupts, "The thing is, we really need your help."

She pulls her eyes to his. "Help with what, exactly?"

"To do something incredibly important—and incredibly dangerous," Rys says. He steps forward, handing her a small silver box similar to the ones the Cicadas came in. Whispering a few words to her, he waits while she nods her head.

Kyra looks at me for a moment before stepping toward me. She extends a hand and touches my cheek as if to make sure I'm real. "I'm so sorry, Ash," she says. "I don't know how I could ever have mistaken her for you."

"It's okay. I was almost taken in, myself. She's pretty convincing."

"So convincing that Finn agreed to marry her," she says with a smirk. "But that won't happen, will it?"

"Not if I can help it," I reply with a cynical chuckle. "But if I want to stop him, I need to let him know I'm alive. I need to speak to him."

Kyra looks into her palm at the silver box and turns to Rys. "You really think this will do the trick?"

"I certainly hope so," he says. "Ash just needs a few minutes to speak to Finn. Can you do this for us?"

Kyra glances at me once more and nods. "Of course. I'll do whatever it takes to help. You know that." She bites her lip and adds, "I...I think Kel knows."

"You do? Why?"

"He's stand-offish with the other Ash. Cold, even. I've never seen him cold with you. It's like he can smell it on her or something. He would never say it—that kid is too smart to give himself away. But I think he's known it for a long time. That boy is smart as hell."

At that, I step forward and hug her tight. "Thank you for saying that," I tell her, grateful beyond words to her for confirming my suspicions. "You don't know how I needed to hear it."

"Oh, I can imagine," she half-laughs into my shoulder. "But your brother knows you, Ash. He loves you."

Backing away, she holds up the silver box. "I'm on it," she says. "I'll do what needs to be done. I promise."

After Kyra has left, Rys tells me a little more about his plan. "At eight o'clock, I'll bring you to the party's location. You'll want to make good use of your time when we're there."

"What does that mean?" I ask.

"If all goes well, you will have a very small window to speak to Finn. Make him believe you're...well, *you*. Make sure he understands fully what's going on."

"Seriously?" My heart surges in my chest and I leap forward to hug Rys. "I can't believe this is actually happening. I can't thank you enough."

"I can't promise anything," he says, pulling back as if the hug is an over-commitment. "Except that I'll do everything I can to get you to him."

I nod excitedly. "Finn is the key to everything," I say. "If I can convince him, and I know I can...then maybe this nightmare can finally end. We can get the Bishop out of here, and..."

It hits me then.

If we take down the Bishop, that's all well and good for the Arc. But what about the Behemoth? What about the thousands of innocents still imprisoned in his horrifying pods, their lives stolen from them, their bodies stolen from their still-anxious families?

I know in that moment what needs to be done. I can only hope that somehow, I can find a way to do it when the time comes.

"One step at a time, Ash," Rys says, reading my mind again. "I know there's a lot to tackle, but we'll begin with tonight and work our way forward, okay?"

I nod again, sucking in my lower lip in an attempt to silence all my raging thoughts. *I want to kill the Bishop. I want to tell the world what he is, what he's done. I want to get Illian back, to restore the Arc to what it should always have been—a bright, happy place filled with the potential for a better world.*

I want to finally start living the life that Finn and I have always dreamed of. To find our way to a small house on the ocean, to bring Merit and Kel with us and start a new existence, free from the shackles of cruel oppressors.

But first, I need to see him face to face.

PARTY

WHEN 7:45 ROLLS AROUND, Rys hands me an outfit — a Consortium uniform, complete with the symbol of a circle crossed by two swords—an image inspired by my father's signature on his old landscape paintings.

"This won't be enough to convince anyone," I warn him. "I'm even more a wanted fugitive now than when the Directorate was in charge of the Arc."

"Ah, but I haven't added the final touches," Rys says, pulling a small box out of his pocket. After opening it and fidgeting with its contents for a few seconds, he opens his palm to reveal a small, clear object, the size and shape of a contact lens.

My jaw drops open when I see it.

"A holo-veil?" I ask, dumbfounded. "How did you get your hands on this tech?"

Rys nods over his shoulder to where Atticus is perched on a nearby chair, innocently preening his silver feathers.

"While you were in the Behemoth, Mr. Owl over there had some downtime," he says. "He went on a few missions which included swiping a couple from a local manufacturer. I'd almost forgotten he had them, until he reminded me this morning."

"Well, I'm glad one of us is making intelligent moves." I step over to Atticus and stroke his head. "Clever bird."

"Thank you very much," Atticus replies, and I let out a laugh. I'm about to embark on a dangerous, foolish quest to see Finn, but I can't help but feel a little giddy right now. Things are finally looking up.

"Now, it won't disguise your voice, as you know," Rys says. "But then, I don't think you'll want to—not if you're to convince Finn. Just don't let the Bishop hear you."

"Or see me," I say. "That guy can recognize a holo-veil from a mile away."

"Good point. Okay, listen—I'm going to be bringing you to a small room—a storage unit not much bigger than a closet. When the time comes, you'll need to get to Finn as fast as you can. Clear?"

"Very."

"Then let's get ready."

Rys hands me another device—a small, black metal tube. "An Illuminator," he tells me.

"You mean a flashlight?"

"No, smart-ass. A flashlight projects a beam of light. When you twist this on, it gives you just enough of a glow to make out your immediate surroundings, but it's not visible more than ten feet from you. Only use it when you're confident it won't give you away."

"Got it."

I pocket the Illuminator and adhere the holo-veil's activator to the patch of skin just behind my right ear. I press it, watching in the mirror as my face alters to that of someone I don't recognize. All of a sudden, my eyes are dark brown, my hair a rich red, my cheeks rosy and round.

I look entirely different from myself and from my twin... and for that, at least, I'm grateful.

Rys, too, dons a disguise, changing himself into a threatening-looking man of twenty-five or so. His hair is bright blond, and he's got two parallel vertical lines forming angry crevasses between his brows.

"You look like someone who should be named Bruiser," I tell him as I study his square jaw and scowling features. "I wouldn't mess with you."

"Uh, yeah, that's kind of the point," he laughs. "I don't want anyone talking to me. People suck."

"Agreed."

When we're ready, he guides me to the nearest Conveyor, instructing it in a gruff, lower than usual voice, to take us to the Royal Grounds.

"Security Clearance Required," a woman's tinny voice snaps.

My breath hitches and I inadvertently reach for Rys before pulling my hand back, in case anyone is watching us.

"Delta Five-Seven-Six-Three," Rys says calmly. "Simmons and Kraft on duty."

Of course he knew this was coming.

I want to laugh, but stifle the urge as the Conveyor shoots us up to the Arc's top level, where the doors open to reveal a veritable fairy tale.

Tiny, hovering lights flit this way and that, like a random, churning sea of fireflies. Some wrap themselves around well-coiffed trees that line a gravel path leading up to the large estate that used to belong to the King and Queen.

The artificial night sky above us is dotted with shining

stars, and I'm almost surprised when I look up to see that no one has arranged them into the words "Ashen Hearts Finn."

"This place looks different," I say under my breath. "I think I liked it better when it was basically the King's private militarized zone."

It's slightly horrifying to see it like this, to know this is the place where Finn's engagement party is occurring.

For a moment, doubt assaults me. Is there any chance that he really is happy about all this? Could it have been his idea?

Has he become one of them? A true Aristocrat, reveling in opulence while the lower classes wallow in squalor?

No. Finn would never turn. He couldn't.

But I need to know for sure. I need to look into his eyes, to hear him say the words. I need to know the truth, once and for all.

Rys brings me up to the large manor house, where we're escorted in by a couple of young Consortium guards who look terrified of my companion's glaring face. They back out of the way on our approach, bowing their heads in submission, which is enough to force me to stifle another chuckle.

We stride down a long corridor until we reach the ballroom where the festivities are to take place, but Rys stops me before I can make my way through the doors.

"We'll go in through the side door via the service corridor," he says, nodding toward the growing crowd inside. "Too risky to walk straight in."

Guiding me down another hallway, he leads me into the ballroom through a back entrance, and along the far wall until we reach yet another door. This one, painted the same light blue as the wall, is all but invisible.

"This is a storage unit," he tells me, opening the door, leading me in and turning on an overhead light. He wasn't kidding; it's hardly bigger than a broom closet. "You need to stay in here until the time is right. Keep the door slightly open and watch for Finn. Make sure you know where he is at all times—that's very important. You'll need to move fast."

"Move fast? When?"

"When you see the signal."

"Rys…" I moan. "Can't you be a little more specific than that?"

He gives me as sympathetic a look as he can under the guise of a grumpy bouncer. "The second you can safely get to Finn, trust me—you'll know. I'm really sorry, but I have to leave you here. I have something to look after in another part of the house."

"You're sure this is going to work?" I ask as he begins to turn away.

"Trust me."

"You keep saying that."

"And do you?"

"Of course."

"Good." With that, he finally leaves, half-closing the door behind him. I watch him go, amused by his new appearance. There's something so dominant-looking about him, so assertive.

The Rys I've always known is handsome, to be sure. But he's boyish and goofy in his way, too. This version of him is all business, and looks like he could take on a fast-moving bus with little more than a thrust of his rock-hard fist.

I pull the door almost shut, turn off the closet's overhead light, and wait as people begin streaming into the ballroom, dressed in their elegant gowns and tuxedos.

It's hard not to be painfully aware that I'm witnessing the guests at Finn's engagement party—an event that should have been my own cause for jubilation, but is instead celebrating a fraud.

Illian and Kurt show up after a time, chatting with guests and looking perfectly content in their own finery. It's all I can do not to fling the door open and run up to them both. I want to shake the Bishop's charm and manipulation out of Illian's mind, to shout, "After all this time, don't you see what's happened to you? It's me! It's the true Crimson Dreg, for God's sake!"

But instead, I wait, my body tightening, a moan escaping my lips when Finn strides into the ballroom. He's dressed in a pair of perfectly cut tails, my evil twin on his arm.

She's wearing a strapless white dress that looks a little like a cocktail dress version of a wedding gown.

My hands clench so hard into fists that I have to pull one to my mouth and bite my knuckle to keep myself from screaming with frustration.

Finally, I wait and watch as the Bishop strides in with the latest phony version of Naeva on his arm. She looks calm and collected, a smile plastered to her lips despite the abuse the Bishop inflicted on her last night.

The Bishop greets his fellow guests with nods and handshakes, smiling and charming them with his usual flare.

At one point while he's chatting with a middle-aged man, he turns to face me and I find myself retreating to the farthest shadowy reaches of the closet for fear of being spotted. It seems I succeed, because he turns away almost immediately and resumes his conversation.

"Where's the signal, Rys?" I ask under my breath as the guests drink, dance, and make endless speeches. I watch, writhing in mental agony as old friends of Finn's family wish him and his young bride well. I wince as they regale the couple with tales of their own marriages, of the wonders of being bound together eternally.

It's enough to make me retch.

Finn and the fake Ashen are standing twenty or so feet from me, champagne flutes in hand as they listen to the saccharine speeches. My doppelgänger clings tightly to Finn, only releasing him to cheer the praise being heaped on them both.

At one point, I spot Rys striding along the ballroom's far wall with something in his hand. I'm almost certain I see a small creature flying through the air behind him—something no bigger than a moth.

But the second I try to focus on it, it's gone.

I'm about ready to give up hope on Rys's so-called "signal" when the Bishop heads to the microphone to make a speech of his own. Finn and my doppelgänger stand to one side, maybe fifteen or twenty feet from where I'm positioned.

In the distance, I see Rys standing against the far wall, staring at me. He issues me the slightest nod as the Bishop begins to speak.

"Was that it?" I hiss, trying to catch his eye when he looks away. "Was that the signal? Help me!"

But he doesn't turn back to me. Instead, he focuses his gaze on the Bishop and smiles, his arms crossed over his chest like he's just won a masterful game of chess.

What the hell is going on with you, Rys?

"Ladies, Gentlemen, friends of the handsome couple," the Bishop says, his smooth voice booming through the large room. "We are gathered here to celebrate the...the—"

Before he can utter another word, he falls to his knees. I watch as a small creature—one no larger than a moth—flits away from him.

22

SEVEN MINUTES...

THE CONSORTIUM GUARDS scattered around the room rush toward the Bishop, who now lies unconscious on the floor. But just as they get near him, the room falls into darkness.

Without a doubt, the blackout was Kyra's doing. Which means it's time to make my move.

Clutching the Illuminator Rys gave me in my hand, I hurl the door open and dart over to where Finn was standing a moment ago, barely making out his broad shoulders in the shadows even as the other Ashen spins around, calling his name.

When I grab his arm, he drops his champagne glass and tries to pull away, so I lean in close.

"Finn—it's me," I whisper. "It's Ash. The *real* one."

He gives in then, almost as if he's been expecting this moment to come.

"Quick," I hiss under my breath, pulling him toward the storage unit. Once we're inside, I close the door, twist the Illuminator into a dull glow, and watch as Finn presses back against the wall. Stepping closer, I deactivate the holo-veil hiding my true face and hold up the device so Finn can see me.

"Ash," he whispers, stepping close and cupping my cheeks in his hands. "Oh, thank God. I hoped...I hoped so much. But I had no way to be sure..." He looks toward the door. "I can't believe Rys's plan worked."

"Wait—you *knew* about it?"

"I knew what he was hoping to do, but pulling anything over on the Bishop is nearly impossible, as you know."

Outside the storage room, people are shouting now, scrambling to figure out what's happened. I take advantage of the mayhem to ask, "How long have you known about Repliks?"

Finn looks genuinely pained as he answers. "I began to suspect that they existed some time ago, but I hadn't seen any evidence."

My hands clench nervously when I say, "You didn't answer my question. When did you know?"

"A month ago. Maybe two."

My stomach turns over. I want to be sick. "You're telling me that until then, you...you thought she was me?"

I don't want to think about what they might have done together over the months. The shared intimacy, the kisses, the...everything.

He shakes his head, and my courage returns shard by shard, morsel by morsel, as I look into his eyes. The light may be meager, but I can still see his beautiful features, his exquisite eyes staring into my own with an expression of quiet desperation melded with desire.

It's a look I suspect he's never given the other Ashen.

"I may not have known about Repliks back then," he tells me softly. "But I promise you, Ash—on some level, I knew she wasn't quite you." Finn takes a deep breath before continuing.

"You remember when we were in Santa Fe—when nanotech was eating away at my mind?"

"Of course," I tell him. "I couldn't forget a thing like that."

For weeks, Finn struggled against a gruesome, cruel power inside him—one that subjected him to painful flashes of a devastating future. He lived a daily nightmare from which he couldn't escape, and nothing I said or did helped him. It was as though part of him had been torn away and replaced with someone else.

"You and I were together," he says, "but we were also a million miles apart. Because I couldn't allow myself the pleasure of being with you. I was afraid of hurting you. I was afraid I'd lost myself, which meant losing you, too."

"What does that have to do with…" I begin, but slowly, it starts to make sense. "You're telling me she…the Replik…feels like another person, even though she looks identical to me."

"Yeah," he replies, looking over his shoulder toward the door. "The morning we left New York, I knew something was strange. But I thought maybe the Bishop drugged you for the flight, or something. I need you to believe me when I tell you I had no idea she was another version of you, Ash. Like I told you, I didn't even know Repliks existed. The Bishop had been so careful to keep that aspect of his work from me."

"I believe you," I tell him. "He kept it from me, too. And so much more, Finn. Horrible things."

"I know about them now," he says with a nod. "But back then, I still thought you were on board with the Bishop's work. You spoke about it so genuinely—you seemed so happy in the Behemoth, so excited. And then, when we came back to the Arc, you were still excited—but you'd changed. Only in small ways at first, but over time, it became obvious you weren't yourself.

At first I couldn't figure out what was off, exactly—like I said, I thought you were drugged or brainwashed, or who knows what else? You were too chirpy, too excited about *everything*."

"That should have been a dead giveaway," I tell him, almost allowing myself a smile.

"It was, more or less. I know you, Ash. Even at your happiest, you're still a little untrusting and cynical. It's part of why I lo—"

Finn stops himself and grinds his jaw. We haven't seen each other in months, and now, it seems, he's not sure if he can bring himself to say the words that are lingering on the tip of his tongue.

"It's why I love you," he finally whispers, reaching a hand out to touch my cheek. "I'm so sorry I haven't gotten to say it to you until now. I'm so sorry."

I want to reciprocate, to tell him I love him and that I've missed him, too. I want to express that this separation has been torture for me.

But part of me is livid that he didn't search for me—that he didn't tear the entire Arc apart looking for me.

"Tell me more," I say, my tone chilly.

"Over time, I realized I was spending my days with a stranger," he says. "Her scent was similar to yours, but not exactly the same. Her hands—the way she touched me. If I looked at her fingers, they seemed right. But they *felt* wrong, if that makes any sense. But still, it never occurred to me... Ash, I would never have left you in New York if I'd known the truth. I would have died fighting the Bishop to get to you. I need you to know that. I need you to know I wanted to find you, but he made it impossible. He was watching me at every moment. He was paranoid, suspicious."

"But you still figured it out. At some point, you figured out she was a Replik," I say, my voice on the verge of shattering.

He nods, and I see now that tears are welling in his eyes. "I started digging deeper into the files where the Bishop's genetic research is stored and little by little, I pieced it together. I never exactly had *evidence* that she was a Replik, but I knew, deep down."

"Then why, Finn? If you knew she was an imposter, why didn't you seek me out?"

"You know why," he says.

I'm about to tell him he's wrong—that there's no excuse he could possibly give me that would justify his behavior.

But I know my words would be a lie.

There's one reason, and one reason alone, that Finn would choose not to hunt for me.

And I know exactly what it is.

23

...IN HEAVEN

"HE THREATENED OUR BROTHERS," I say, my voice catching in my throat. "Merit and Kel. Didn't he?"

Finn takes my face between his hands and holds on as though he's terrified to let go. "Not in so many words—not directly. But he made it all too clear that he would hurt them if I stepped out of line. And as much as I love you—as much as I wanted to find my way to you—I knew you would never forgive me if Kel suffered for it. And I would never forgive myself."

"Does the Bishop know...?" I nod toward the door, toward the Replik beyond it.

Finn shakes his head. "That I know what she is? No, I don't think so. I've been careful to play-act all these months, at least, as much as I could. I've pretended to be excited about her, about the wedding, all of it. But the Bishop suspects something—I know he does."

"Why do you say that?"

"Because," he says, touching his lips gently to mine as he

speaks, "I wouldn't kiss her." He pulls back and looks down into my eyes.

My heart dances in my chest as I say, "Really?"

"Really. Not on the lips, not after that first time—the morning we left New York. For a time, I tried to be affectionate with her, to give her what I could. But like I said, she felt so...wrong. And I'm certain the Bishop saw it in my body language. It was obvious that I didn't want to be intimate with her. Even before I knew what she was, I felt, somehow, like I was cheating on you by being with that version of you. But there was one day when the Bishop came by the residence to check up on us. That was when I realized I needed to up my game—and when I realized he was worried. He watched us intently, like he was studying our behavior when we were together."

I nod, trying not to picture it too clearly in my mind's eye. "What did you do?"

"I tried to be just affectionate enough with her to satisfy him. You know, to put on a good show. She played right along, of course, because as far as she's concerned, she *is* you. That's the weirdest part. She wants to kiss me, to hold me all the time. She doesn't understand why I'm cold to her, because in her mind, she's Ashen Spencer, complete with all the memories and emotions you've ever had. As far as she's concerned, I love her deeply. But she doesn't realize my heart belongs only to one person—and while that person may share a lot of her characteristics...there is only one Ash. Then again, she's convinced she *is* that Ash."

I start to protest, but Finn shakes his head. "You and I both know she's a fake. But understand that she really doesn't see herself as a usurper here. She thinks she belongs in this world, just as you and I do."

I swallow a strange, twisted emotion, and ask, "How did the Bishop react when he saw you together?"

"He didn't. I mean, he didn't do anything specific, not at first. He seemed satisfied that everything was as it should be. I thought he was going to leave without incident…until he saw Kel and Merit sitting on the living room couch. He marched over and sat between them with his arms around them both. He asked if they were happy." Finn lets out a quick breath, then says, "They both said yes. The Bishop looked me in the eye, put a hand on the back of each of their necks, and wrapped his fingers around them."

When he sees me flinch, he reassures me. "He didn't hurt them, Ash. It was purely for my benefit. He looked into my eyes, and I knew without any words passing between us that it was his warning to me. A caution that if ever I got any stupid ideas in my head, he would end both the boys without a second thought."

My heart sinks and rises at once. If it's even possible, I hate the Bishop more now than I ever did for daring to lay a finger on my brother.

But I also love Finn more than ever for protecting the boys from that bastard.

"Kel and Merit were staying in the large residence with the Replik and Kyra for their own safety," Finn explains. "It was part of my plan to convince the Bishop I trusted the other Ash —that I truly believed she was you. I never worried they were in danger with her. Remember—she loves Kel, just like she loves…"

"You," I say softly, pulling Finn close and kissing his lips. "Just like I love you."

He nods, pressing his forehead to mine, and says, "I would never, ever abandon you or Kel. You know I would never let any harm come to those boys—and even though I wanted to find you, I suppose part of me knew that if you were with Rys, at least you were safe."

I nod, pulling myself to his chest and pressing close to him, exhaling only when I feel the security of his arms around me.

"Finn," I say, "I don't know if you know, but your mother...she..."

"I know," he replies, his tone solemn. "She's probably dead. The Bishop told me, though he lied about the circumstances. He said she'd had an 'accident.'"

"No," I reply. "It was no accident. I left her on the roof. She wasn't in very good shape. I'm sorry. I didn't want it to end that way. I wanted to bring her to justice. To put her on trial and hold her accountable for her crimes."

He bows his head slightly, then shakes it. "I'm just glad you escaped," he says. "When I found out you'd been replaced by a Replik, I thought...I thought my mother had killed you, Ash. Or else that the Bishop had."

I shake my head. "You know he doesn't do the dirty work himself. Look—I know why the Bishop wants you to marry the...other one. It's not for the good of the Arc. He wants to torture me, to draw me out of hiding. We can't let him keep us apart. You need to come with me, right now. We need to get away from here..."

"We can't. The Bishop's Acolytes took Merit and Kel before this party—hid them somewhere. He said they were just 'babysitting,' but I know better. He'll have them killed if I don't go through with tonight. He needs this wedding to happen, Ash. It's a distraction, a celebration to mask all the evil he's doing behind the scenes."

"Have you talked to Illian and Kurt? Can't you tell them what's going on?"

"You know I can't." Finn taps the back of his head. "The Bishop's neuro-implant. He watches me—at least, while he's conscious. Talking to Illian and Kurt has been nearly impossible—and even if it were, they're too far gone. They both believe in their hearts the Bishop is some kind of savior."

"That's madness," I retort. "Illian is too smart to believe something like that!"

"You and I are intelligent people. And look what we believed when we were in New York."

My shoulders sag as reality sinks in once again. He's right —I believed the Bishop to be something greater than most humans.

The sad truth is, he's simply crueler.

"I have one bit of good news," Finn tells me, slipping his fingers under my chin.

Beyond the closet's door, the crowd has calmed down. Voices are no longer shrieking in a frenzied communal panic, and somewhere in the distance, I hear my own voice calling Finn's name.

The Replik is hunting for him, and I have no idea what she'll do if she doesn't find him.

"Tell me the good news," I urge. "Quickly."

"Like I said, the Bishop surveils me through the neuro-implant," Finn says. "But I have ways of garbling the signal for a few minutes here and there. It's been enough to do some surreptitious research under his nose."

"Will he be able to see this conversation?"

"No. Not while he's unconscious. The transmission is automatically disabled—we made sure of that."

The commotion beyond the door crescendoes, distracting me for a moment, and my heart rate quickens.

My eyes shoot toward the door then, and I think of the

Bishop falling to his knees and wonder if there's any chance at all that Rys's tiny drone dosed him with enough drugs to end his life.

Somehow, though, I doubt it.

"Ash," Finn says, "I'm going to get us out of this mess. I promise you that." He kisses me gently, then strokes his thumb over my chin. "Hmm," he says.

"What is it?"

"Your scar—"

"Oh, yeah. It's gone," I nod. "To make me look more like the Replik, and the Replik look more like the real me. At least, that's Rys's theory."

To my surprise, Finn smiles. "Shame. I always loved it. It's time we brought it back, don't you think?"

I cock my head, puzzled by his meaning.

"Look—two can play at the Bishop's game."

"How?"

He smiles again, and it's seductive and mischievous at once.

He reminds me suddenly of a benevolent version of the Bishop, and I want nothing more than to kiss him long and deep, to savor every bit of him while I can...but the din of voices just on the other side of the door warns me that our time is coming to an end.

Finn twists around and pulls his eyes down to the narrow space below the door. "The lights are back on," he says, turning back to face me. "Look—give me a few days to put my plan into action. I should warn you—the Bishop is stronger than either of us knew when we were in New York. He's a walking weapon of mass destruction, and if we don't stop him, he *will* destroy the lives of every person in this place. But as long as he continues to believe I'm happy to be marrying his little Ash-clone, I'll be able to keep working my way toward my endgame. I just need a few vital components."

"I don't know, Finn. After tonight, he'll be on high alert. Maybe it wasn't the best idea to drug him."

Finn shakes his head and lets out a low, quiet laugh. "I beg to differ, Ash. I needed to see you—the *real* you. You don't know how much. It's feeding my soul, my mind. I was so worried…honestly, I was terrified I'd have to go through with that sham of a wedding."

"How the hell are you planning to get out of it?"

Finn's lips curl into the most delicious smile as he says, "You'll find out very soon, my Ash. I promise you that."

Once again, I hear my own voice in the distance, calling frantically for Finn.

"You should go," I say, my heart aching with the thought of losing him again.

"I know." Finn steps toward me and kisses me hard. He cups my face in his palms and looks into my eyes when he whispers, "Ash—I want you to know, I have never slept in the same bed as her. I've never kissed her lips since the day we left the Behemoth. The only lips I ever kiss will be yours, and yours alone."

After one final, gentle touch of his lips to mine, I watch him slip through the door to slink back into the ballroom filled with panicked party-goers. He leaps over to where the Bishop is still lying on the ground and cradles his head. When the other Ashen rushes over to join him, his eyes veer momentarily to my own. He nods once, and I close the door, lean against the wall and let myself slump to the floor, prepared to wait as long as I need to while the party unwinds.

24

WAITING

WITH MY HOLO-VEIL REACTIVATED, I crack the closet door open as the commotion carries on.

Now that the guests can see, a group has gathered around the Bishop, trying to figure out what to do with him. I make out shouts of "Don't lift him! He could have a head injury!"

But after a few minutes, the Consortium's men finally lift him onto a makeshift stretcher and transport him toward the nearest Conveyor.

More than an hour passes before Rys knocks on the door and pokes his head in.

"All clear," he tells me. "The happy couple has left to be with the Bishop when he wakes up—you know, to make sure everything is okay and that he doesn't, say, suspect that one of them had something to do with his collapse."

I nod and rise to my feet. "Any talk about who did this terrible thing?" I ask with a sly smile.

"I spoke to a few Consortium members. One of them speculated that maybe it was the escaped Ashen lookalike and that scoundrel Rystan Decker, but another said they were seen fleeing from Sector One some time ago. Others confirmed that appalling rumor. They even showed me video to confirm it. So now, they've chalked it up to a group of disgruntled Dregs who are jealous of the Bishop's fortune."

"Wait—back up a minute." My eyebrows meet in a baffled expression. "You said the Ashen lookalike and you fled? How is that possible?"

Rys puts his hands on his hips and frowns, which, in his current version, looks almost hilarious. "Why do you always insist on underestimating me?" he asks. "I'm a living god. A real one, too—not like that Bishop doorknob."

His casual insult to the Bishop makes me snort-laugh.

"Also," he adds, "I have the ability, thanks to my clever stealth-drones, to create moving holographic projections that look like they're…"

"Fleeing into the mountains," I laugh. "That's why they're not searching for us in the Arc? You could have told me!"

"I suppose I should have. I was saving it for a special moment. And look how happy I've made you."

Still chuckling, I add, "Well, it'll keep the hounds in the Arc off our trail for a while, I guess."

"That's the idea."

I punch him gently in the shoulder and let out a chuckle.

"Physical assault?" Rys laughs. "Someone's in a good mood. I take it your Seven Minutes in Heaven went well?"

"We weren't making out in the closet," I protest. "We were…scheming."

"Scheming. Is that what the kids call it nowadays?"

I punch him again. "Finn has a plan. I'm not sure what it is. All I know is that we might need to make further use of your holograms to keep the Bishop's eyes on the mountains. He'll be on high alert after tonight. Whatever the Consortium may tell him, he'll suspect *everyone*."

"He may," Rys shrugs. "Or he may not. In the meantime, I'm going to keep up my secret communication with Finn. By the way, I managed to talk to him after he left you in here."

"What? How?"

"Kyra walked by and 'accidentally' spilled an entire glass of Merlot on the Fraudulent Ashen's pretty white dress. It was a shame, really."

"So clumsy of Kyra. I'll have to remember to thank her for that later."

"Definitely. Anyhow, Finn and I have a cunning plan."

"Great. Tell me what it is."

"Soon."

"Rys!"

He shoots me a playful look and says, "Ash, more than anyone I know, you deserve for something good to happen to you. Finn and I are two guys who happen to care about you a lot. Let's just say your best days are coming."

"I have no idea what that means, and frankly, I'm terrified."

"You probably should be, honestly," Rys says with a shrug. "Meanwhile, let's go get ourselves changed into something— or some*one*—more comfortable. These holo-veils are creepy as hell."

Rys escorts me back to the residence, where we remove our fake faces and change our clothes. I tell him about the conversation I had with Finn, and he listens intently.

"Finn knows things," Rys replies. "More than I suspected. In a few days, when we put the wheels in motion, we're going to have to face reality."

"Which is what, exactly?"

"We're looking at an uphill battle. The Bishop's followers

are intense and loyal—and the Bishop still has thousands of people confined to pods here and in the Behemoth. You and I managed to escape our induced comas in one piece—which means those people can do it, too. We need to help them, and for that, we need people like Kurt and Illian on our side. Though I have to say, it would help if there wasn't a cult of brainwashed loyalists fighting for the bad guy."

"Ugh," I groan. "Why can't people just use their minds and realize they're all being brainwashed on a daily basis?"

"Because sometimes, it's easier to follow than to think for yourself. Humanity has proven that millions of times over the years. If someone comes along who seems to know what they're talking about, we're only too happy to leap on board and praise them for taking charge."

"It's more than that," I reply. "The Bishop may be charming, but he uses other tactics. Blackmail. Mind-altering chemicals. When Finn and I were in the Behemoth, we were sure he piped something through the vents to make us all happy and compliant. Whatever he does, it works wonders for his cause. Look at Illian and Kurt, and how easily swayed they were. Illian has willingly trapped himself in a world he's convinced is real. The Bishop is creating a false hope, an idealistic image of a world that doesn't really exist. As far as Illian is concerned, the Arc is on an upward trajectory." I bow my head when I add, "It's a weakness, I suppose. Proof that none of us is strong enough to lead."

Uncharacteristically, Rys reaches out and lays a gentle hand on my cheek. "It's not a weakness to want a better world, Ash. Most of us want the exact same thing, and when someone like the Bishop comes along—someone who promises to deliver that world with all the glorious bells and whistles—it's hard as hell to resist the temptation to believe them."

"*You* resisted," I say. "You were never charmed by him. You saw my Replik for what it was. You knew all along that something was off."

Rys shrugs and pulls his eyes away. "I suppose," he says almost bashfully. "But remember—I had an owl watching the city from above, which means I saw the world through a very different lens. I saw Scorp drones, spying on innocent people. I saw frightened civilians. And I didn't inhale any happy-gas or whatever it was the Bishop was inflicting on you guys."

"Still, how were you so sure all along? Even Finn wasn't totally sure the other Ashen was a fake. But you and Atticus," I say, looking over to where the silver owl is perched on top of a bookshelf on the other side of the room. "You two weren't taken in for a second."

"I've told you," Rys says, pulling his eyes back to mine. "You're all the family I have in this world. Your pain hits me like a stone thrown at my chest. When your mother…" He stops, swallows, and winces before continuing. "When she died, I felt it, just like I felt the pain and loss when my own parents were taken. The thing is, when you hurt, I feel it. It's selfish, I suppose—but it's why I've worked so hard to protect you every step of the way."

I allow myself a moment of tenderness, of vulnerability, when I reply, "You haven't only protected me. You've protected everyone and everything. Quietly, stealthily. You've kept so many people from harm over the months."

"But too many others have been lost." He sets his jaw when he adds, "I'm going to talk to Finn and sort through our plan. I promise you, I can do better. And together, we're going to help more people. But in the meantime, I need you to lay low and trust me one last time."

I do trust Rys.

But the next few days are an agony of drawn-out anticipation after the sliver of time I got to spend with Finn. Trapped as I am inside Piotr's old residence, I pace about for hours on end while Rys toils away in one of the bedrooms with Atticus by his side. He's secretive in his work, though he knows how desperate I am to know what progress he's made—and, more particularly, what his and Finn's master plan is.

On occasion, he sends his Cicada drones through the Arc's ventilation system and tells me they're "running reconnaissance missions," but still, he refuses to reveal what he's learned.

Four days pass before he finally announces that he's managed to connect with Finn, and that everything is going swimmingly.

"The Bishop has recovered, and he doesn't suspect a thing," he tells me the morning before the wedding is to take place. "At least, not about Finn's part in any of it. The wedding is going ahead as planned."

"Kel and Merit? Are they all right?"

"Totally fine, and back in the residence. Kyra is with them as we speak."

Relieved as I am, I scowl at him, irritated to have been kept in the dark for so long. "Well, I don't believe the Bishop isn't suspicious. The one thing I know about that man is that he sees way more than we think he does. He knows things.

Sooner or later, he'll find out what happened to him, and when he does, he won't rest until he's had his vengeance."

Rys counters my gripe with a grin. "Let's hope it's later, for all our sakes."

"Fine. Let's say it takes him a while to figure it out. Tell me, why should I be happy that this wedding is proceeding? It's a freaking nightmare, Rys."

"The morning of the wedding," he tells me, his grin intensifying, "all will be revealed."

It's all I can do not to throttle him. "What? We can't wait until the morning of the wedding to make our move!"

"Are you worried that Finn will marry your Replik?" Rys asks with an impish smirk. "Because I'm pretty sure that won't happen."

"Of course I'm worried about it!" I snap. "If he doesn't…"

I force my voice to halt in its tracks, too afraid to finish the thought out loud.

If he doesn't, both our brothers could die.

"I know what you're afraid of," Rys says, the grin altering to a look I don't see on his face often: one of true sympathy. "Kel is like a brother to me, too, Ash."

"Then you know we can't afford to screw this up," I retort. "So I don't understand why you and Finn are keeping secrets from me. Just tell me what's happening, so I'm prepared for it. What is it we're going to do?"

"We're going to get you and Finn back together, where you both belong. But first, we need to give you back your scar."

I narrow my eyes, and this time I allow myself a snicker. "Finn said the same thing when we were in that damned closet together. Fine. Give me back my war wound, and keep being cryptic until I punch you so hard that you can't breathe for three days straight."

Rys rubs his hands together, then calls to Atticus, who flaps over and lands a few feet from me.

"This might hurt just a little," Rys says, leading me by the hand to sit in front of Atticus. I watch as the owl's belly opens up and a small, metallic arrow-like object emerges.

"Umm," I grunt. "Are you sure this is a good idea?"

"It's the only way," Rys says. "Tru—"

"I know, I know," I interrupt with an exaggerated eye-roll. "Trust you. I will if you tell me—how do you know exactly where to put the scar?"

Atticus turns his head ninety degrees and projects an image on the air. I don't need to study it to realize I'm seeing my face projected in perfect clarity.

"Your doppelgänger," Rys says. "She's in his memory banks."

"Pity. We'll have to erase her soon."

"Agreed. Erasing her is the best possible plan."

Atticus turns back to me and the metal object comes toward my face. "Stay perfectly still, please," he says and I close my eyes, waiting for a jolt of pain or whatever else is about to assault me.

To my surprise, all I feel is a brief stroke of heat, then it's over.

"A masterpiece," Rys says.

I open my eyes to see smoke rising before them. "Um..." I say, reaching for my chin.

"Don't touch it! It needs a few hours to fade, but when it does, it will look like your former scar."

"Fine!" I tell him, raising my hands in surrender. "Thank you, Atticus."

"You're welcome," the owl replies with a bright blue flash of his eyes.

"What next?" I ask, slapping my palms to my thighs and rising to my feet.

"Next, we wait," Rys says. "And I work. We have to execute our plan perfectly, or you and I will both end up dead."

I let out the deepest sigh of my life before I reply, "Sounds fabulous."

25

MORNING

When the morning of the wedding comes at last, I find myself standing in front of a mirror, examining the "scar" Atticus so skillfully gave me last night. I have to confess, it does look identical to the one I lost, and I have no idea how he managed to copy it so perfectly. Then again, I understand very little about how Rys and his drones work their particular brand of magic.

I'm still in the dark about Rys and Finn's plan for this momentous—and tumultuous—day.

All I know is that Rys woke me early and told me to drink as much coffee as my bladder could bear, and as I begin to work my way through my second mug, I find myself thinking once again about Finn.

Butterflies migrate from my chest to my belly as I imagine his eyes, his touch, the way his fingers feel against my skin. I miss the constancy of him, the warmth of his affection. I miss the feeling of wholeness that engulfs me when we're together...and I can't wait to be with him again.

But almost greater than my desire to see Finn is an aching

need to see my brother. I want so badly to put my arms around him, to make sure he knows I'm still here, still myself. For all I know, he's convinced that his sister has morphed into someone other than her former self.

The thought of us losing what we once had breaks my heart.

"Will Kel be at the wedding?" I ask Rys when he steps into the kitchen and takes a seat next to me.

"I imagine so," he tells me. "It *is* his sister getting married, after all. I mean, sort of. Oh—by the way, Happy Birthday."

I'm in the midst of taking a sip of coffee when the last two words hit my ears, and I spit brown liquid all over the kitchen table.

"What?" I blurt out, wiping my mouth with the back of my hand. "It's not my..."

I realize even as I'm protesting that I have no idea what the date is. My entire sense of time was skewed when we came out of our induced comas.

Rys nods. "Today's the day. Mine was a few days back, but I'm choosing not to be offended that you didn't get me anything because, you know, there's a lot going on in that Ashen Spencer head of yours."

"Holy crap. I had no idea..." I feel my cheeks heating with a startling realization: I'm eighteen years old today.

I'm officially an adult.

Then again, my birthday is hardly what has brought on any inkling of maturity. The last year of my life would be enough to convert any child into a perverse version of adulthood. I've experienced death, destruction, cruelty, and multiple attempts on my life—not to mention that I have been robbed of my entire identity and any meager autonomy I once possessed.

Seeing my distress, Rys reaches a hand out, and when I take it, he guides me into the living room, where a small, sad-looking cupcake is sitting on the coffee table, a candle poking out its poorly iced top.

He lights it with a device he pulls from his pocket before saying, "I'm not about to sing. But you should definitely make a wish."

I look into his eyes for only a moment before I crouch down, blink my own eyes closed, blow out the candle, and wonder if there's any chance my wish could possibly come true.

"Please, please, please…" I whisper.

Rys lays a hand on my back. "My second gift to you on this momentous day is one I think you'll enjoy," he says. "But first comes the gift you won't love quite so much."

"Oh, no," I moan. "What are you going to do to me?"

He slips over to a side table and extracts something from its drawer—a device that looks similar to a gun. I've seen such an item before, when I first came to the Arc. One of the Directorate's employees used it to inject me and my fellow Candidates with wrist implants so that they could track our emotions as well as our movements.

"What are you doing with that?" I ask.

I may trust Rys, but I've learned the hard way to be skeptical of anything that looks like it might have come from the enemy.

"This particular gift," he says, "is from Finn. One of my drones picked it up after he left it in the lab for me. Inside its chamber is a nano-implant—one that will enter your bloodstream, if you'll allow me to inject it."

I'm not sure how to feel about this. The last time Finn provided me with an implant, I discovered he'd gifted me with the Surge—a weapon so powerful I almost killed him with it.

"If it's the Surge," I say, "it won't help me. By all accounts, the Bishop is strong enough to resist it. And my doppelgänger already has it in her own bloodstream, so at best, it would just make us equals."

Rys shrugs. "Equal is better than defenseless," he says. "Look, if you turn me down, I'm not going to force the implant on you."

I chew the inside of my cheek only for a moment before relenting. "Fine. Go for it. If it's from Finn, he's probably got good reason to have sent it your way. But for the record, I'm not a fan of surprises."

"Then this day might prove a little challenging for you, Ash," Rys tells me as he pulls the neckline of my shirt down, presses the gun to my nape, and clicks the trigger. I feel a slight sting in my flesh, then I'm fine.

A few seconds later, a knock sounds at the residence's door.

I gasp and turn to Rys, who calmly says, "I suppose we should see who that is."

"You don't look worried."

"That's probably because I'm not."

As I conceal myself behind the couch, Rys leaps over to the door and I hear him yank it open.

"Come on in!" he says. "Ash will be so happy to see you."

When I hear the door close, I dare a peek around the corner.

The face I see—the luminous smile and beautiful, lively eyes—is enough to make me leap forward and throw my arms around the visitor.

"Diva!" I cry, squeezing her tightly enough to elicit a happy squeak. "What on earth are you doing here?"

I met her on my first day in the Arc. On the train that transported me from the Mire to the Hub, she styled my hair and makeup in preparation for the Introduction Ceremony, where the Candidates were judged for our placements within the Arc's social hierarchy. She wove fluttering blue butterflies into my hair and made me feel beautiful.

Unfortunately, she also led me to believe those who resided inside the Arc would prove decent, empathetic human beings, because she believed it herself.

She and I were wrong about the last part—but Diva has always been a loyal friend and ally, and I've grown immensely fond of her.

"I'm here to do your hair and makeup, of course," she tells me, giddy with excitement. "And I can't tell you how happy it makes me!"

My mouth drops open, and I freeze. After a moment I turn to Rys, my eyebrows raised. "I don't understand," I say. "Why would I need my hair and makeup done…"

"You'll find out in about thirty seconds," Rys says, looking at a projection in his palm. "Twenty, actually."

"This all seems pretty sketchy," I say, turning back to Diva, who issues me an enigmatic, toothy grin.

Sure enough, a few seconds later, another knock sounds at the door. Rys silently gestures me to conceal myself in the kitchen, and he follows suit while Diva opens the door.

"Hi there!" I hear her say in her usual sing-song lilt. "Come on in! I've been waiting for you!"

"Thank you," a familiar voice—that of a young woman—says.

My stomach lurches with the realization that it's *my* voice.

HER

"WHAT THE—" I begin to stammer before stepping out of the kitchen to confirm my fear.

Sure enough, my Replik is standing by the door. Draped over her arm is a garment wrapped in an abundance of red plastic—something I can only guess is a wedding gown.

"You!" she says when our eyes meet. "They said you'd fled the Arc. That you'd..."

"Escaped," I reply. "Yeah. I know."

My Replik turns to Rys, then looks at Diva, a look of almost naive panic in her eyes. "I was told to come here to have my hair and makeup done. I don't understand what's happening." She hesitates for a moment, then looks like she might drop the dress and flee for her life. "I can summon guards," she warns nervously. "I can have you all arrested..."

"No, you can't," Rys says, stepping between her and the door to block her escape route. "And for the record, the implant connecting you to the Bishop was disabled this morning. Finn told him you wanted privacy on your wedding day, you see, and he was given permission to disconnect you. You may not recall, as you were unconscious at the time."

She lets out a horrified gasp, looking as though she's been violated.

And, perhaps for the first time, I understand how she feels.

In her mind, she's the real Ash. She's not a synthetic reproduction of me; she is me. As far as she's concerned, she deserves to marry Finn. She deserves my life, because it's her life, too.

This is her wedding day...and we're ruining it.

For the first time, I understand that her motivations don't come from a place of cruelty, but from a place of trust. She trusted the Bishop, just as I once did. She trusted Finn, because her mind told her he loved her.

Inside her is every memory accumulated during the course of my own life—memories of my father, my mother, Kel, our home. Memories of the evening I laid my eyes on Finn at the Introduction Ceremony, when I looked into his eyes and fell instantly for him.

"Guards or no guards, I can't let you two get away with... whatever it is you're trying to do here," the Replik says angrily, stepping toward me. "I have the Surge. The Bishop told me to take you down if ever I should see you again."

I throw a fearful glance toward Rys, who looks oddly calm as he crosses his arms over his chest and smirks, as if he doesn't have a worry in the world.

My eyes go wide as the other Ashen thrusts her hands out, palms toward me. Again, I look to Rys, my mouth opening to issue a panicked plea for help.

But no words come, and Rys just chuckles.

I expect a blinding flash of light—a violent blow, knocking me back into the wall.

But nothing happens.

The Replik freezes in place, as confused as I am by the strange silence in the room.

"What's going on?" she asks. "Why didn't it work?"

"I'd like to know, too," I reply.

"What's happening," Rys says, stepping toward me, "is that the world is beginning to shift back toward what it's meant to be. This *person*, if you can call her that, was never meant to steal your power from you. She was never even meant to *be*, Ash. And she sure as hell wasn't meant to marry Finn. Not today or any other day."

The Replik turns to him, her face contorted in pain, and says, "You don't mean that! I love Finn!"

"You don't feel love," he snarls. "You feel only what is programmed in your systems—in your memory banks. You understand the chemical reaction that is human attraction, but only on its most fundamental level. You are incapable of emotion, despite what that jackass the Bishop might have told you."

A crazed, feral snarl erupts from her throat, and she leaps at him. But Rys throws a hand into the air between them, and before she can reach him, she collapses to the ground, her body sapped of all strength.

As I stare at her limp, lifeless form, a tiny hummingbird-like drone flits away from her, and I understand what's happened.

"She's sedated," Rys says. "For now."

"Rys," I say, my voice trembling. "Why exactly did you summon her here?"

"Because it's time to deactivate her," he replies, striding toward her. "Diva, help me pick her up, would you?" he adds, slipping his hands under her arms. "We'll lay her in the guest bedroom."

"What happens after we...deactivate her?" I ask as Diva takes the Replik's legs and helps Rys lift her.

Rys and Diva exchange a knowing look and smile in unison.

"You will go to the Royal Grounds," Diva says, "and marry Finn in her place."

"What?" I blurt out. "Are you joking?"

"Not at all," Rys replies with a smile. "Happy Birthday."

My eyes shoot to Diva, who nods and says, "It's true, Ashen. I'm here to get you ready for your big day."

27

MAKING THINGS RIGHT

What I feel at that moment is an indescribable, tremulous combination of hope, joy, and pain.

All of a sudden, everything makes perfect sense. I'm going to marry Finn right under the Bishop's nose.

It's why Rys gave me back my scar.

It's why we're about to deactivate my doppelgänger.

I can have my life back. My identity.

Finn.

Kel.

It's the greatest news I could ever have received.

And yet, it feels surprisingly bittersweet, given what's about to happen.

I watch Rys and Diva carry the Replik into the bedroom and lay her on top of the covers. She looks peaceful, as though she's fast asleep, dreaming contentedly.

When I pull my eyes to my Replik, I see myself mirrored in features. Though she's unconscious, I can feel my own pain in her face, in the tightness of her frame. I saw it when she failed to activate the Surge, too. A fear that her life would soon end.

It's a fear I recognize all too well, one I have felt too many times to count.

"How will it happen?" I ask softly, overcome with a sudden, inescapable sympathy for this creature I've despised since the first moment I laid eyes on her.

"How will we destroy her, you mean?" Rys asks.

He doesn't utter the word "kill," but he may as well.

"Yes," I say.

"That's up to you." He tightens, his eyes locked on me. "Ash...I thought you'd be happy about this. Or at least relieved."

"I *am* relieved," I tell him, though I'm sure my face doesn't convey the emotion. "It's just...she has my memories, Rys. My feelings. She's absolutely convinced she loves Finn every bit as much as I do. To her, *I'm* the one who doesn't deserve to exist. Right now, it's hard for me to see her as anything other than human. Maybe that doesn't make any sense, but it's the truth."

"Sure. But it's that sort of sympathy the Bishop is counting on for every one of his Frankenstein creations. He's counting on people seeing them as better versions of ourselves. But don't forget—they're not. They're versions that he's skewed and adapted for his own purposes. They're an army of subordinates doing his bidding."

"All the same, I want to know how we're going to do this. I don't think I can bring myself to..."

Stab her? Shoot her? All the things the Directorate used to try and force me to do to my classmates?

Human or not, she bleeds, like me.

"There is a way to deactivate Repliks without causing them pain," Rys assures me. "Finn told me about it. He's been studying them since he discovered they exist."

"What is it?" I ask him, my eyes locked on the Replik's chest as it eases slowly up and down.

Rys pulls open a drawer on the nightstand and extracts a small hypodermic needle. "Simple. Easy. Painless. I promise."

What's about to happen is necessary, and I've always known it. With her gone, I can speak to Illian once again, and to Kel. I can be free, provided I can fool the Bishop just long enough to marry Finn.

There's no question in my mind of what needs to happen.

But it's not going to be easy.

"You can do it, if you'd like," Rys tells me, offering me the needle, but I shake my head.

"I don't think I can. I'll save my bloodlust for my true enemies—not for their creations."

"I get it," Rys says, turning to face the bed. Diva stands to the side, watching in silence as he presses the needle into the Replik's neck.

To my horror, my clone's eyes pop open as she feels the sharp jab. She looks up at Rys and says, "What time is it?"

"Ten a.m.," he replies.

Her face looks panicked when she squeaks out, "My wedding...It's in two hours..."

"Yes, I know," Rys replies gently, but as he speaks, he turns to lock his eyes on mine. "And I'm sure you're looking forward to it, Ash."

"I..." she replies, but her eyes close before she can finish the thought.

A few seconds pass before her features alter, her skin turning gray and dull, her hair losing its sheen. To my relief, in a mere moment, she's ceased to look anything like me. She doesn't even look human anymore.

It's as if an exquisitely crafted holographic illusion has been switched off forever.

"Is she..." I begin, but I can't get the words out.

"She's been permanently deactivated," Rys says. "Every component of her has been shut down."

"It's for the best," says Diva. "She was never real. She was an illusion."

"I know," I nod, turning away from the strange, inhuman corpse. I sigh before I repeat, "I know."

Finn is mine once again. I am his.

We will face what is to come together, with all our combined strength. We have a great deal yet to do—we need to dismantle the power structure the Bishop has created. We need to find a way to release his numerous prisoners, both from the Arc and from the Behemoth.

Our work begins today, with our wedding, our vows to one another, and a bond that will never again be broken.

"I suppose it's time to get married," I say, wiping away a tear inspired more by joy than pain.

"Are you sure?" Diva asks, seeing my blotchy cheeks and red eyes. "This is a lot to spring on you all of a sudden. We could tell the Bishop Finn got cold feet..."

"He would kill Finn for less," I tell him, my tone grim. But I smile and add, "To be honest, so would I. I've wanted this since the moment I met Finn. Not necessarily a big, lavish wedding, maybe—but I always wanted to know what it would feel like to begin our *forever* together. And today, I'm going to find out."

Rys makes a gagging sound, and I turn to see he's still standing by the bed, where he's pulled a white sheet over the Replik. "Oh, sorry," he says. "Did I say that out loud?"

"Were you practicing your best man speech?" I ask with a mocking scowl.

"You know I can't be a best man. I'm supposed to be at large in the mountains, remember?"

His words inflict a jolt of pain in my chest. He's right—he can't be there with me, watching over me protectively as he has for so long.

Rys, too, looks suddenly pained. "Speaking of which..."

"What is it?" I ask.

Diva interjects then. "I'll be in the living room," she tells us both. "Whenever you need me."

"I have to go," Rys says when she's left us. "Now that we've implemented this part of the plan, I have to leave the Arc, or else I'm putting you and Finn in danger, Ash. I need to get as far from here as possible. It's easier to draw the Bishop's eyes away from the Arc if I'm out there."

"I don't want you to go," I say, devastated by the pending loss. "Can't you stay here in the Arc? Can't you and Atticus keep hiding?"

Rys shakes his head. "I want this day to be perfect for you, Ash—as well as all the days to come. That means I need to create a trail for the Bishop's people—one they can follow properly. I need them convinced that you and I really did leave the Arc, or they'll piece together the truth, and all our planning will have been for nothing. If I stay here and they find me..."

"They'll figure it out."

"There's a good chance of it, yes. Besides, I have work to do—other than leading the Bishop's followers astray, I mean. You're not the only one who has plans for a happier future."

I tilt my head and narrow my eyes. "That sounds like something a mysterious superhero would say."

"I'm no superhero. But I do have a vague plan of action. In the meantime, go to Diva, get your hair and makeup done. Get ready for your spontaneous wedding. I give you both my blessing."

My blessing.

Words normally associated with the father of the bride. But my father is long gone, and I suppose Rys is the closest I have to a senior family member.

I step toward him and throw my arms around his neck, pulling him into a bear hug. He squeezes me back, his chest tight when he says, "I'm happy for you."

I pause for a moment before replying, "There's a real risk the Bishop will know I'm not a Replik, isn't there?"

Rys backs away, stroking a finger over my chin. "Not as much as you think. We fixed your scar. I even gave you Finn's implant, remember?"

"You never told me what kind of implant it is."

"Honestly, I'm not entirely sure. Part of it is a chip the Bishop puts in every Replik—a sort of identification module. Finn and I have a theory the Bishop has a scanner in one of those godawful silver rings of his, and that he can scan people simply by passing a hand over them. It may also be a key to some of his control. If he *does* scan you, though, you will show up as the very Replik who's lying under that white sheet." Rys nods toward the bed. "Anyhow, you should be able to fool the dickhead just long enough."

"Long enough for what?"

Rys doesn't reply, at least not in words. He simply smiles knowingly then leans forward, kisses me on the cheek, and says, "Enjoy your wedding day, Ash."

I let out a laugh and wipe away the fresh tear that's now making its way down my cheek. "A few years ago, if you'd told me I was going to marry anyone before I hit twenty, I would have told you you'd lost your mind."

"But now?"

"In the past year, I've learned to appreciate every good moment—and if I can marry Finn today, if I can find happiness, even for a few precious minutes—I'll take it. I only wish…"

I reach out and take Rys's hand in mine.

"I know," Rys says. "I wish I could be there, too. I'll tell you what, though—when this is all over, and trust me, Ash, it *will* be, one day—we will have another ceremony for you. A small one, on the beach you've always dreamed of."

"I'd love that," I say, glancing over at Atticus, who's perched on the dresser at the far end of the room. "Is he going with you?"

Rys shakes his head. "Not just yet. I'll be bringing other drones as my companions on this particular journey. Atticus will stay and watch over you. He knows you, knows the way you move and think. Plus, he has that invisibility thing going for him."

I smile. "Thank you. I don't begin to imagine how Finn and I are going to take down the Bishop, but we could use all the help we can get."

"Consider Atticus your wedding gift, then," Rys says with a smile I can only describe as wistful.

"Rys! No! I couldn't…"

"Of course you could. You can. Take him, please. He's more attached to you than to me, anyhow."

I glance over at the owl, whose eyes flash blue then green, then red, and back to blue.

"You're sure?" I ask Rys.

"I'm sure. Who knows? You two may need a guard-owl on your honeymoon."

"Honeymoon," I repeat, my chest pounding. "Oh...God."

I haven't even thought of a honeymoon. Could it really be that the Bishop would permit us such a luxury? Can we possibly fool him long enough to get away with it?

"Ashen Spencer," Rys scolds, taking me by the shoulders. "Enough with the doubt and fear. If you look scared today instead of happy, that bastard will know it's the human version of you he's looking at. You need to smile and act like his best friend and closest ally. And for God's sake, act like you're excited to be marrying the man of your dreams. Got it?"

I let out a grim sigh. "You're right, I know you are. And trust me—if we manage to pull off this stunt today, I will be all smiles. But the Bishop is so annoyingly good at reading people. He's perceptive beyond most anyone's imagining. I don't see how I can carry on the charade long enough to survive until the honeymoon."

"I do. You're marrying Finn Davenport, damn it. Hell, I'm not into guys and even I would be giddy with delight if I got to say 'I do' to that tall drink of water. Just...let yourself be happy until it's time for the next phase of Finn's plan."

"What's the next phase?"

Backing away, he winks and says, "That's for Finn to tell you. For now, go. Get ready with Diva. I know she's eager to make you beautiful—not that it'll take much effort."

As I turn away from him, I remember my doppelgänger lying on the guest room bed. "The other Ashen...Am I going to wear her wedding dress?"

"Of course you are, Ash," Rys tells me. "It's *your* wedding dress. It always was."

28

PREPARATIONS

WHEN I'VE FINALLY SUMMONED the courage to move away from Rys, I step into the kitchen, where Diva is awaiting me.

The moment she sees my expression, her face sinks into a look of worry.

"Everything okay?" she asks. "You don't exactly look like the glowing bride-to-be I'd hoped for."

"I will," I assure her. "Let's just say I'm suffering from conflicting emotions."

When she pulls a chair out from the table and gestures me to take a seat, I do so without hesitation, grateful to have put some distance between the Replik and myself.

Diva runs her fingers through my hair and says, "Ashen, we have all suffered from conflicting emotions for so long that I'm not sure any of us knows what it is to feel pure joy anymore. There's always a shadow in our minds—a memory of someone we've lost, or something we've seen that we wish we could erase from our minds. If we don't try to savor the small, shiny points of light that flicker in an otherwise grim world, we'll all lose it."

She's right. Our lives since the Directorate took control of our world have been a mish-mash of pleasure and pain, even for those who, like her, were afforded the luxury of living in the Arc from the beginning. Diva has seen brutality, just as I have. She knows the cruelty our leaders are capable of.

She was with us in Santa Fe when men, women, and children were murdered horrifically before our eyes.

"There are so many people we need to save," I say in response. "People Finn and I can help. They're trapped, imprisoned, comatose. So many don't know they're even alive, and I want to free them. I want to see them reunited with their families."

"And you will. I *know* you will. But for right now, I want you to try and relax. Remember what's about to happen. Not only are you about to marry the man of your dreams, but you're about to do it right under the Bishop's perfect, stupid nose."

At that, I let out a laugh at long last.

"You're right. Let's do this. I can forget about saving the world for one day, right?"

"Damn right."

Diva works her usual magic, styling my hair, applying various types of makeup I never knew existed, and crafting me into someone I'm sure I'll barely recognize when she's finished.

But even when she's finished with my hair and makeup, she puts a hand up and tells me to freeze.

"Nuh-uh!" she says, waving a chastising finger in my direction. "No looking at yourself in the mirror. First, the gown. Trust me, it's magnificent."

I wait as she fetches the dress the other Ashen—the Replik

189

—carried in with her and slowly pulls its red plastic covering away to reveal something I wasn't expecting.

It's not the plastic that's red.

It's the dress itself.

It's long, flowing, a sea of scarlet, and it's the most beautiful garment I've ever seen in my life.

"A dress fitting for the Crimson Dreg," Diva says triumphantly as she holds it high enough for me to see it in all its glory.

The gown is every bit as exquisite as I would expect from someone who essentially shares my mind. Its fitted bodice, boned and embroidered, looks as though it must have taken weeks to stitch. The skirt is accompanied by a long train of flowing layers of silk as beautiful as the rest of the garment.

"So strange," I breathe as I stare at it. "I couldn't have picked out a more exquisite dress myself." An odd sense of sympathy, even affection, pulses through me for the twin I've lost.

"She isn't—*wasn't*—all bad," Diva replies. "Just *created* by someone bad."

"I know."

I take the dress from her and, glancing toward the door, drape it over the nearest chair.

"I'll make sure Rys doesn't come in," Diva promises. "While you get into it."

I slip out of my clothes quickly, and when I'm ready, Diva helps me into the gown. She fastens the buttons at the back then guides me to the bathroom so I can finally look at myself in the full-length mirror.

I inhale a breath, holding it inside as I stare at the young woman reflected back at me.

My dark hair is half pulled back, half flowing down my shoulders, and Diva has tucked small white flowers in here and there. My makeup, as always, is flawless and tasteful at once.

Not surprisingly, the dress is tailored perfectly for my body, and it's difficult to hold back a torrent of happy tears.

"I know it should be a white dress," I say. "But I'm so glad it's red. I'm glad there's some of me in it—of what Finn and I have been through together. But...is it weird that I feel like I'm stealing someone else's day?" I ask, forcing away the emotions.

"No. Because you're Ashen, and it's just like you to feel so much for an imposter. But this day is rightfully yours, and deep down, I think you know it."

After a minute, Diva purses her lips together and lets out a whistle. A few seconds later, Rys pokes his head in, then steps into the room, crosses his arms, and lets out a strange, low growl of admiration.

"Well, Ashen Spencer, you look incredible," he says. "Finn is a lucky man, but it's not like I didn't already know that."

"Thanks, Rys," I reply with a shyness I didn't expect. "I appreciate it."

"I'm sorry, you two, but it's time to get this show on the road," Diva says. "Come on, Ashen. We need to get you to the Royal Grounds and get you married before you turn into a pumpkin."

"I'm pretty sure it's a carriage that turns into a pumpkin in the fairy tale," I tell her. "But I get your meaning."

As we turn to leave, I throw one last glance toward Rys, trying not to remind myself what this moment means for our friendship.

"Go!" he says with a wave of his hand. "You crazy kids have

fun. I'll be sending Atticus to watch in secret, so don't worry—
I'll be seeing everything through his eyes."

"When will I get to speak to you again?"

"Soon," he says. "But hopefully not *too* soon. You've got a
honeymoon coming, and a life to plan. When the time is right,
we'll meet up. I'm sure of it."

I give him a final smile before turning and following Diva
out of the apartment. With my real face on full display, I feel
oddly naked, but the elegant dress and my companion both
grant me a sort of legitimacy, and we walk with intent toward
the Conveyor.

When I hear the flutter of wings, I turn just in time to see
Atticus disappear into stealth mode behind us as he slips out
of the residence.

"Remember," Diva says as we walk down the hall. "You
requested my services for your hair and makeup—meaning
the *Replik* requested me. Your behavior from here on in has to
be *her* behavior. No suspicious glances, no accusing looks
thrown at anyone today. You're supposed to be the happiest
you've ever been, and utterly oblivious to anything bad. As far
as you're concerned, you've won at life."

I let out a laugh and say, "Why do I have the feeling Finn
told you to say all that?"

"Because you know him well," Diva replies with a chuckle.
"Of course he told me to. He wants you safe. Whatever plan
he has for you both involves you making it through the day in
one piece. Your future husband loves you."

"Future *husband*," I repeat.

It seems like such an adult word. But after all, an adult is
what I am. I may never have experienced what many
teenagers or young adults do—driving a car, drinking ridiculous amounts of alcohol, university or college—but I've been

through a rapid-fire succession of harrowing experiences most adults have never had to endure.

I suppose I deserve the privilege of calling Finn my husband.

"You excited?" Diva asks as we make our way onto the Conveyor.

I nod. "I am. And if I'm being honest, I'm terrified, too. Though I'm not sure if that's wedding jitters or *I may die today* jitters."

"Fair enough. But no talk of death, okay? You never know who or what might be listening at the ceremony."

It takes only a couple of minutes to reach the Royal Grounds, but when the Conveyor doors open, Diva tells me to conceal myself against the wall. "Sorry," she says. "I just want to make sure no one important sees you before the big moment."

She peers out, then turns back to me. "We're good," she says. "All I see are Consortium members headed up toward the manor house."

I follow her out of the Conveyor, hearing only the faintest flutter of Atticus's wings as we make our move. Diva waves to a Consortium guard who approaches, beaming when his eyes land on mine. "Congratulations, Ashen," he says with a nod. "You look lovely."

"Thank you so much!" I tell him, attempting to emulate my Replik's bubbly demeanor.

"Your carriage will be here in a moment," he tells us both.

I shoot Diva a look, but she shakes her head almost imperceptibly, reminding me that I shouldn't be surprised by anything that occurs in this place. *After all, I planned it all myself.*

Within a few seconds, I hear the sound of hooves on

gravel. Looking to my right, I see a black horse pulling an ornate red and gold carriage that must once have belonged to the Arc's King and Queen.

Not quite my style, but at least I can conceal myself inside.

When the guard has opened the door, Diva helps me in, taking care not to let my dress get caught before slipping into the seat beside me.

"We'll head straight to the venue," she says. "The ceremony will be quick. Finn's request."

"How many guests are coming?"

"A few hundred, I think. Mostly Consortium members, Illian and Kurt, of course, and a few old friends of Finn's family—some of the few Aristocrats who aren't in the Hold for their crimes. But no one you need to worry about, except..."

"Except for one," I say.

The truth is, I'm looking forward to seeing Illian and Kurt. I'm eager to speak to them, though I'd be more eager if the Bishop weren't breathing down my neck.

"What about Finn?" I ask.

"He'll be here, of course," Diva laughs.

"I mean...will he be waiting for me?"

"I suspect so," she says, nodding in the direction we're heading. "You'll see for yourself in a minute."

"Do I have bridesmaids?" I ask, slightly panicked at the possibility that the Replik made friends while I was in a comatose state for all those months.

"Only Kyra. She's your maid of honor. Merit and Kel are co-best men. I suspect Finn orchestrated all of it."

"I don't know how I'll be able to keep myself from losing it when I see Kel. All I'll want to do is hug him, pull him close, tell him I'll never leave him again."

"It's okay to be a little emotional, you know. It is your wedding day. Just...try not to blurt out that you haven't seen him in months."

"I'll do my best."

I expect the carriage to bring us to the manor house, but instead, it bypasses it and takes us directly to a large, white structure that looks like a gigantic tent set in front of the backdrop of rolling green hills and woods beyond.

"What's this?" I ask, craning my neck to see.

"Something new—a place Finn had constructed just this past week. He told me it's a holo-chamber, a sort of alternate reality room where any setting can be conjured, complete with smells, precipitation, wind—you name it."

I smile when I say, "I know exactly what he's talking about."

Finn and I spent a night in such a place inside the old hotel known as the Palace in Manhattan. A night gifted to us by the Bishop. It seems an odd choice for our wedding, but I trust Finn completely. If he had this place built, he must have had his reasons.

"I have to say, I'm excited to see what he has in store for you both," Diva tells me. "I suspect it will be pretty fabulous."

"Here's hoping," I say with a nervous smile.

When the carriage stops and its driver steps down and opens the door for us, I wait for Diva to step out, then join her on the gravel pathway. She walks me to the tent's entrance, and when I take a peek inside, I see a crowd seated some distance away in elegant white chairs. Their backs are to us, and, as my eyes scan them, the ground beneath their feet morphs into white, pristine sand.

"Oh..." I say softly as the ocean appears beyond the gathered guests, waves lapping in eager white caps against the sand.

As the scent of salt meets my nose, a beautiful sense of calm washes over me, a small voice in my mind assuring me that everything *will* be fine.

"Look!" Diva whispers, pointing to something on the beach. A white arbor crawling with rose-covered vines. Under the arbor, awaiting our arrival, are Finn, Merit, and Kel.

As I watch, another figure sidles up next to them—one who sends a chill along my flesh.

"I thought you said Merit and Kel were the best men," I tell Diva with a shudder of disgust. "What's the Bishop doing up there with them?

"Officiating," a voice says from behind me.

29

THE BIG EVENT

I TURN around to see Kyra behind me, in a dress of light blue silk that matches the ocean perfectly.

After deciding it's an appropriate gesture, I give her a quick squeeze and whisper, "You can't be serious about the Bishop officiating."

"I thought you knew. Rys said—"

When I pull back, the look on her face speaks volumes. But I smile and squeeze her hands, forcing myself to act like the naive Replik I'm meant to be.

"Rys probably thought I'd refuse to come if he told me," I reply, breathing deep to get hold of my emotions. "This is going to make the ceremony a little more challenging."

"Ashen," Diva whispers, leaning in close to push a strand of hair away from my cheekbone. "Breathe. Ask yourself how your Replik would behave. She doesn't have your hatred of the Bishop, remember—for whatever reason, however he did it, he programmed her to adore him. They're best pals. *Act like it.*"

I nod, forcing my smile to expand as I turn to look at the

Bishop. When he looks my way, I offer up a little wave of excitement before turning back to my friends.

"Oh, great," Kyra says under her breath. "The Tree crowd has arrived."

"The who?"

She nods to my right, and I turn to see a small crowd gathered by the inner wall of the tent. Twenty or so serious-looking men and women are standing in a line, dressed in gray tunics with silver trees emblazoned on their chests. The Tree of Life—the symbol of the Bishop's followers.

Though they don't appear to be holding weapons, something about them feels threatening, as if they're waiting for a signal to make their move and take down anyone who should prove disloyal to their beloved leader.

"Right," I whisper. "I'm going to ignore them. If I don't, I'll freak right the hell out."

"Good plan."

Once again, I look toward the arbor. Illian and Kurt are seated in the front row, the seats my parents or Finn's would normally occupy.

Despite everything that's happened, a swell of affection warms my chest as I watch them turn to each other. Illian reaches up and pushes a tendril of Kurt's hair out of his eyes, and Kurt presses close to his partner to whisper something in his ear.

After all is said and done, I can't deny how happy I am to see them together and healthy.

I only hope the Bishop lets them stay that way.

"It's time," Diva says, holding out a bouquet of white flowers for each of us. I don't know where she got them, but I happily accept the larger of the two, grateful to have something to keep my fingers occupied.

When a pretty, familiar piece of classical music begins to play, Diva commands, "Kyra, you go first. Ashen, give her five seconds, then follow."

When Kyra is halfway down the aisle, I begin to walk forward, butterflies swarming maniacally in my stomach as my emotions clash inside me.

I'm about to marry Finn. I'm going to see my brother up close for the first time since before I went to New York.

And the whole time, I'll be standing next to the Bishop.

As Kyra takes her place opposite the boys, Kel, who seems to have grown several inches since I last saw him, grabs hold of Merit's arm and yanks on his sleeve, pointing at me.

In the same moment, Finn's eyes shoot to mine. At first, he looks vaguely apprehensive, his jaw set tightly.

I read his thoughts instantly. He's studying me, trying to figure out which version of Ashen he's seeing. Wondering if Rys was successful this morning—if the Replik has really been disabled.

When I offer up a broad smile, he lights up with a relieved grin, bouncing a little on his toes in anticipation of my arrival.

I'm glad you know it's really me.

I can only hope the Bishop doesn't.

Soaring orchestral music begins to play—some famous piece or other, probably chosen by a wedding planner. It's pretty, but a little militaristic for my tastes. I feel as if I'm marching off to war instead of into a lifetime of bliss with the man I love.

My legs nearly give out under me as it hits me how surreal and twisted this moment is. *I'm pretending to be a version of me who was simulating me.*

As I glide down the aisle, my perma-smile adhered to my face, it takes all my strength not to look at the Bishop. If he sees me wince for even a split-second—if I let on in the tiniest way that I am repulsed by his presence here—he'll know beyond a shadow of a doubt what's happened.

This moment is the most important of my life so far. I *need* to make it down the aisle. I need to exchange vows with Finn, to...

Oh, God.

The vows.

Am I supposed to know what to say? Did my Replik have a plan? Was I supposed to memorize a speech?

As I ask myself the questions, panicking while trying to maintain my happy glow, a voice slips into my head.

"Don't worry, Ashen. There's nothing to fear."

That voice—it belongs to Atticus. He's somewhere overhead, watching like a shadow against the artificial sky. How he read my thoughts, I can't say.

Or maybe he simply read my body language. Shoulders tightening. Pace slowing.

"Can you hear me, Atticus?" I ask silently, sending my silent words into the ether.

But he doesn't reply, and I tell myself I simply imagined the voice in order to calm myself.

It's true, after all. There is nothing to fear. Finn would never set up something as intricate as this wedding and forget to tell me to write vows.

Besides, if it comes down to it, I can speak for hours about my love for him. About how I feel when I look into his eyes. How much I love his affection for his brother, for Kel. How I adore his protective nature. How I want to spend every day and night for the rest of my life by his side.

As those thoughts weave their way through my mind, my smile grows with each step. In a moment of weakness, I let my eyes move to the Bishop, whose chin is high, his eyes assessing me. But for once, he doesn't look suspicious.

If anything, he looks pleased with himself, as if he's proudly responsible for the miracle that's about to occur.

As his eyes slip over my features, they settle on my chin, and his smile deepens. No doubt the Bishop has seen my newly reinstated scar and confirmed that I am indeed his creation.

When I finally step beneath the arbor, it's all I can do not to reach over, grab Kel, and pull him to my chest. I'm convinced he's grown six inches since I last saw him in person, though it seems impossible. How much of his life have I missed? How much joy, how much sadness?

He stares at me with a goofy grin, elbowing Merit as if to say, "Isn't my sister pretty?" and I let out a quick laugh before doubt creeps in and I ask myself if the Replik would have reacted in such a way.

I slam my mouth shut and focus on Finn.

He reaches out, offering me his hands. I hand my bouquet to Kyra and take them, staring deep into his eyes.

I turn briefly to my right and smile at the guests. Illian's eyes are locked on mine, and he's smiling, too. But something in his face looks blank, vacant, as if his mind isn't entirely present.

For a nervous moment, I wonder if there's any chance I'm looking at a Replik—after all, the Bishop could have done to him what he did to me. Replaced him with someone who would happily do his bidding and turn the Consortium into something close to a cult.

But as I study him and Kurt, I'm certain they're human. Flawed, taken in by a man with quiet, insidious powers and a level of cruelty that's impossible to fathom—but human.

As the thought swirls through my mind, I tell myself to snap out of it. I need to focus on the here and now, on Finn, on the hands that hold my own, anchoring me to reality and to our future.

I focus on his eyes, pulling myself closer.

"You look beautiful, Ash," he whispers as the Bishop looks on.

"Thank you. So do you."

I didn't think such a thing was possible, but he looks even more handsome than he did the night of the Introduction Ceremony. My heart flutters in my chest as I look at him, and I find myself wishing we didn't have to go through with this public display. I'd give anything just to run away into the mountains. To say goodbye to Arcologies and civilization forever.

But a voice draws me back to reality.

"Are you two ready?" the Bishop asks with an unreadable smile.

Finn and I nod in unison, our eyes locked. "So ready," Finn says, and this time, I allow myself the sort of giggle I've heard from the Replik more than once.

"Me, too," I chirp as the ocean waves hit the shore mere feet from where we're standing.

"Dearly Beloved," the Bishop begins in a booming voice that projects itself to the back of the assembled crowd, "We are gathered here to support a union long in the making, and crucial to the well-being of the Arc—and indeed of the entire world. The Crimson Dreg is marrying her love today, and I am so very proud to have been asked to officiate."

A chorus of cheers and applause erupts from the gathered crowd, and I turn to see the Bishop's Acolytes beyond the seated guests, throwing their hands in the air, whistling, and shouting.

"When this union is made official," the Bishop adds, "I look forward to working with these two wondrous individuals to improve the lives of us all. Ashen and Finn will lead us to a new age of prosperity, longevity, and advancements the likes of which the world has rarely seen." He locks eyes on the people in the front row and says, "Do you not agree, Illian?"

What's he doing? Why would he ask that in the middle of our wedding?

I jab myself internally, reminding myself to keep up the act even as I turn to face Illian and Kurt, who look suddenly glum and pale. For the first time, I wonder if some part of them understands what's happening.

"Yes," Illian says, his voice strained. "Of course I do."

"Good," the Bishop replies. "Then I ask, Ashen Spencer and Finn Davenport...do you agree to be joined in Matrimony, to commit to one another as long as you both shall live?"

His delivery of the last few words feels drawn out and menacing, and sends a cold tremor along my flesh.

"We do," Finn and I both say, our hands tightly clasped together.

I feel light and heavy at once, like this is a dream that should be wonderful, but has far too much potential to turn nightmarish.

"Ashen," the Bishop says, forcing my eyes to land on his own. "Do you give yourself freely to Finn, to love and to cherish, as long as you both shall live?"

"Yes. Of course I do."

"And Finn?"

"I do," he says.

"In that case, before all these witnesses, I now pronounce you husband and wife. Kel, Merit...please."

The two boys step forward on cue, and Kel hands me a gold ring. Merit hands a similar, smaller one to Finn. Silently, we slip them onto one another's fingers before clasping our hands together once again.

Triumphant, the Bishop calls out, "So begins a new age, and a new world. From this day forward, nothing will be the same."

Forgetting my act for a second, I tighten, my eyes widening as I pull them up to Finn's. *What does he mean by that? What is he planning to do?*

But before anyone has a chance to notice my reaction, Finn pulls me close and kisses me passionately, deeply, his arms wrapping protectively around me. He's sealing our bond and solidifying our union. But he's also shielding me, preventing me from exposing my true self.

The crowd explodes into uproarious applause as I surrender, my tension fading with the touch of Finn's lips, the taste of him. It's a sensation I've craved desperately for so long—one I've had to deny myself.

Just before he pulls away, Finn whispers against my cheek, "I love you, Ash. I have a wedding gift for you, and I think you're going to like it. Now, let's get out of here."

30

RECEPTION

As we make our way hand in hand back down the aisle with Kel, Merit, and Kyra in tow, Finn leans in again.

"We will talk about everything, I promise," he whispers. "But not right here, not right now. For now, we have to carry on the act."

"Act?" I whisper back, looking up at him with a genuinely amused smile. "And here I thought you were happy to be marrying me."

With a laugh, he pulls me close and again, he kisses me, to more cheers from the onlookers. "I couldn't possibly be happier," he says, shooting a look toward the Bishop. "Okay, maybe there's one thing that could make me *slightly* happier. But you know what I'm saying."

"Yeah, I get it." I nod, grinning from ear to ear.

I don't know what horrible things our enemy has planned for us. All I know is that Finn and I are together, my Replik is gone, and things are looking up. I'm not about to let my guard down, but at least I can breathe slightly easier than I could a few days ago.

As if on cue, the cloud hanging over us in the form of the Bishop strides up to us, clasps a hand onto each of our shoulders, and says, "Congratulations, you two. I am more delighted than I can say to see you lovebirds joined at last. I have wished for this from the very first time I met you both."

You mean you've wished for Finn to marry the Replik, I want to say. *You never wanted me happy. You wanted to torture me the second you decided I wasn't useful to you.*

As the waves lap at the shore in the distance, I find myself wishing we were standing on the edge of a cliff so that I could push him off.

Just as I'm fantasizing about the Bishop's demise, Illian and Kurt walk over to wish us well. As Kurt gushes about what a handsome couple we are, Illian pulls me into a bear hug.

"Congratulations, Ashen," he says quietly. I can hear the sincerity in his voice, but there's something else, too; a sort of distant sadness.

Pulling back, I look him in the eye.

"Are you all right?" I ask.

He stares at me for a few seconds, his sorrowful expression softening, a smile invading the corners of his eyes. "Ashen, I…" he says softly. "Yes. I'm just fine. Thank you."

I turn to Kurt and study him for a moment. Like Illian, he looks a little off-kilter, like something has slightly disoriented him. "And you, Kurt?" I ask. "You're doing well?"

Out of the corner of my eye, I watch the Bishop. He may be wondering why a Replik would ask such a question, but if he's confused, he doesn't show it.

"I'm doing great," Kurt says with a smile, stepping forward to kiss me on the cheek. "But this day isn't about us. It's about you, Mrs. Davenport."

"Mrs. Davenport," I repeat, looking to Finn. "I like the sound of that."

"Or I could call myself Mr. Spencer," Finn replies with a laugh. "I know my name isn't exactly your favo…"

I stop him with a hand to his chest. "I love it," I insist, planting a kiss on his lips before he has a chance to bring up his mother's name in front of the Bishop.

I'm married to Finn. This is supposed to be the happiest moment of my life. The last thing I want right now is to think about the Duchess.

There's only one thing that could make the moment better, and he leaps at me, his arms twisting around my waist.

Kel.

I squeeze him tightly, trying against all my instincts not to let on how excited I am to be in his presence at long last. When I pull back, I try to read his expression. Does he know? Is he aware that the Ash he's spent the last several months with isn't the one who's looking at him now?

If he does know, he's doing a hell of a job of hiding it.

"Happy Wedding-slash-Birth-Day!" he says. "My present is with the other ones in the ballroom."

"Ballroom?" I ask.

"Yeah," Kel laughs. "You know, where the reception is going to be! Did you forget or something?"

"Of course not!" I blurt out. "I'm just a little distracted, Little Man. But I'm looking forward to opening your gift with Finn later."

Merit sidles up next to Kel. He looks temporarily sheepish before he, too, moves in for a hug. "Congratulations," he says quietly.

"Thank you, Merit," I tell him, hugging him tight. When he

pulls away I study his expression, then peer at Finn, who drapes an arm around his brother.

"He's missing our parents," Finn says, and I nod solemnly.

"I get it, Merit. I miss my parents, too."

I can't tell him the truth of it—that I don't know if he still even *has* two parents.

"I'm sure they miss you," I tell him.

"I doubt it," Merit replies with a scowl. "In case you've never noticed, our parents aren't exactly Mom and Dad of the Year award winners. I still wish they were here, though."

Finn takes me by the hand, abruptly changing the subject. "Should we make our way to the ballroom, then?" He asks. "Sorry—this is my first time getting married. I don't know how things work."

"First time? Are you planning on more weddings?"

"We'll see how this one works out, I guess." Finn lets out a snicker, then says, "Actually, first, I think you and I should walk around the gardens a little. I want you all to myself, just for a few minutes."

"Sounds great."

I gather my long red dress about me and accompany him out of the tent, where the scent morphs immediately from salty air and seaweed to grass and flowers.

"That is an amazing achievement. The tent, I mean," I say. "I kept forgetting we weren't actually on the beach, which is some kind of miracle."

"Do you think so?" Finn asks. "Good. I'm glad. I have exciting plans for that technology. I've been hard at work on something special."

I give him a curious side-eyed glance, but don't dare ask what he means. I'm still acting, after all—still supposed to be the slightly oblivious, happy Replik who never asks too many questions.

Finn takes my hand and guides me down a set of stone steps toward a long gravel path that leads into the perfectly groomed garden that once belonged to the King and Queen.

"I wonder where the owners are now," I say.

"I can only imagine," Finn says. "It's entirely possible they're dead. The Bishop has taken everything from them, and he's not one to keep ambitious people around if they don't offer him something in return."

"Speaking of the Bishop..." I reply, but Finn shakes his head and whispers that I need to wait a minute. We walk a little farther, stopping only when we reach a stone bench set at the edge of a pretty, blossoming orchard.

When we sit down, I hear a flutter of wings and a moment later, I see Atticus come out of stealth mode and land a few feet away on a tree limb.

"Atticus," Finn says, seemingly unsurprised by the owl's sudden appearance. "Block any and all transmissions to and from this specific location."

The owl lets out a low hooo before reverting to stealth mode.

I look over and spot the Bishop wandering among the wedding guests, Naeva on his arm. Occasionally, he sends a curious glance our way, but to my relief, he doesn't make his way over.

"I don't think he's listening in," Finn tells me. "But just in case..."

He leans forward, brushes my hair back, and kisses me. "I'm so sorry, Ash," he whispers.

"Sorry?" I ask. "For marrying me?"

"For leaving you in New York. For losing you like that for

so long. For letting myself be taken in by that monster. I'm so sorry I failed you. You must have thought..."

He doesn't finish. Then again, he doesn't need to. I know exactly what he's thinking.

I reach up and stroke my fingertips over his dark layer of stubble. "I thought exactly what you would have thought in my shoes—that the Bishop screwed us, took advantage of us, and hurt us both deeply. You were a victim, just like me."

"Rys saw the truth," Finn says, lowering his chin remorsefully. "He knew about the Replik. He's the one who saved you from my mother—and it should have been me. Like I said, I failed you."

I shake my head. "Rys wasn't near the Bishop. He wasn't brainwashed like we were," I tell him, taking his hand in mine. "But it doesn't matter anymore. We're together now. We're *married*, Finn—which is crazy. I mean, this wasn't how I ever thought things would end up, but look—Merit and Kel are here. We're bound together. We even get to go on a honeymoon, right?"

"Which I'm pretty excited about, to be honest."

"Me, too," I confess, my face heating.

Finn presses toward me, cupping his fingers under my chin. "I wish I could take you somewhere far away. To Greece, or Italy, or somewhere just as amazing. But I promise you, we'll get to those places one day. We will have the life we've dreamed of."

With a nod, I smile up at him. "I know we will," I tell him. "But I also know we can't leave here just now. Things are too volatile in the Arc."

"Not only that," Finn tells me. "But things are about to get *more* volatile."

I glance around, wary that someone could be listening in

spite of Atticus's help. "What do you mean?" I ask under my breath when I'm confident we're alone.

"The Bishop has something planned," he says. "There are Aristocrats and Directorate members in the Hold—the ones Illian put there ages ago. He's promised to free them, but only if they're willing to join the ranks of his cult. He's hoping to expand his numbers here—to get the rich and powerful behind him and overthrow the Consortium."

"I don't get it. To what end? He already took the Behemoth in New York. I don't understand why he's even here anymore. Does he really need to destroy another Arcology?"

Finn clenches and unclenches his jaw. "I can't say for sure, but I think something has happened out east. Something momentous. I've only heard whispers about it between the Bishop and a few of his Acolytes. But I'm pretty sure he's lost control of the Behemoth."

"What?" I blurt out, my jaw dropping open. "How is that even possible? You and I both saw that place. We know what kind of hold the Bishop had over it. Everyone inside was kept separate, isolated. He was the only one who controlled the mag-lifts and the residences. How could someone possibly take it over?"

"I don't know yet. But I can't imagine your friend Adi and her band of rebels managed to barge in and take over. So whatever coup may have happened must have been from the inside."

"A coup might not be such a bad thing," I say with a smirk. "Maybe the Wealthies inside the Moth have banded together somehow, now that he's far away. Anyone would be better than the Bishop—and if someone's taken over the Moth, maybe they're planning on freeing the prisoners from that horrible silo. If they did that, they'd have a potential army—thousands of people on their side."

"Maybe," Finn says, but he looks a million miles away, his face lined with worry.

I take his hand in mine, pull him to his feet and put my arms around him, pressing my face to his chest. "We're supposed to be euphoric today," I tell him. "I'm supposed to be acting like my giddy Replik, and you're supposed to be ecstatic to be marrying her. So no more worrying, okay? We have our whole lives ahead of us. Plenty of time to freak out. How about for today, we just pretend life is perfect?"

Finn lets out a low chuckle, kisses my forehead, and says, "You're absolutely right."

Turning to his left, he calls out, "Atticus, you can go ahead and stop blocking the signal. It's time for us to socialize."

A quick hoot greets our ears in response, then Finn and I start heading back toward the manor house, where the gathered crowd is making their way inside.

As we make our way to the ballroom, Kel comes running up to me again, and once again, he throws his arms around me.

"Ash?" he whispers, pulling me close.

I press my ear to his mouth and ask, "What is it?"

"It's you," he says softly. "Isn't it?"

So, you do know about the Replik.

I can't help but be proud of my brother for hiding his suspicions so well from the Bishop.

I nod against him and whisper, "Of course it's me. Don't say anything about that, okay? It's our little secret."

"Of course."

I take Finn's arm as we step into the ballroom, and it's the Bishop who approaches next, taking me by the arm and turning me his way. He's not gentle in his touch as he pulls me away from Finn.

"Congratulations, Ashen," he says. "I'm sure you two will be very happy together." He presses close to hug me and says, "You remember what I said, yes? The honeymoon is the perfect time to gather information. You will see what you can find out—what your handsome husband has been up to. You will report back to me the second you know anything at all. Understood?"

My lips curve upward and I have to stifle a laugh. So, he really *does* think I'm her.

Can this possibly have been so easy?

Instead of letting doubt flood my mind, I pull back and nod. "Yes, of course," I say with a smile. "I'll tell you every-thing, just like I always do."

"Good. We're very close to the next stage of our plan, and I don't want anything to go wrong."

I'm tempted to ask what he means by "next stage," but something tells me he and my Replik have already discussed it. Asking questions would likely be the kiss of death.

I throw a sideways glance in Finn's direction, and the Bishop says, "Go to him. We'll discuss this further later. Enjoy your special day and your honeymoon. I'll be seeing you very soon."

His tone is ominous, even a little threatening, but I chalk it up to his strange brand of arrogance. Nodding, I step over to Finn, relieved to be free of the Bishop's touch, his breath, his scent. I'd almost forgotten how grotesquely appealing he is— like a beautiful, inviting flower waiting for its unsuspecting victim to approach so he can devour them whole.

When I once again hook my arm through Finn's, he escorts me to a long table coated in a white cloth, an abundance of roses arranged into an exquisite centerpiece. We seat ourselves, our fingers woven together in a silent vow never to allow ourselves to be separated again.

"Food!" someone shouts jubilantly. Kel, Merit, and Kyra rush over to seat themselves at our table, as does Diva.

"There aren't going to be speeches, are there?" I ask, leaning in nervously to Finn.

He shakes his head. "We're going to eat and get the hell away from this place. That's all."

The guests have begun taking their own seats at various tables, all of which are decorated with name tags. Illian and Kurt are at a nearby table, sitting with a few Consortium members from the Santa Fe faction. They look tense, and I notice Illian and Kurt exchanging whispers here and there as they look over to the place where the Bishop is sitting with Naeva and flanked by a few of his uniformed Acolytes.

"Don't worry," Finn tells me, reading my expression. "I promise you, this will all be over soon."

I'm not sure if he means the wedding or the nightmare that is the Bishop. But as if in reaction to Finn's words, the Bishop's head whips around and his eyes land on mine, narrowing into an accusing look.

Under the table, I slip a hand onto Finn's thigh and my fingertips dig in, desperate to anchor themselves in something solid.

A few minutes ago, I was utterly confident that Finn and I had pulled this plan of his off.

But I'm not so sure anymore.

HOPE

WHEN WE'VE CONSUMED a feast of roast beef, a plethora of vegetables and a delicious hunk of dark chocolate wedding cake, Finn and I entertain the masses with exactly one dance, which is projected on a series of screens around the ballroom and, according to a few Consortium members, is being broadcast to the entire Arc.

The tale of the Aristocrat boy and the Crimson Dreg, it seems, has been wrapped up with a tidy bow and put on display for all to see.

As I press close to him, our bodies swaying on the polished oak dance floor, I look up into Finn's eyes, recalling the night almost exactly a year ago when we danced together at the Introduction Ceremony.

Finn must be thinking of it, too, because he says, "Happy Birthday, Ash."

"You remembered," I reply with a smile.

"Of course. So much has happened in the space of a year, but this date is one that will always be momentous to me. The day you came into this world and made it glow bright."

He leans in to kiss my lips, and I feel myself losing my center of gravity for a few seconds, blissful and at peace.

But even as we pull apart, memories of the past year take my mind captive.

So much death, I think. *So much cruelty. And here we are, at the center of all of it, still unable to make it stop. The King and Queen may be gone, and the Duchess. But the Bishop is still in charge—still threatening our friends, our shrinking family.*

"How are we going to end this once and for all?" I ask him softly, tears in my eyes. "This cycle of cruelty?"

"With help," he says. "With strength. With determination."

"You make it sound so simple."

"It won't be. You and I haven't fought a war—yet. And with any luck, we won't have to. But we both know what's coming, and how brutal it will be. I can only hope all my planning won't turn out to be pointless."

As he finishes speaking, the music comes to an end. Illian approaches us with two glasses of champagne and hands them to us, turning to the crowd.

"Please raise your glasses to the Davenports—the new Duke and Duchess of the Arc! May they live a long and happy life together!"

I'd almost forgotten the titles newly bestowed upon us by the Bishop—titles that feel like an injury inflicted with deliberate malice.

The crowd, oblivious to my discomfort, cheers and does as he says, lifting glasses and swigging whatever it is they may contain. I take a tentative sip of champagne, and Finn downs his quickly, more trusting than I am.

"You want to get out of here?" he asks me, and I nod.

I turn Illian's way. "I don't want to be rude, but..."

He puts his hands up and says, "Far be it from me to keep

you two from beginning your honeymoon." He chuckles, glances toward the far end of the room where the Bishop is standing, and quietly leans in to hug me. "Ashen," he whispers, "I'm so sorry."

"Sorry?" I ask, jerking back. What is he apologizing for? What has he done?

I look around at all the people drinking champagne and wonder if someone has slipped something into their glasses.

But Illian shakes his head. "You don't understand. I'm sorry for letting myself be taken in. I promise you—I'll make it right."

He steps back, smiling, and bows his head. "Go, you two. Enjoy yourselves. I will keep an eye on you, but only from a distance. I have disabled any and all comms systems that could potentially be hacked into on the level where you'll spend the next two weeks. So there won't be any monitoring of your activities by a third party."

"Understood. Thank you, Illian," Finn says, taking my hand and kissing it. "Come on, Ash—we have somewhere to be."

He escorts me to the nearest Conveyor, and I'm careful to ensure my dress's entire train is inside in case the door whooshes shut.

I hear the faint flapping of wings, and breathe a sigh of relief to know Atticus is with us.

"I don't have any luggage, a toothbrush, anything," I say with an amused realization.

"All that will be provided for you, don't worry. And if you want to see Kel in the next few days, that will be possible, too."

As the doors close, I spot the Bishop in the distance, his eyes once again locked on mine—and once again I get the feeling he knows more than he's letting on.

When we're finally sealed in, I turn to Finn. I smile, but he can see the worry in my eyes.

"Two weeks is a long time," I tell him. "The Bishop will be able to…"

"The Bishop doesn't have long in this place," Finn says mysteriously. "Take my word for it. In the meantime, I have a favor to ask of you."

"Anything."

"Give me twenty-four hours. Twenty-four hours when we don't speak of him, of suffering, of death, of how we're going to save humanity. That's all I ask."

For a moment, his words jar me. Am I really that wretched? Can I not go for a day without lamenting about the ills of the world?

But after a second, I let out a laugh. "You've got it," I tell him, kissing him. "Twenty-four hours it is. But after that, I'm going to become insufferable."

Finn takes the flowing fabric of my dress between his fingers and says, "I would expect nothing less from the Crimson Dreg."

When the Conveyor stops and its doors open, my breath catches in my chest, and I freeze in place, unsure if I'm living a dream.

I haven't asked Finn where we're to spend the next two weeks. There is, after all, much of the Arc I've never seen—the building itself is three hundred levels high. But somewhere deep inside was a hope that we would find ourselves in a place that meant something to us. The Grotto, where we used to hide from his mother and swim together—though I'm not sure I'd want to be confined to what's essentially an underground cavern for two weeks straight.

This place, as it turns out, is even better.

We're on the Escapa Level—the immense adult playground that features replicated versions of cities and other places around the world. Paris, Rome, Istanbul, Bali, Rio, and more. Any location that a tourist might want to see is represented here, in graphic, painstaking details. For years, after all, the Arc was a prison keeping its wealthy tenants trapped inside "for their own protection," and many of them craved occasional escape. So they would come here and spend days or weeks in the Escapa's hotels, sipping cappuccino on patios or roaming long hiking trails, the scents, sounds, and sights rendered to perfection.

Right now, Finn and I find ourselves looking out onto a long, broad Parisian street, the Eiffel Tower looming in the distance. A sea of lights twinkle around us as if we've changed time zones and night had suddenly fallen.

The scent of fresh bread and savory spices hits my nose, and I want nothing more than to wander down the street, taking in every inch of every stone building, every façade of every restaurant.

The world around us has turned exquisite—but the most remarkable thing is the lack of people. I've only ever seen shoulder to shoulder crowds in the Escapa, and now, it seems, we have it virtually all to ourselves.

"Where is everyone?" I ask, holding Finn's hand and taking a tentative step forward.

"The crowds are gone for the next few days," Finn says. "A little gift from Illian and Kurt. They shut down the Escapa to tourists just for us. We will have waiters and so on—the employees in the hotels and restaurants have remained behind to help us. But there are no tourists. The streets are ours. Anywhere you want to go, anything you want to see—there will be no waiting in line. No tickets to buy. The Escapa is our playground, Ash."

I spin around, letting the red dress flare around me, my arms outstretched. It's a rare feeling, but I am, without question, happy.

Atticus, coming out of his stealth mode, flies up and perches on top of a lamp post, his eyes glowing blue as he scans the area.

I leap into Finn's arms and kiss him again, hardly daring to believe this is happening. "Thank you," I say. "I genuinely don't know how you managed all this. This...magic. With the Replik. With me. With Atticus..."

I pull my eyes up to look at the silver owl, who issues a quiet hoot.

"Do you suppose Rys can see us through him?" I ask, my arm around Finn's waist.

"I think so—not that he'd spy on us. Would you, Rys?" Finn asks with a twinkle in his eye, looking up at Atticus.

The owl shakes his head slowly, but surprisingly, I don't hear Rys's familiar voice saying something smart-assy. I miss him suddenly. "I wonder where he is."

"I'm sure we'll find out soon enough," Finn assures me. "In the meantime, no talk of worries or wretchedness, remember? We're supposed to be celebrating, not getting stressed out."

"Right. I did make a promise."

We walk along the street, our eyes veering left and right to peer into shop windows and restaurants, until we come to an elegant hotel with large glass doors. Finn leads me inside, and a man behind the desk hands him a key.

"Everything you requested is in your suite, Monsieur," the

man says in a thick French accent. "Let me know if you are in need of anything at all."

"Thank you."

Finn picks me up and leaps toward a nearby set of stairs, climbing until we come to a long corridor on the second floor. He carries me to the end, then manages to unlock the door and step over the threshold, and doesn't set me down until we're inside.

The suite that meets our eyes is unbelievably beautiful— polished wooden floors, sixteen-foot ceilings, and windows taller than Finn himself, looking out toward the Eiffel Tower and the Seine beyond. If I didn't know any better, I would be convinced we'd somehow ended up in the *true* Paris.

Finn sets me on my feet, steps up behind me, and wraps his arms around my waist, his chin resting on my head.

"To think the world once felt like this," he says, his tone wistful. "This carefree. This natural. When did it all go wrong?"

I spin around, taking his face in my hands, and kiss him. "No wretchedness!" I chastise. "You and I are supposed to fix the world, aren't we? Us, and Rys, and Atticus, and..."

"And..." Finn says. "Yes. We'll fix it, you and I. And you're right. No wretchedness."

Taking his hand, I skip my way into the bedroom, which is even more stunning than the living area. On the bed are two expensive-looking white robes and a small plate with an assortment of delectable-looking chocolates.

I dash over to the closet, where I find an array of clothing hanging tidily in wait, both for Finn and myself. I let out a happy sigh and turn back to face my husband.

Husband, I think, a happy shudder running through me.

"I know we're not supposed to talk about it," I say, "but I do have one question."

"What is it?" he asks, slipping close to me and laying a hand on my waist. His eyes stare hungrily into mine, and he leans down to kiss my neck, which takes my mind entirely off the words I was about to ask.

It takes every ounce of my strength to pull away and look at him.

"Do you really think we can come out on top, after everything we still have to face? There are still people trapped in the Moth and the Arc. There are still brainwashed young women being used as incubators for Wealthies. And the Bishop..."

He raises his chin and scrutinizes me, then lets out a sigh.

"Ashen Spencer. I love you," he says, combing his fingers through my loose strands of hair. "But you're incorrigible. And in answer to your question: I have no idea, but I hope we can make things right. In the meantime, what say we take our lives one day at a time? We're together now, after far too many months apart, and I don't know about you, but I want to make up for lost time."

I nod, smile, and, surrendering my mind and my body, let him guide me over to the bed. He kisses me then, an unrelenting, famished kiss, and my fingers twist their way through his hair as his tongue finds its way past my lips.

Once again, I feel what it is to fall, weightless and helpless, knowing that I may collide hard with the earth.

But this time, I am not afraid of what is to come.

This time, I am hopeful.

THE SUITE

WE SPEND the night living a fantasy I had never dared dream. A whirlwind of emotion, sensation, need, hunger. We are entwined in one another's arms, one moment glistening with perspiration, exhausted to the point of collapse, and the next moment, we are energized anew. We taste every inch of one another's skin, experience every tingle of every nerve ending imaginable...including nerves I never knew I possessed.

To say the night is a happy one is the greatest understatement ever uttered, and yet I can't begin to find the words to describe the flurry of excitement that sends my heart into a rapid-fire drumbeat in my chest.

We are married, but the ceremony, the quick vows, the witnesses are irrelevant. What matters is that we are now bonded. We are one.

By morning, I feel as though I've run several marathons, but somehow, I'm eager and fully prepared to run many, many more.

I lie on my side, the white sheet half-draped over my body

as Finn runs a lazy finger over the curve of my waist. The smile on his lips is one that I never want to vanish.

"I have a question," I tell him.

His smile threatens to fade as he pulls his eyes away from my body and says, "Go ahead."

"Was it his idea or yours? The wedding, I mean?"

Finn looks away only briefly before meeting my eyes again. "It was mine," he tells me. "The Bishop was doubting my feelings for the…other Ashen. When I suggested a wedding, it was in the hopes that it would convince him that I was fully on board. He jumped at the idea. He loved it. So I basically led him to think it was his idea all along. The man is a walking ego trip." He pulls back a little and asks, "Why? Do you wish it hadn't happened?"

Without hesitation, I shake my head. "I've spent the last year of my life waking up every morning—that is, when I wasn't in a coma—unsure if I would survive to see another day. Nothing has changed, not really. I'm still not sure if something catastrophic will happen to us both, or to Kel, or Merit. But the one thing I'm sure of is that I love being married to you."

"Good," he says, playing with the ring on his finger. "Because I'm pretty sure we consummated our marriage about eighteen times last night."

I push him down, laughing, and climb on top of him, kissing his mouth, his neck, my hands slipping over his broad chest. I let out a contented moan as I feel his body under my own.

"You are mine now," I tell him, "in every conceivable way."

I've heard all my life that marriage is a quick way to ruin a couple's intimacy, that it stifles excitement and desire. But in this instant, I find it impossible to believe. The one certainty in my life is my bond with Finn, and that is enough to give me hope, to fill me with an excitement I've never known before.

We spend the next several hours in bed, covering ourselves in our robes only when a knock sounds at the door sometime in the early afternoon. Finn strides over to find that the hotel has sent up a very late breakfast for us: coffee, croissants, eggs, and an assortment of French pastries I couldn't begin to name.

For some reason, looking at the tray of amazing food makes my eyes well with tears.

Once Finn has laid it down on the table, he steps over and takes me in his arms.

"What is it?" he asks. "What's wrong?"

I shake my head, letting out a half-wail, half-chuckle. "My family," he says. "My parents. They never got to experience anything like this. They never had money. Never had privilege." I look into Finn's eyes, wiping my tears away. "There are thousands of people out there who need our help, and here I'm standing in this amazing hotel room, living a moment of absolute luxury. It feels so wrong...but there's still a part of me that never wants to go back. Part of me wants to wave my hand and tell them all to sort out their own mess, so you and I can just keep being happy."

"I hate to tell you, Ash, but this is how a lot of Wealthies have lived for hundreds of years," Finn says, his tone cynical. "I should know—I was part of it. My parents never worried about their status, about money. But it didn't make them good people."

"I know," I tell him. "And I would never abandon those who need us. But I hate that I'm even a little tempted."

"It's the fact that you fight the temptation that makes you

different. That's what makes you so powerful. It's why I love you so much."

He steps back, wipes the remaining wetness from my cheeks, and kisses me. "I have something for you today. Something I think you'll like. A part of the Escapa you've never seen."

"Oh?"

He nods. "I hope it makes you happy."

I grin, still forcing away thoughts of our dubious future, of the Bishop and his frightening followers, of the Consortium's crumbling leadership. I try not to let my mind stray, telling myself instead that Finn and I have an opportunity to grow our strength over the next several days. To conspire, to come up with a plan to take down the Bishop. But for now, I tell myself, it's okay to allow myself a modicum of pleasure. After last night, it's remarkably easy to melt into bliss and shove away the nightmare that has consumed me for so long.

Finn advises me to bring winter clothing along for our outing—a strange request, given that it's practically summer, and besides, everywhere I've ever been in the Escapa is climate controlled. Still, I oblige, packing a tote bag with a puffer jacket, a hat, mittens, and a scarf, all of which are sitting in wait in the suite's walk-in closet.

I pull on a pair of jeans, a light sweater, and a pair of leather boots.

Finn dresses similarly, his athletic physique looking more appetizing than ever in a cotton sweater, dark jeans, and a pair of brown ankle boots.

"The place we're going is some distance away," he says. "So we'll be taking a ride."

"Not a Conveyor?"

He shakes his head. "Actually, I thought it might be more

fun to take a train. You'll be able to see more of the countryside that way."

"Train?" I ask, laughing. "I didn't know there was one on
this level!"

"It's not used all that often," Finn tells me. "But it exists. It's
mostly just a novelty item, but can be pretty handy. Come on
—it's time."

With the tote bag slung over my shoulder, I accompany
him to the hotel's foyer, and when we step out into the street,
we find the train waiting for us. It's small—a sort of miniatur-
ized version of an old-fashioned passenger train with five or
six cars.

"It's not on tracks," I laugh.

"No. Like I said—it's purely a novelty item." Finn takes my
hand and guides me into one of the cars, and almost instantly,
the train begins moving fast through Paris's empty streets.

I take a seat next to Finn, leaning my head on his shoulder
and watching out the window as we leave the replica of Paris's
downtown and make our way into what looks like a hilly
countryside.

Before half an hour has passed, snow-capped mountains
are rising up before us; massive, intimidating peaks even
larger than the familiar Rockies.

"Are we in the Alps?" I ask.

Finn nods. "I thought you might like to see the world from
up high."

"How is this possible, though? The Escapa's ceilings aren't
high enough to contain entire mountains. It's got to be some
sort of optical illusion."

Finn lets out a laugh that reminds me that every single
thing in the Arc is basically an illusion.

"Right. Holo-this and fake that. I almost forgot how this

place works," I tell him, recalling how much I've seen in this enormous building that turned out to be nothing more than projected fantasies.

"This illusion is special, I'll admit," Finn says. "While you were..." He stops, clears his throat, and shifts his eyes to look out the window. "While that bastard had you and Rys imprisoned for months, and while I was trying to figure out how to get us both out of the mess the Bishop created, I did some work with a few of the Consortium's tech scientists. They taught me a lot about simulations and Alternate Reality— about how it's all used to deceive the mind and convince us we're seeing and feeling one thing, while the opposite is true. It was interesting, to say the least."

"Something tells me we're not just going into the mountains to breathe in the fresh alpine air," I reply. "This is something you've been planning for a while, isn't it?"

Finn nods and turns my way. "It is. You trust me, though —right?"

"Of course I do," I chuckle, thinking how much he sounds like Rys right now.

"Good. Let's just enjoy the day while it lasts."

His choice of words sends a trickle of nervous energy shooting through my body. "What do you mean, while it lasts?"

He leans in and kisses my forehead, slipping an arm around me. "Sorry. Bad choice of words. I just meant we got out of bed kind of late, in case you'd forgotten."

I press against him, feeling a little unsteady, and sink into his warmth. I tell myself he didn't mean anything; that he, like me, is simply trying to make the most of our precious time together.

As the train shoots its way into the mountains, it begins

snaking up a winding, hairpin turn-filled road that leads us up to one of the peaks. I look down toward the road where we started and back to the Escapa's various, distant cityscapes beyond, and then stare up at the sky, trying to figure out where exactly the illusion begins. How is my mind so easily convinced that we've climbed so high when I know it's impossible? How is it that my body feels that we're at a higher altitude than we were only a few minutes ago?

"Strange, isn't it?" Finn asks, and I nod.

"Almost creepy," I tell him. "Maybe one day…"

I don't finish the sentence. For some reason, the idea of concluding it fills me with apprehension, as if forecasting the future will guarantee that it fails to come true.

"Yes. Maybe one day we'll go see the real thing," Finn promises.

"How?" I ask, my voice tight. "Finn—we may be on our honeymoon right now, but our wedding was a political stunt. You and I don't have control over our fates. It's always someone else pulling the strings, using us, manipulating us. I became the Crimson Dreg because the Consortium needed me to be. Whether you like it or not, you're essentially the Bishop's prisoner, and as far as he's concerned, the real me is still fleeing for her life with Rys right now. He and his people will never give us a moment's peace."

"Yes, they will," he says, his tone determined. "We won't give them a choice."

"We don't hold the cards," I tell him as the train finally pulls to a stop. "We never have."

Finn takes my hand and guides me silently outside, where a swell of chilly wind prompts me to open the tote bag, pull on the puffer jacket and gloves. Finn wraps his arms around me and holds me close as we look out over green valleys and flowing blue rivers far below. Wooden chalets dot the foothills, and in the distance, I see the tiny pinpricks of people skiing down snow-coated slopes.

"What would you say," Finn asks, "if I told you this mountain—this entire landscape—was entirely my creation?"

I jerk backwards, stunned. "Your creation? What does that even mean?"

"It means I built it while sitting in front of a holo-screen. I designed it—the ecosystem, the winding road, every nook and cranny. I built it for you. For this moment."

Laughing, I reply, "First off, I suppose I would thank you for going to all that trouble. Secondly, I would ask if you've turned into a fully-fledged deity. I'm pretty sure mountain-building isn't on most humans' résumés. Not even the clever ones."

When he chuckles, I add, "I'm not kidding. How did you do this without anyone knowing?"

"Oh, they knew," Finn says. "When I first talked to the Bishop and Illian about a wedding and a honeymoon, I asked if I might be allowed into the holo-imaging labs to create my dream vacation. So it's not like they weren't aware of what I was doing."

"Well, color me highly impressed. It's incredible."

"I'm glad you think so," Finn says, snapping his fingers. Immediately, the chilly air dissipates. "Because there's something else I want to show you."

The snowy mountainside disappears, and we find ourselves standing inside a plain white room.

The air is stagnant and suddenly warm, and I remove my jacket.

"Where are we?" I ask Finn, looking around for the train, which has also vanished.

"A special place," he tells me. "Like the one in the Behemoth—the *Enhanced Illusion* room I used to create the artificial beach for our wedding. Any room, any hallway, any closet in the Arc can be turned into an E.I. chamber, given the right technology. It's just a matter of creating a portal."

"Portal?"

"The door or opening that a person steps into to get inside the E.I. Once they're over the threshold, the illusion begins. For you and me, it happened when we stepped into the hallway leading to our suite. Everything we've set our eyes on since then has been a construct, a world mapped out first in my mind, then through code to make it into something that appears incredibly real."

I look around, blown away by how thorough, how multidimensional Finn's deception was.

"I don't like being misled," I tell him, laughing. "But as lies and deceit go, this is pretty cool, Finn."

"I'm glad you like it," he says, beaming. "So—where would you like to go next?"

I ponder the question for a moment. Part of me wants to return to our bed, to curl up with Finn, lean my head against his chest, and breathe in his scent.

"I want to go to Sector Eight before it was destroyed," I tell him. "I want to see my home."

"Are you sure?" he asks.

I nod. "Just one last time," I tell him.

He slips away from me, raising a hand to the blank wall. A holographic screen appears before him, and he flicks his fingers over its symbols until the walls disappear and we're surrounded by a street lined with welcoming houses.

Mine sits among them—not decrepit as it was in the final years, but freshly painted a cheerful blue with white trim. Its lawn is groomed, the garden planted with tulips of various colors.

On the porch, I see my parents—both of them—sitting on a swing. They look young and happy, and I realize as I stare that this projection is from a time before my brother and I even existed.

My eyes well with tears, and Finn says, "I'm so sorry—I couldn't exactly control the timeline," but I shake my head and take his hand. "This was in the databanks…"

"It's perfect," I tell him. "Absolutely perfect. Thank you."

As I stare at my parents, I say, "When I look at them, I just want to make them happy. To give Kel a chance at a future. I want families like ours to return to something like normal. I want the lies to stop—the lies about disease, about aging and illness, about everything. I want people to be able to live without the constant threat that those they trust will betray them."

"That's a tall order," Finn says. "The world is corrupt, and always has been."

"I know," I sigh. "It's only a dream—like what we're seeing right now."

I issue my artificial parents a final, lingering look before I ask, "Do you think we could go back to the hotel now?"

Finn nods and, flicking a hand through the air, returns us to our suite. Emotionally spent, I trudge into the bedroom, lie down on the bed, and curl myself into a ball. Finn slips in behind me and holds me, kissing the crown of my head.

A few minutes later, an alarm—a piercing, terrifying bleat on endless loop—begins to sound.

"What the hell is that?" I ask, leaping to my feet. Finn does the same, looking around at the lights in the corners of the room that are flaring to life in angry red blasts.

"Something has happened," he says. "That's the Consortium's alarm. Illian set it up ages ago—he told me about it. It was before we returned from New York. Before the Bishop…"

"Before the Bishop took this place over," I conclude. "You don't think…"

"I don't know."

A projection appears at the center of the room. Illian's face, looking grave.

"Ilian?" I call out. "Can you see us?"

But he doesn't reply.

"It's a general announcement," Finn says gravely. "An emergency broadcast for everyone in the Arc."

"My friends," Illian's voice booms. "I am sorry to bring you ill news. There is no easy way to say this, so I'll just tell you—"

I reach out and take Finn's hand, squeezing tightly. "What's going on?" I mutter.

"It's happening," Finn replies. "The Arc is under attack."

MAYHEM

"THE ARC and its residents are in danger," Illian's voice echoes. "Many of those who were prisoners of the Consortium—some of them former Directorate Guard and Aristocratic leadership—have been freed and supplied with weapons. They have been asked to fight on behalf of the man you've come to know as the Bishop."

A strange, icy numbness sets itself into the marrow of my bones as Illian's words penetrate my mind.

I was happy. I was whole. I was at peace.

And while I knew it couldn't last, I'd hoped for a few more hours of pleasure before all hell broke loose.

"To think most people believed the Bishop was really using our wedding to unite the Arc's residents," I say, sneering.

"It looks like his time as Mr. Charming has come to an end," Finn replies with a nod. "No surprise there."

Illian is still talking, and I cross my arms as I listen. "Allies, Consortium members—all those who are loyal to our cause— we need you to take up arms. Prepare to fight for your lives.

The Bishop's followers intend to take many of you prisoner, to use you in ways too horrific to divulge."

"So," Finn says softly. "Illian has finally broken through the brainwashing. He's seen the Bishop for what he is."

He sounds more pleased than panicked, which baffles me.

"It's too late!" I retort. "There will be bloodshed, Finn. We've seen the Bishop's cult. There are thousands of them, all ready to throw themselves on the sword if their dear leader commands it."

"True. There *are* thousands."

I have to fight to stabilize my voice when I ask, "Why don't you sound more upset about this?"

"Because there's a funny thing about cults. They can't exist if there is no leader," Finn says the words cryptically, and I turn and glare at him. He seems eerily calm, given the mayhem that's clearly unfolding before us and the panic in Illian's voice.

"Finn—why does it seem like you knew this was about to happen?"

He pauses only for a second before nodding. "I suspected," he tells me. "I've been watching the Bishop for some time— watching his patterns, his interactions with the Tree of Life Acolytes. They've become more and more aggressive over the weeks and months. It was only a matter of time before they decided to commit a coup."

"Atticus!" I croak out, hoping he's somewhere close by.

The owl appears before me as if I've summoned him from thin air. "Do you have eyes on what's going on in the rest of the Arc?" I ask.

"No. However, some of Rys's surveillance drones do," Atticus replies, issuing a projection of one of the market levels, where fighting has already begun between civilians and the men and women dressed in the Bishop's gray Tree of Life tunics.

The battle is violent and bloody. People are beating one another with anything they can find—pieces of wood from display cases, steel tubes, hammers. I'm grateful when I realize I can't see too much detail—the last thing I want is to watch my fellow Dregs get slaughtered in the streets.

"How the hell did this happen?" I ask, turning to Finn. "Why did he feel the need to attack? He's got all the power in the world! What more does he want?"

"He knows he's *losing* his power," Finn says slowly, and once again, I get the impression he's not surprised.

"What are you not telling me?" I ask, desperate. "Please, Finn."

He takes me by the shoulders, kisses my forehead, and says, "I love you. I want nothing more than to protect you—to protect our future. Do you believe that?"

"Of course I do."

"Good. Because I have some bad news."

He puts a hand on my cheek and gently turns my head so that I'm facing the bedroom doorway.

When my eyes meet the sight before us, I instinctively press myself to Finn.

The Bishop is standing in the doorway, his chin down, eyes locked on mine. Behind him are two guards, each carrying a high-powered rifle.

I freeze, hoping Atticus has concealed himself. Something tells me those rifles would blow him to pieces.

As if they're reading my mind, the guards pull their guns into position and ready themselves to fire.

The good news is that Atticus is nowhere to be seen.

The bad news is that the weapons are aimed directly at Finn and me.

Reminding myself that I'm supposed to be a Replik and not the human version of Ashen who longs to see the Bishop dead, I smile and step forward. "What's going on?" I ask sweetly. "Finn and I are still on our honeymoon...aren't we?"

The Bishop issues me a grim smile. "I allowed you a night. I allowed you a little pleasure. But if you think for a moment that I was not aware of what you two did..." He steps forward, takes my chin in his hand and strokes a coarse fingertip over my scar. "If you don't realize how poor your attempt at conceal-ment really was, then you don't know me as well as I thought, Ashen. I know everything. I see everything. And you are a fool."

Finn steps toward us, attempting to thrust himself between the Bishop and me. But the Bishop glares at him and lets out a wicked, feral snarl.

"Think twice before you instigate anything, Davenport," he barks. "You have no idea what you're getting yourself into." He squeezes my face hard, drawing a high-pitched yelp from my lips.

To my surprise, Finn backs off, raising his hands in defeat. "You're right," he says. "You win."

What?

I thought Finn had a plan to take the Bishop down. I thought he'd found some weakness in this far-too-powerful man.

Apparently, I was wrong.

"You two are coming with us," the Bishop says. "I have plans for you both, now that you've outlived your usefulness."

"Does Illian know about this?" Finn asks.

I shoot him a puzzled look. Why does Illian matter? After

all, the Consortium leader has proven unable to stand up for himself, let alone anyone else.

The Bishop lets out a laugh and asks, "Do you really think Illian is concerned with the likes of you two? He's got a civil war on his hands. He doesn't care if you live or die…or disappear."

"Disappear," I repeat angrily. "What is it this time? Feeding us to wild dogs? Having one of your Repliks tear us limb from limb? Honestly, I'm surprised you're not planning a public hanging like you did in New York. The Royal Gardens would make a picturesque spot for a gallows."

At that, the Bishop balks for a moment before tightening his jaw and saying, "Believe it or not, Miss Spencer, I, too, wish to keep the peace."

Miss Spencer. The words are meant to be a weapon, to convince me the wedding wasn't real.

But they have the opposite effect. Finn and I are one. We are strong and powerful, and we will not be separated again.

Only, when I glance over at Finn, he looks defeated. His shoulders are slumped, his lips downturned.

"Forgive me," I retort. "I didn't realize having armed guards shove rifles into people's faces was a peaceful gesture."

Finn shoots me a look of warning and says, "Ash—be careful. We should just do what he asks."

What?

Why isn't he fighting back, or at least protesting a little harder?

We were on the verge of starting a life together, and now he's just abiding by the Bishop's wishes, telling me to accompany the bastard to who knows where?

Then it hits me.

The Bishop must have drugged him again. I don't know

how, I don't know when. But Finn has suddenly turned complacent, lethargic. The resolve I saw in him only a few minutes ago is gone. The spark in his eye—the passion when he looked at me as we lay in bed together—gone.

"We can't let him do this!" I tell him, grabbing him by the hand. "We have to think about Kel and Merit! Don't you see that?"

Finn shakes his head. "They'll be safe." Turning to the Bishop, he adds, "Won't they?"

"Of course. I would not hurt such promising young men. I have never intended to do them harm. I have plans for them. You have my word."

"See? It'll be fine," Finn says.

"Fine?" I shout. "You're taking this asshole's word for it? Since when is the Bishop an honorable or honest man? Finn, what the hell is wrong with you?"

He shrugs. "Nothing. I just know this is an unwinnable fight, Ash. Surely you see that."

"What are you talking about? I have—"

I'm about to announce that I have the Surge at my disposal, but Finn shakes his head slightly, silently warning me against any impulsive acts. But why?

All I can think is that he knows something about the Bishop that I don't. Is he resistant to the Surge? Is his skin made of some bizarre material that will reflect it back at us?

I pull my hand away and turn to the Bishop. "Fine," I say. "Take us wherever you need to. Clearly we aren't going to put up a fight."

The Bishop, grinning malevolently, thrusts a finger under my chin, forcing me to look him in the eye. "You and I could have been something," he tells me. "A combined force to be reckoned with. But you were always too willful, Ashen. Too unwilling to bend to the winds of change."

He turns and gestures the guards to bring us along. Each of them grabs one of us by an arm, and I find myself sullenly avoiding Finn's gaze as we make our way along the corridor to the stairs. We stumble down and out into the street, trudging along until we reach a Conveyor.

When its doors open, the guards shove us inside. The Bishop follows, commanding the Conveyor to take us to "Training Quarters B-15."

I'm all too familiar with the Training Quarters, the large rooms where we used to endure long hours of combat classes. They're isolated, soundproof, and can easily be locked from the outside to keep non-compliant Candidates and others confined.

Whatever the Bishop has planned, it's probably not going to be pleasant.

Silently, Finn and I stand, heads down, in the Conveyor until it comes to a stop. When the door whooshes open, the Bishop takes my upper arm and drags me into a large white room, followed by Finn, then dismisses the soldiers, who head back onto the Conveyor.

The doors seal up, and we find ourselves alone with our enemy.

"So," the Bishop says, extracting a small, flat device from his pocket, "I expect you will try to overpower me now. Just so we're on even ground, you should know that one slip of my finger will bring each of you to your knees."

"How?" I ask.

The Bishop snickers. "At yesterday's sham of a wedding, I implanted a small neuro-device in each of you—one that is currently making its way through your bloodstreams. One click of this little apparatus, and you will feel pain like nothing you've ever known."

Panicked, I look at Finn, whose chin is still down.

"Finn? Is he serious?"

His shoulders begin to shake, and for a moment, I'm convinced he's crying.

But when he lifts his face and stares into the Bishop's eyes, defiant and proud, I find myself more baffled than ever.

"It's funny," he says.

"Oh? What's that?" the Bishop asks with a scowl.

"You talk about bringing us to our knees. Even if that were true, the thing is, it wouldn't matter. Ash and I aren't going to hurt you. Someone *else* is."

FATE

"Finn?" I breathe, desperate to make sense of what's happening.

Did Atticus manage to accompany us silently and invisibly from the hotel? Is he the one who's going to hurt the Bishop?

"Remember what I told you on the mountain?" Finn replies.

At first, I'm not sure what he's asking. But then I remember what he said about the Enhanced Illusion chambers and the portals that lead into them—portals that can be used to create any illusion, however large or small.

"Yes," I tell him. "But…"

Finn holds up his right hand and snaps his fingers, which instantly transforms the white room around us into a cold, confining prison cell.

The door to the Conveyor disappears only to be replaced by iron bars, and the Bishop's head whips around, a panicked look in his eyes.

With an angry snarl, he presses his thumb to his device and Finn falls to the ground, doubled over in pain.

But I feel nothing.

No shock of agony. No piercing trauma.

Why not?

Finn cries out as the Bishop presses the device again.

"Let him go!" I cry. "You can have me—you can torture me, whatever you want. Don't hurt him!"

"How sweet that you adore the boy so much." The Bishop steps toward Finn, who's on his knees, his palms pressed to the floor. "What did you do to her?" he hisses. "How is she immune?"

Finn pulls his chin up, his eyes red as he struggles against the pain. "I gave her a new implant. A gift to protect her from you," he grunts. "You think you know everything, you bastard, but you don't. And I've got news for you. I saw your plan from a mile away."

"Lies!" the Bishop says, inflicting another round of agony. "Mr. Davenport, cease this charade, this illusion. Bring us back to the Training room. Impressive though this may be, I do not have time to waste on tricks."

"That's too bad," Finn says through a wince, pushing himself to his feet and wiping his hand over his chest. "Because I have a lot of them in store for you."

The Bishop presses the device again, but instead of doubling over, Finn grabs it from him.

"Oh," Finn says. "Did I forget to mention I implanted myself with the same inhibitor I gave Ash? Your trinket doesn't hurt me one bit. I was faking it, just as you fake every aspect of your pathetic existence."

Finn flings the Bishop's device to the ground and crushes it under his heel.

His eyes wide with terror, the Bishop backs away. For once in his life, he looks vulnerable.

No.

He looks *defeated.*

"You stole Ash from me, but worse than that, you stole her life from her," Finn growls. "And I could kill you for it right here and now. So could she. But I have something else in mind for you, you goddamned psychopath."

For the first time in his life, the Bishop cowers, his fingers trembling, his mouth open, lip quivering. He looks small, thin, frail, even, like a delicate bird trapped indoors with no recourse but to slam himself against a window in a futile attempt at escape.

"Whatever you're doing," he says, his voice coarse, "you should think about it. My followers…"

"Your followers will be fine," Finn says with a chuckle. "Because their dear leader will be fine."

The Bishop looks instantly relieved, as if Finn has just opened the door and waved him to freedom.

"Oh, I wouldn't look so excited if I were you," Finn cautions. "That's the beauty of my plan, you see. I said their dear leader would be fine—but I didn't say *you* would."

"I…don't understand."

"What's that saying?" Finn asks. "*Good writers borrow, great writers steal?* Well, I stole your idea. I hope you don't mind…"

As Finn's words sink in and his intentions grow clear, it's all I can do not to let out a triumphant shout. And I can see from the Bishop's expression that he, too, understands exactly what Finn has planned for him.

"You wouldn't," he murmurs. "You didn't. It's not possible."

Finn smiles, stepping toward the Bishop, who backs toward the cold stone wall, pressing tremulous white palms to its surface.

"I thought you were strong," Finn tells him. "You gave the

impression of being so powerful, and I assumed for a long time that your bloodstream was swimming with nanotech. So I didn't dare mess with you. You threatened Merit and Kel. I was afraid you would hurt them. So imagine my surprise when I figured out just how weak you really are."

The stone wall disappears, and the Bishop almost falls backwards, stumbling several steps. All of a sudden, he is standing on a floating platform, a harsh wind beating at his sweat-streaked hair.

I'm not sure how, but Finn and I are standing on another platform entirely, several feet from our enemy. All around us is darkness and high above, stars twinkle brightly in the sky. Below us…is nothing.

The air feels thin, as if we're high up, though I'm not sure if we're on top of the Arc or somewhere else entirely.

Suddenly fearful, I reach for Finn, taking his arm. "Where are we?" I ask softly.

"Don't worry," he replies. "We're safe."

The Bishop seems to hear the calming words, because he begins to stride determinedly toward us, but just as he reaches the platform's edge, Finn puts a hand up. "I wouldn't do that if I were you," he says.

"We're in a damned *simulation*," the Bishop retorts. "Nothing will happen to me if I take another step. We're in an E.I. chamber, that's all."

"Are you sure about that?" Finn asks. "You're very confident in that assessment. But go ahead—take another step or two. See how it works out for you."

The Bishop, looking taken aback once again, freezes in place and glares daggers at Finn. "What have you done?" he snaps.

"Nothing you didn't teach me. You're the master of deception, after all." Finn turns to me and nods once before adding, "You left Ash on top of the Behemoth with a woman who wanted her dead. You left her to be burned alive—and I was too brainwashed, too far gone to know your plan. But you were arrogant, Bishop. You thought I wouldn't figure out that you'd sent me home with an imposter." Finn meets my eyes, a look of pain on his features. "But when I *did* figure it out, I put a plan into action. I stole your genetic material. Your secrets. I stole the means to build something greater than anything you've ever developed."

"Impossible," the Bishop spits.

"Is it?" Finn steps closer to him, raises his chin, and says, "You sleep very soundly, you know—thanks to Naeva's Replik."

The Bishop looks like he's about to reply, but instead, he seals his mouth into a tight line.

"When the Directorate spread the Blight around, they did so with tiny micro-drones. So small that most humans never noticed them coming. I decided to use those same drones to extract samples from you. And do you know what I discovered?"

The Bishop scowls, but fails to reply.

"Your *name*," Finn says.

I tighten, shocked. The Bishop has always been an entity larger than life—a man without a name, one who defies such banality.

"What is it?" I ask. "Who is he?"

Finn lets out a laugh. "Eustace," he says. "Eustace Smith. He is no one and nothing. He's a man who figured out how to game humanity's system, and for a time, he did it very well."

"Lies!" the Bishop shouts. "Eustace Smith is long dead. You

know full well that I am so much more than that man ever was. I am a force to be reckoned with."

"Not dead," Finn says. "You were born nearly eighty years ago. You have defied time with your endless experimentation, I'll grant you that—experiments, I might add, that were the work of scientists and not the product of any genius whatsoever on your part. You may not be a Replik, but every inch of you—every bit of skin, every cell—is fake. You're an artificial being, one made up of disparate parts cobbled together from thousands of humans you destroyed in the process. You are a murdering fraud—but then, we all knew that."

"A fraud with powers unlike anything you'll ever know," the Bishop snarls. "And you're about to witness some of what I can do!"

He thrusts his hands toward Finn as if he's expecting a miraculous, devastating magical spell to erupt from his fingertips.

I brace myself, suppressing a cry of warning. All I know about the Bishop—all I've known since the first moment I laid eyes on him—is the power he exudes. His ability to control others, his daunting, charming nature.

From that first moment, he filled me with simultaneous fear and excitement.

And in this moment, I fully expect an explosion of devastating proportions to burst from his body.

But nothing happens.

There is no blast, no flame, no shock of electricity.

There's nothing but awkward silence and a man standing before us who looks uncharacteristically frightened. The look of haughty malevolence, of pure arrogance, has been eradicated from his eyes and replaced with a dullness that's almost pitiful.

"What have you done to me?" he wails.

"No more than you did to Ash or to so many others," Finn replies. "You gave me the blueprints. The roadmap to this moment where we stand right now. You taught me to steal gifts from others, Bishop, so that's what I did. I stole every gift you've ever bestowed upon yourself. You are nothing more than a frail man now."

"You're hoarding my power for yourself, no doubt," the man called Eustace snarls like a feral beast. "Thieving monster."

But Finn shakes his head. "Not for myself, no. I've already given them to someone else—someone very special. I think you'll like him."

With that, he flicks a hand in the air. Through the darkness, I see a flash of silver as Atticus appears, soaring toward a door that's just appeared at the far end of the Bishop's platform.

The door slides open, and as Atticus hovers in the air, blocking the Bishop's view, someone—a man, from the looks of it, steps onto the platform to join him.

"What is this?" the Bishop asks, his voice a desperate screech. "What have you done?"

I reach for Finn, taking his arm questioningly, but say nothing.

Atticus rises into the air, disappearing into the darkness above like a silent, ever-present sentinel. The other man strides toward the Bishop, stopping a few feet from him.

When I see his face for the first time, I cup a hand over my mouth, hardly able to believe what I'm seeing.

NARCISSUS

THE MAN STARING at the Bishop...*is the Bishop.*

"That's...a Replik?" I whisper.

Finn nods. "Sort of. More than a Replik, really. He's a highly intelligent, weaponized version of our friend here. One with as much charisma and charm—and every ability the Bishop was keeping secret." Finn nods toward the new arrival and says, "Welcome to the product of Project Narcissus. Please, Replik, tell us what you're here to do."

The second version of the Bishop turns our way, smiles the mischievous, alluring grin I've seen so many times, and says, "I'm going to steer my followers away from their rebellion. I will order them to help me free those who are wrongfully imprisoned—to help the Arc work its way to greatness. They will be honored to help me, of course. They'll do anything I ask."

"And?" Finn asks. "Was there something else?"

The man, who looks every bit as real as the Bishop ever did, turns to his twin and nods once. "I'm here to end him."

"Will you ever reveal to anyone what you're about to do?"

"No. Of course not. I'm no fool."

"Good," Finn says, clapping his hands together. "Please—be our guest."

The Bishop—the real one—backs toward the edge of the platform, no doubt debating whether or not to leap off and risk the potential fall. I can see in his eyes that he knows what his doppelgänger is capable of.

And he's terrified.

"What's he going to do?" I ask, my heart throbbing. I despise the Bishop for too many reasons to say, and part of me wants to watch him suffer a long, drawn-out death.

But I'm not entirely sure I've turned into a sadist just yet.

"There are several choices," Finn replies. "Before he imprisoned you with my mother in the Behemoth, the Bishop treated himself to a sample of her special power—her ability to conjure heat and flame. But he had other tricks up his sleeve. I've given the new version of him an entire arsenal of weaponry—which, by the way, I can disable at any point."

I swallow and tense up, half hiding behind Finn as if to shield myself from whatever is about to happen.

"Ash," Finn says, reaching for me. "You don't have to watch this. You can leave, if you'd like."

I shake my head and say, "No. I need to see it. He can't be allowed to live, not after all he's done."

"Are you sure? Because what's about to happen here—you might not be able to unsee it."

I press my forehead into his shoulder and nod. "I'm sure," I tell him. "I'm just grateful it's ending. I thought…"

"You thought I'd gone weak," he says quietly. "I'm sorry for putting you through that. I needed *him* to believe it, just for a few minutes. I needed him arrogant, cocky. And for that, I needed you to be worried. Ash, if you knew how long I've wanted to destroy him for what he did to you, to us…to so many people. I feel no pity for him. I despise him."

"I know," I reply. "So do I."

"Ashen!" the Bishop—the real one—calls out, reaching his hands toward me. "Talk to him! You have the power to stop this. It doesn't need to end like this. You and I were friends once. We were close. You admired me. Surely you remember those days."

"I only admired you because you messed with my head," I sneer. "You can't charm me anymore. Just because I'm not excited about the prospect of watching you meet your end, doesn't mean I think you deserve anything less than to rot in Hell."

"You heard her," Finn says, gesturing to the Replik. "It's time to do what you were created to do."

The Replik raises his hands toward the Bishop, palms out. At first, the air feels thick, the silence around us growing heavier as my breath traps itself in my throat. Finn, too, tenses, waiting for the moment of truth.

All I can think is, *This is too easy—too simple. Something has to go wrong.*

It always does.

But my mind swirls with contradictory thoughts. It wasn't easy or simple at all for Finn to pull this off—to create a replica of the Bishop without the man himself learning of it?

That's a *miracle*. A work of art.

Something only a true genius could have accomplished.

The Replik stares at his target, a grim smile on his face that makes me wonder if he's simply a more powerful version of our enemy.

He's enjoying this, I think with a shudder.

No. He's hesitating.

He seems to be waiting for something, though at first, I'm not sure what.

The Bishop sees it, too. A lack of willpower in his twin, who looks ready to attack, yet makes no move to harm his foe.

Emboldened, the Bishop takes a step toward his doppelgänger, challenging and aggressive. Then another step.

All of a sudden, I understand.

"He won't attack unless he's threatened," I say under my breath.

"True," Finn replies in a whisper. "I thought it would be safer to ensure he's not aggressive. He's programmed to defend himself and others, but not to kill for his own pleasure, and never to issue orders to harm anyone. But our buddy Eustace doesn't need to know any of that."

The Bishop leaps at the Replik, seemingly convinced his twin is helpless to fight back. He reaches for his opponent's throat, hoping to choke the life out of him.

But the instant his hands wrap themselves around the other being's neck, the blast comes.

A surge of blinding light illuminates the entire chamber where we're standing like a streak of lightning. High above us, I spot Atticus, his eyes staring down at the action, prepared to swoop in and protect us.

The blast hits the Bishop square in the chest. It's powerful enough to tear a hole in his flesh and send him shooting backwards through space. I cry out involuntarily, convinced he's going to fall to his death...

But Finn snaps his fingers and the strange void where we've been standing morphs into a Training room once again.

The Bishop lies lifeless on the cold floor. His face is white, his eyes locked on the darkness above him. His chest is smoking and blackened, and no part of him gives off any sign of life.

The Replik steps over to stand above him, then turns to Finn. It's eerie to see the Bishop's twin with the same intense look in his eyes, the same knowing grin...and yet to know he means us no harm.

"Do you wish for me to dispose of the body?" the Replik asks.

"Yes. You can't leave any evidence that he ever existed. Understood?" Finn replies, and we both watch as his creation shoots another blast at the Bishop's lifeless form. This time, the body seems to light up for a moment, then disintegrates inch by inch, until nothing remains but a minuscule pile of ashes.

Relieved and traumatized at once, I collapse onto my knees, and Finn crouches next to me, holding onto me as I stare, baffled, at the sight before us.

I have seen enemies fall before. I know I should feel a sense of victory, even of joy. But all I feel, looking at those ashes, is pain. The Bishop left behind an Arcology filled with prisoners. He destroyed so many lives in his greed, his selfish pursuit of eternal life, and now he's simply...gone.

In the end, maybe he didn't suffer enough.

With his work done, the Replik turns to look at Finn, his expression expectant.

"Thank you," Finn says. "That will be all for now. You know your next task. Go meet with your followers. Tell them their focus is now going to shift to rebuilding the Mire and helping those in need. You will also free any and all who are in Sensory Deprivation Chambers, and see to it that they receive the medical care they require."

"Of course." With that, the Replik turns to head back through the door where he first emerged, but Finn stops him.

"Bishop!" he calls, and a chill runs its way down my spine. I tell myself it's natural that he would respond to that name. In his mind, that's who he is.

"Yes?" the Replik replies, spinning back to face us.

"Tomorrow, after the dust settles, we will meet with Illian as we discussed. It's time to move on from all this."

"Very good. I'll be there."

"Oh, and when you see Naeva, treat her well. If I ever learn you've hurt her—if ever you should defy your programming-- I will end you."

Once the Bishop's disturbing twin has left, Finn flicks a hand through the air and the room shifts into our hotel suite. Clean, elegant, perfect.

But no part of me is able to relax for a second.

"We need to leave," I say, striding toward the bedroom to put together a bag of clothing. "We need to make sure the boys are safe."

"They're safe," Finn says. "Don't worry."

"How can we know? The fighting in the Arc looked pretty serious. Illian seemed so worried..."

"Did he?" Finn asks, his tone remarkably casual. I turn to face him, to assess his expression. On his face is a grin that I would call smug if I didn't know him better.

"What are you saying?" I ask.

"I guess I'm saying when Illian's done with this leadership gig, he might want to consider a career on stage."

I feel my eyes widen, my mouth dropping open.

"I want to punch you right now," I tell Finn. "You're really telling me it was all an act?"

"Um, yeah. We scheduled that so-called broadcast to blast

through this place the second the Bishop came for us—which I knew would happen. It was only a matter of time. I'd hoped he'd allow us a little more honeymoon time first, but then, generosity was never that man's strong suit."

"What about the fighting? Atticus showed it to us, not Illian. He said it came from…"

Finn grins when he says, "From Rys's old drones."

I reply slowly. "Because you and Rys were in on this whole damned scheme together. You two are cruel!"

"Hey, now—we just rid the Arc of a major bad guy. I'd say we did something good."

"Illian knows about the Bishop's Replik, right?" I ask, unsure how uneasy I should feel about being so entirely out of the loop.

"Yes," Finn replies. "But he's sworn to secrecy, of course. He and Kurt, both. The four of us—and Rys—are the only ones who know."

There's a part of me that feels tense, even angry that they didn't let me in on any of it—the wedding, the fake coup. The fake Bishop, for that matter.

But I can't deny that Finn pulled it all off masterfully.

"You could have told me, you know," I say. "You can trust me."

"I trust you more than anyone in this world, Ash. I suppose I wanted it to be a surprise. I *told* you I had a wedding gift for you."

"Quite the gift," I reply, finally allowing myself to laugh. "Never, ever do that again."

"Create a virtual clone of a psycho dictator intent on destroying the world to grant himself eternal life? Okay, I promise."

I punch him in the shoulder as I've done to Rys a thousand

times. "When did my husband become so good at subterfuge, sleight of hand, trickery?"

"When he spent months pining for you," he replies. "My anger fueled me. I wanted—needed—you back, and for good. I was not going to let that man take you from me again, Ash. And, like I said, he taught me well."

"Too well."

I'm torn between admiring him and fearing him, though the look in his eye—the concern, the pure affection I'm seeing right now—reminds me I have nothing to fear.

"I know what you're thinking," he says. "Some of it, anyhow. We still have so much work to do—freeing the prisoners in the Behemoth, for one thing."

I smile. "With the Bishop gone, will it even be possible? You know how hard it is to get into that place…"

I don't want to say what I'm thinking: that maybe we should have kept the Bishop around to extract information from him, but it seems Finn is one step ahead of me.

"Everything inside the Replik's mind is a memory taken from the Bishop," he assures me. "Just as he stole your thoughts and implanted them in your Replik. The only difference is that I've made a few small tweaks."

"Tweaks?" I repeat, hesitant to feel hopeful.

"As I said, I took away his aggression and malevolence. The new Bishop is our ally, Ash. I promise you that. And if he ever develops enough willpower to defy me or anyone else, I can immediately shut him down. Illian has that power, too."

At last, I allow myself a quick, relieved exhale, and I step forward, taking Finn in my arms. "I can't believe he's really gone," I tell him. "You took so many risks." I pull back, look him in the eye, and say, "I'm serious. Don't ever do something like that again, not without telling me."

"I won't," he says with a grin. "I swear. I only kept it from you because I know you would have tried to talk me out of it, and honestly, you would've been right to do so. You're so good, Ash. So kind. And I love you for it."

He kisses me then, and for a moment, I almost forget all that's just happened.

"I don't know how you pulled any of this off," I tell him when we've finally moved apart. "But Rys always said you were the genius around here, and he was right. You pulled off a coup of your own, Finn."

"*We* did. Together."

"Hardly." I shake my head, laughing bitterly. "I failed at my part. He saw right through me, even with the scar on my chin. But you were one step ahead of him all along, which I didn't think was even possible." For a moment, I bask in his achievement.

But it's not long before a dire thought infiltrates my mind. "I wonder where Rys is."

Looking around, I search the suite for Atticus. I call his name, and finally, he appears, flying over to a desk by one of the large Parisian windows.

"Yes, Ashen?" he says in the voice that is neither human nor entirely mechanical.

"What do you know about Rystan's whereabouts?"

Atticus seems to ponder the question for a moment before replying, "I'm not entirely sure. I lost contact with him several hours ago. I can, however, tell you he was headed east. He said he had business to attend to in Brooklyn, to help Adrastos and the others to rebuild. He planned to bring an entire army of drones along with him, and from what I can gather, he was successful."

"Oh. That's good, I suppose."

Part of me feels sad to know he's headed so far away. With the Bishop gone, he could be here with us, working toward a new life in the Arc or the Mire.

But maybe he'll be happier in New York for a time. If there's anyone who can figure out how to rebuild the parts of the city that are destroyed, it's him.

"But let me know when you hear from him. I'm worried."

"Of course I will."

With that, Atticus disappears, and I hear the faint sound of wings flapping at the air as he leaves the room.

I throw myself down on the couch, my head squished into the cushions, and moan, "Why do people always end up trying to kill each other?"

"Because it's in our nature," Finn replies. "We step on ants when we're children simply because we can. It's cruel, but we find ways to rationalize the behavior. Only later in life does it occur to us what sadists we once were, and all the while, we forget we're the same now as we were then—we're just more quiet and measured about it."

"I don't crave killing," I protest. "I don't want to hurt people. Or ants."

"Maybe not. But you want to stop the ones who are hurting others. Sometimes, violence really is necessary to stop a tyrant."

Closing my eyes, I say, "Maybe, just maybe...we should stop *giving* power to tyrants."

PEACE AND QUIET

On the third day of our honeymoon, the Bishop's cult followers gather to meet with the man they believe to be their leader in a large park in Sector Two. Atticus helps us to spy on the proceedings, which go better than I could ever have expected.

Finn and I watch the owl's video feed from the comfort of our Parisian hotel room. Our little vacation, after all, is far from over—though it has been significantly marred by the events of the past twenty-four hours.

"I came to the Arc to help make our world a better place," the Replik announces to the crowd of men and women wearing the Tree of Life insignia. The "new" Bishop's chin is down, his eyes focused and narrowed slightly. He manages to look handsome, menacing, and strangely benevolent, all at the same time. "To that end, I wish for you, my loyal Acolytes, to set an example for those who live inside the Arc. We will rebuild the Mire from the ground up. We will restore every house in every Sector to its former glory, and we will ensure that every man, woman, and child has a home, food, and medical care."

A few Acolytes exchange surprised glances for only a moment before a few begin to cheer, which inspires the rest to join in.

"They're so easily manipulated," I observe with a smile when the "Bishop's" speech is done. "And for once, I'm happy to see it."

"People like to have a purpose," Finn replies, stroking his fingers through my hair. "Sometimes that purpose is fueled by rage, sometimes by kindness. But ultimately, I'm not entirely sure it matters to the individual, as long as they feel they're part of something."

"And what is your purpose, Mr. Davenport?" I ask, unwilling ever to call him *Duke.*

"To make you happy, Ashen Spencer," he replies, just as reluctant to curse me with his surname. "To protect you and the boys—while bearing in mind that you could probably kick my ass if you wanted to."

"Let's hope we never find out," I laugh.

"Amen to that."

We're standing by a large, open window that looks out onto a Paris street. A cool breeze strokes my cheek as I thread by fingers behind Finn's neck and let out a contented purr of pleasure.

"This is the life," I sigh. "I could do this forever, honestly."

"As could I," he says, kissing my neck before pulling up and looking me in the eye. "But…"

"Oh no."

"It's nothing bad," he chuckles. "Illian wants to meet with us and asked if it would be all right to get together downstairs for a cup of coffee."

"When?"

Finn calls out for Atticus, who flaps over from the next window, where he's been staring out at the street below.

"Yes?" the owl asks.

"What time is Illian arriving?"

Turning his head ninety degrees, Atticus stares out the window. "I believe he's coming up the street even as we speak," he says. I lean out the window to see Illian, headed for a café across from us. He stops and waves, and I wave back.

"Shall we, then?" Finn asks.

"Let's," I tell him, taking his arm, grateful to have gotten dressed this morning.

We head down to street level, where Illian is already seated at a small, round table, a café americano sitting before him.

Finn and I pull up two chairs and squeeze in around the table. I try to assess Illian's expression, which seems to be a combination of pain and joy.

"The gathering in the park went well," Finn tells him. "The new Bishop is as charming as the old one, but without the subterfuge."

Illian laughs. "Or the mind-bending manipulation," he says, and his smile disappears. He turns to me, his mouth tightening into a thin, worried line. "Not that it's an excuse. Ashen…I owe you an explanation."

I put up a hand before he can say anything. "I understand, Illian. I've been there, remember? I'm the one who made videos singing the guy's praises from New York. I meant every word. I thought he was some kind of messiah. You don't have to explain a thing."

He shakes his head. "I do, because I didn't only fail you. I failed the people of the Arc. A true leader would have seen that infiltrator for what he was. He would have listened to you when you warned me what he was doing. I was blinded."

"It's not the worst thing in the world to be blinded by love," I tell him, laying a hand on his own. "You thought Kurt was going to die. You were traumatized. Then suddenly, he was all right. It's natural to be grateful to the man who saved him."

"It's kind of you to say. But I proved myself unworthy by allowing love to cloud my judgment," Illian says, looking to Finn then, as well as me. "Just as a leader is unworthy if they can be weakened by hatred. Like I said, I've failed. And I feel that we need new leadership. In fact, I'd say we need to give the people a chance to *elect* their next leader."

Finn shakes his head. "It's too soon. So much has happened in such a short time—throwing more change at the residents might be too much. Besides, there's no one who can lead the Consortium like you can, Illian. And there's so much to be done. We need to free the people the Bishop imprisoned in those chambers, for one thing—and that needs to happen before any talk of an election."

"Perhaps. But I was thinking that perhaps you two should run for office," Illian replies, eyeing me and then Finn. "Both of you. King and Queen. Duke and Duchess. Whatever you want to be called. You two could lead this place to a new era."

Finn and I exchange a look, reading one another's minds.

No way in hell.

Neither of us wants to be a leader. We're both exhausted, depleted.

"All Ash and I want is peace and quiet," Finn says. "And running for election is the opposite of that. Ash can speak for herself, but the last thing I want is to throw myself into the fray."

Illian clasps his hands on the table. "Let's ponder it for a time," he says. "In the meantime, this can't get out, not to anyone. If the residents of the Arc begin to think they're floating in a rudderless ship, all hell will break loose. We need to rebuild the Mire, and to help set up a city government down there. We need strategies, infrastructure. We need to give the people their freedom back, first and foremost. They've been living under dictators for far too long."

Finn nods, a solemn look on his face. "Agreed."

"There's one thing I'm wondering about, though," Illian adds. "The Bishop—the new one. You have faith that he won't rebel? If he's implanted with the other Bishop's thoughts and memories, isn't there a chance he will betray us?"

"The real Bishop was a complicated man," Finn explains. "His mind was clouded by a toxic ambition. When I implanted the Bishop's memories into the Replik, I streamlined his thinking a little. Ambition and greed aren't possible for him." With that, he looks my way. "Just as love wasn't truly possible for Ash's Replik. As clever as the Bishop was, he never did figure out how to replicate deep human emotion—which, it turns out, was a good thing."

"Good to know," Illian replies.

"So," Finn says, pressing his palms to the table. "It's high time we fix what's broken once and for all. In the meantime, I'll speak to the Arc's science and medical wing about extracting the Bishop's victims from their pods. It's too bad Rys isn't here—he got himself and Ash out, and obviously knew what he was doing."

"Atticus can help," I reply. "He helped us. He knows what to do."

"Where *is* Rystan?" Illian asks. "I was expecting him back

in the Arc after everything. I would have liked to apologize to him in person."

"New York City," Atticus replies as he comes in to land on the next table over. "Brooklyn, to be precise."

"You've found him?" I ask, grinning.

"Yes, Ashen Spencer. He is currently staying with your friends, Adi and Cillian. They're working on a plan to infiltrate the Behemoth and to free its many prisoners. As we speak, a small group of the Trodden are gathering to help."

The Trodden. I'd forgotten the name of the rebels in New York—those who knew the Bishop was no friend of theirs.

"Does Adi know?" I ask. "About her sister? Does she know the girl she brought home is a Replik?"

Atticus's eyes close for a moment, silver lids taking their place. A whirring sound fills the air, then he opens them again. They flash briefly red, then blue.

"I am not certain," he says. "I'm sorry."

Finn and I exchange a look, and he takes my hand and pulls it to his lips. "Rys will help her get the real Stella back," he says. "He'll help get them all back."

I eye my husband proudly. He sounds so mature, so adult. Then again, after everything we've been through, it's no surprise.

When we've said goodbye to Illian and left the café to head back to the hotel, I take Finn's hand and pull it to my chest.

"I'm proud of you," I tell him. "I know things have been weird and confusing between us—understatement of the century." I let out a laugh. "But I'm truly happy. I think we're going to be all right, and this might be the first time I've said that out loud since the first day the Blight hit."

In the middle of the silent street, Finn stops walking, pulls me into his arms, and kisses me in a way that sends me reeling. For a moment, I'm sure I'm going to lose my balance, but he senses my dizziness and keeps me on my feet.

"I'm not perfect," he says softly, his chin resting atop my head. "I've made so many mistakes, Ash. But I hope you never doubt that everything I have done has been out of love for you, for the boys."

"I will never, ever doubt that, Finn Davenport," I tell him, taking his hand and leading him toward the hotel's front door.

By the time we're making our way along the corridor to our suite, I'm busily contemplating who should run for office. There are a few possibilities, of course—various Consortium members who have stood by Illian's side and managed to navigate the Bishop's madness without succumbing.

As Finn lifts me into his arms, pushes the suite's door open, and once again carries me over the threshold, all I know is that he and I will never, ever be poisoned by the sort of ambition that drove his mother and the Bishop.

The only goals I have in life are happiness. Not only for us, but for our brothers, too.

"Finn," I say as he sets me down gently.

"Mmm?" he asks, leaning down and pushing my hair away from my neck to leave a trail of kisses in its wake.

"Do you think we could spend the rest of our honeymoon somewhere else?"

He pulls back and looks down at me, concerned.

"What's wrong?"

"Nothing at all," I chuckle. "This is beautiful and perfect and I'm so, so happy to be with you—and the selfish part of me wants desperately to be alone with you forever. But I've missed so much time with my brother. I was thinking maybe you could use that incredible brain of yours and summon a place he and Merit would love."

Finn smiles, kisses me, then says, "I have just the place."

THE FALL

UNSURPRISINGLY, Finn comes through with flying colors...literally.

Within a few hours, he's used the Arc's Enhanced Illusion systems to create a theme park larger than any I've ever seen and summoned Kyra and Diva to bring the boys to us.

Paris has temporarily disappeared in favor of roller coasters, enormous Ferris wheels, pirate ships, haunted houses, and more.

When my brother arrives, his mouth drops open. He grabs Merit and begins to drag him from one ride to the next, pointing out all the perils and pitfalls before he notices me standing to the side, watching him with tears in my eyes.

"Ash?" he says, running over. "What's wrong?"

I grab him by the red t-shirt he's wearing and pull him close. "I'm just so happy to see you," I say. "To know...to know there's no one left to separate us."

"Me, too," he says, beaming as he pulls back. "Do you want to go on the big coaster? The one with all the loops?" he asks, pointing up to one of Finn's creations.

"That thing? It scares the hell out of me!" I reply.

"Is that a yes?"

"Absolutely!"

We spend the day racing around the park. Kyra and Diva laugh as they wave their hands high in the air on every conceivable virtual ride, and despite the fact that I know there's no real risk to any of us, I scream more over the course of a few hours than I've ever screamed in my life.

As the day winds down, Finn raises a glass of soda to us all and says, "Where would you like to go tomorrow?"

"Are you serious?" Merit asks. "We can go anywhere?"

"Anywhere."

The boys contemplate the question, and Kyra gestures to me. "Ash should pick," she says. "She's been through a lot."

"We all have," I tell her, taking her hand.

"Still—tell us where you would be, if you could be anywhere in the world."

I don't have to think hard before replying, "Right here, with all of you. But if I could bring you all *anywhere...*" I hurl a happy sideways glance at Finn. "Remember when I told you about my dream of a cottage on a beach?"

"Of course I do," he says.

With a stroke of his hand through the air, our surroundings change. The theme park disintegrates and the smell of salt hits us all. Sand dunes roll up to our right, tall grasses billowing in the breeze. To our left, the Pacific Ocean stretches out as far as the eye can see.

"Come on," Finn says, offering me his hand.

I take it and we run up the bank until I see a white house with a black roof and round windows looking out to the ocean. A large deck protrudes from a broad set of French doors at the back of the house, complete with several inviting lounge chairs.

"Finn!" I cry out, rushing toward it. "The house—when did you—"

"I've been designing it since the day we spoke of it," he tells me. "I worked on it while you were absent. It's modeled after a house on the west coast—one that is waiting for its new tenants."

I pull my eyes from the house and stare at him.

"You mean—"

He nods. "You, me, Kel, Merit." Looking over at the others, he says, "Kyra and Diva, if they want to come. I know you wanted a cottage, but I wanted to make sure it was big enough to hold all of us and visitors, should they ever show up."

I throw my arms around him, holding back a sob. "Thank you," I say.

"You know this one's not real, right?"

"It's real enough. Let's go inside."

We slip in through the French doors. Beckoning us nearer, laid out on a long wooden table, is an assortment of food and drink.

"Would you like to spend the rest of our honeymoon here?" Finn asks as the others step in behind us.

"Yes, please," I reply, turning to look at my brother. "If it's okay with you guys."

"It's your honeymoon," Kel says, laughing. "I just want to know one thing."

"What's that?"

He turns to Finn. "Is there a speed boat?"

"You can have any and every kind of boat you could possibly want, Little Man," Finn says. "Just say the word, and it's yours."

"Meanwhile," Diva says, taking both boys by the shoulders, "maybe we should head outside and go for a walk along the beach—and leave the newly married couple to some quiet time, hmm?"

"Fine," Merit sighs as Kyra grabs him and steers him out the door. "Let's go look for lobsters!"

She turns back to us and mouths, "Are there even lobsters?"

"I'll make sure of it," Finn whispers, and we watch as they slip out and close the doors.

"Well, then," Finn says, turning my way, "How about if I show you to the main bedroom?"

Three days pass. Three blissful, perfect days spent playing in the ocean, lounging on the deck, eating delicious, fresh food. Diva styles Kyra's hair as the boys make sand castles and play with the motorized virtual toys Finn summons for them.

I lie with my head pressed to Finn's chest, reveling in his touch as I watch the scene unfold. I never grow bored or restless, and all I can think is that I don't want this to end.

On the seventh day, though, the bliss comes to a crashing halt.

Sometime in the mid-afternoon, a silver bullet shoots from the sky to come to an abrupt landing on the wooden deck, mere feet from where Finn and I are sitting.

"Atticus?" I say, staring at him. "What's going on?"

"It's Rystan," he replies. "I'm afraid I have bad news."

"Rys?" Finn says, rising to his feet. "I thought he was with Adi in Brooklyn."

"He was. But there is unrest in the city. A new conflict. And Rystan is missing."

The owl turns his head around to face the cottage's white wall. On it, he projects a video showing buildings on fire and violent clashes in the streets. People whose faces are half covered with bandanas scrap with men who look like uniformed soldiers.

"This is real?" I ask, recalling the time not long ago when Atticus showed me a video of what turned out to be a fake battle between the Tree of Life Acolytes and the Arc's Dregs.

"I assure you that it is," Atticus says. "It was sent to me by one of Rystan's sparrows a few minutes ago, when it was separated from the rest of the drones."

"I'm trying to figure out who's fighting," I tell Finn, squinting at the projection. "It looks like the Trodden on one side. Adi's allies. But—the others don't look like the Bishop's people."

"No, they're not," Finn replies. "There's a symbol on their uniforms. Atticus, can you enlarge the image?"

When the video zooms in, I see what Finn's seeing.

The emblem on the soldiers' uniforms sends a violent shudder through my body.

The symbol, that of a rose, is similar to the one I've seen so many times on Directorate gear. But its stem is tangled with something else.

"Is that a…a crown?" I ask.

"No," Finn says. "Not quite a crown. I think it's a…tiara."

"What does *that* mean?"

The words slip past my lips even as a swell of sickness rises up inside me.

I know exactly what it means.

A rose.

A tiara.

Who do we know who is both a Directorate member and an Aristocrat—someone who would gather an entire army to his or her side and send them out into the streets to attack Dregs?

Finn and I stare at one another, shock on both our faces as we contemplate the unthinkable.

"It can't be," I say quietly. "It's not possible."

"Anything is possible," Finn tells me. "Atticus—what's the last thing Rystan told you?"

"He had assembled his drones in a safe haven in Brooklyn," the owl replies. "He was preparing to use them to infiltrate the Behemoth."

"I don't like this at all," I say. "I should have been in touch with him—checked in. I should have made sure he was okay."

I close my eyes and picture the scene Atticus just showed us. Bodies in the streets. Fire everywhere. Destruction raining down on innocent people, just as it did so long ago in the Mire.

"Finn...what if..."

I can't even bring myself to say the awful words for fear that speaking them might manifest them into some grim, horrid truth.

"If she is alive," Finn says, uttering the words for me, "then Rys, Adi, and everyone else in that city is in grave danger."

FLIGHT

IF SHE'S ALIVE.

The words hang in the air between Finn and me, gruesome lead weights threatening to crash through the earth itself and take us down with them.

I never saw the Duchess die.

I didn't see a body.

But I did leave her on top of the tallest building in the world with no means of escape. How could she possibly have gotten down safely, let alone amassed an entire military force since that fateful day?

Then I remind myself that it's been months since I was last in New York. Months since Rys and I fled in the Eagle. And the Duchess is as conniving and manipulative as the Bishop ever was.

If anyone could accomplish such a feat, it's her.

"She is alive," I say softly. "Isn't she? She's found her way back to a seat of power in one of the greatest fortresses humans have ever created."

"Nature abhors a vacuum," Finn says softly.

I nod my understanding. "When one cruel leader disappears…"

"Another happily takes their place," Finn concludes, his voice betraying a quiet torment.

"We have to go to New York," I say, reaching for him. "We need to find Rys. He and Adi—and everyone else—they're all in danger. And there are hundreds of thousands of innocent people imprisoned inside the Behemoth. The Duchess will never free them." I look into the owl's electronic eyes and ask, "Do you have a way to check in on Adi?"

"I have lost contact with most of Rys's drones," the owl says. "But I will try and connect with the sparrow who sent the video and send a message her way. Perhaps we can acquire a few answers."

"Before you do that, we need a means to get out east. An Air-Wing or other flying vessel. Are you able to secure one?"

Atticus flaps his long wings and takes off, heading away from the cottage. "Consider it done," he calls out. "Meet me in the Royal Grounds in a half hour."

When he's gone, we rush into the cottage, where we find Merit, Kel, Diva, and Kyra playing a game of Scrabble on the living room floor.

I crouch down next to Kel, taking his chin in my hand. He looks so much older than he used to, almost a teenager. It breaks my heart to know I'm leaving him again.

"What's going on?" he asks, a worried look in his eye.

"Finn and I have to go somewhere for a couple of days," I tell him. "But we'll be back soon. Both of us. I promise you that."

"Where are you going?" Merit asks, his eyes shifting from me to Finn and back again. But instead of meeting his gaze, I look at Kyra, who has already read the concern on my face.

"What can Diva and I do?" she asks.

"Look after them for us."

"Of course."

"You didn't answer my question," Merit gripes, and Finn kneels down next to him, giving his brother a quick hug, his eyes landing on mine.

I know what he's thinking.

How do we tell him we're going to New York to see if his mother is alive after all this time? To find out if she's responsible for still more death and destruction?

That yet again, she's leading an army of assassins against innocent people?

We don't even know if our theory is right. All we know is that Rys is missing, and that we need to find him.

So that's what Finn tells the boys.

"We haven't heard from Rystan in a little while, and we want to make sure he's doing okay in the big city," Finn finally says with a smile. "That's all. Once we've made contact, we'll come home."

"Are you sure?" Kel asks, his brow scrunched adorably into a skeptical knot. "The last time you went to New York…"

"Absolutely sure," I tell him with a stroke of his hair. "We'll be back as soon as we can. And maybe when New York City is all cleaned up and rebuilt, we can take you all there on a holiday."

"Really?" Suddenly, Kel has forgotten any and all doubts. "We can see the Empire State Building?"

"Really," I tell him with a faint laugh. "Now, we need to pack and get going. The sooner we leave, the sooner we return. You guys be good to Kyra and Diva, okay? Make sure you help them out around the place."

"We will," Merit says. "Bring us some souvenirs, okay?"

My smile fades when I say, "Of course we will."

Be careful what you wish for, I think darkly. *You don't want to know what sort of souvenir we may end up with.*

As promised, Atticus manages to secure us an Air-Wing to fly to New York. The owl assures us that Rys long since programmed him with the capacity to fly it single-handedly, and that we will be safe.

"I am fully charged, but will connect my power supply to the Air-Wing's so that my energy level doesn't drain," he tells us as he escorts us on board. "You have nothing to fear."

"That's reassuring," I tell him, following him inside the aircraft.

Finn and I are both dressed in the latest versions of our stealth uniforms. And though we'd both hoped never to have to fight a battle again, we both feel strong, thanks to the nanotech swimming in our bloodstreams.

"I can shield us if anyone attacks," he tells me. "We've got pain inhibitors, and the new uniforms are virtually bulletproof."

"Are they fireproof?" I ask, wincing. "Because something tells me Mommy Dearest won't be using a gun."

"Unfortunately, no."

When we've settled into our seats, Atticus navigates the Air-Wing out of a hatch on the Arc's roof, and we begin our flight smoothly, though I still find myself holding Finn's hand so tightly that I'm afraid I might break his bones.

"You okay?" he asks.

"I have this weird feeling," I tell him. "Not exactly fear. Something else. Like things are…I don't know, off-kilter."

Finn takes my hand and pulls it to his lips, gently kissing my wedding ring. "Not with us, I hope," he says.

"No. Definitely not with us. You're the one thing in the world that feels entirely steady right now."

"Excuse me," Atticus says politely as we soar over the mountains. "I have some news."

I try to leap to my feet but realize I'm buckled into my seat. "What is it?"

"A video that Rystan sent some time ago just came through. It seems it was floating in the ether for several days, and it just hit my memory banks."

"Are you able to show it to us and still fly this thing?" Finn asks.

Atticus twists his head around to face us and says, "Of course."

He projects the video in holo-format in the space between us, and I gasp when I see Rys standing at the center of a small park I recognize in Brooklyn. Adi is by his side, equipped with a gun of some sort—a rifle, from the looks of it. Rys, too, is carrying a weapon and facing the camera that's filming him.

"Ash, Finn..." he says, his breath coming in labored heaves. His face is beaded with sweat, and he's looking around warily. "We're under attack. Her army is enormous—they're powerful."

His voice begins to break up, but I can still make out a few words.

"There...thousands...them. I...I think they're...Sss..."

His voice cuts out entirely, then the sound of gunfire erupts. I see Rys ducking, covering Adi with his own body as others flee for their lives.

A second later, the projection fades, then vanishes.

"Atticus," I say, my voice choked in my throat. "Did a drone take that footage?"

"Yes. Another sparrow."

"Where are all the others? Didn't Rys have a whole army of them?"

"He did, yes. I cannot say where they are. I don't know."

"Do you have any idea what he was trying to say to us? That last word—it was something starting with S?"

"I do not know. I'm sorry."

I look at Finn as Atticus pulls his head back to face the front of the Air-Wing.

"Is there a Directorate faction that begins with S?" I ask.

Finn shakes his head. "Not that I know of. Honestly, I don't know what he's talking about. He said there are thousands of soldiers. Where did they come from? The Bishop didn't have that many at his disposal...did he?"

"I don't know," I say, my voice shaky. "He had so much hidden from us, it's hard to say what he did and didn't have in his arsenal. For all I know, the whole of upstate New York was a military complex full of soldiers just waiting for a fight."

"Except their commander is gone," Finn says. "So the question is, who's in charge?"

We exchange a look as the words pass silently between our two minds. Neither of us wants it to be true. Finn has mourned his mother in his quiet way already. He knew, just as I did, that the world was better off without her.

But now, there's a chance she's back and stronger than ever.

LANDING

As we fly, Atticus manages to hook us up with the Arc's communications system, pulling up a video screen connected to Illian's direct line. Kurt is seated next to his partner, and both of them wear grave expressions.

After Finn informs them of our departure, I explain what led us to such an impulsive move.

"There's a new force at work," I tell Illian, who looks distraught. I tell him about the rose and crown on the logo, and though he doesn't say it, I can tell he's thinking the same thing Finn and I are.

"Let's hope our side can keep up a good fight, and that Rystan has survived," he says. "We can send soldiers, but I'm afraid they'll arrive too late to do much good."

"We'll let you know if we think there's any point," I tell him. "Adi and her people are experienced fighters—at least, *some* of them are. I know they'll do what they can to keep Rys safe." I go silent for a moment before asking, "Does either of you know of a type of soldier that begins with S?"

Illian and Kurt exchange a glance, but both end up shrugging. "No," Kurt says. "Not a type. Only rankings, like sergeant, that sort of thing. But that's all."

With a sigh, I thank him and tell both men we'll be in touch soon.

"We will hold off on the elections in the meantime," Illian says. "No point in announcing the plan with you two gone."

With a nod, we disconnect, and I lean my head against Finn's shoulder.

"The longer I live," I say softly, "and the more pain I feel, the more I'm convinced that humans are bottomless pits. Just when I think I've felt as much sorrow as I possibly can in one lifetime…I discover my capacity for it is endless."

Finn kisses my head, slipping an arm around my shoulder and pulling me closer. "I love you, Ash. I can't tell you everything is going to be okay, because I don't know if that's true. But I love you. We will do everything we can to get Rys back and free the Behemoth's prisoners. If I have to kill my own mother to do it, I will."

"I should never have let him leave like that," I moan. "He left the Arc to protect me. But he should have stayed."

"You couldn't have known what would happen. None of us saw this coming. None of us expected my—" He halts, and I can feel the words sticking in his throat. He doesn't want to say it, to acknowledge fully that his mother could really have survived.

"I should have expected it," I tell him. "I learned a long time ago that if someone dies in a movie but you don't see their corpse, chances are they're still alive. The last time I saw your mother, she was coming at me with a fireball the size of my head swirling in the air in front of her, ready to hurl it at me."

"Well then," Finn says with a bitter smirk, "I guess I'm glad you jumped off that building."

After several hours, we land on the street in Brooklyn where Adi and Cillian live. The second we're free of the Air-Wing, Finn, Atticus and I rush toward Adi's place and I pound on the door.

In the distance, we hear gunfire, and smoke wafts from rooftops, portentous and dark.

"Adi! It's me! It's Ashen!" I cry when no one opens the door.

After a minute or so, it finally cracks open. Adi stands before me, looking thin and terrified, but she pulls me in and hugs me tight.

"Ash!" she says. "I can't believe you're here!"

"We got Rys's message," I tell her. "I'm so glad you're okay. Is Cillian—"

"He's inside. A bunch of us are. Come in, quickly, all three of you. It's not safe out there."

I look down the street to see a few people in dark uniforms headed our way. Something about the way they move is familiar, though I can't entirely put my finger on it. I wonder for a moment if they're Repliks.

"Stella?" I ask as Adi shuts the door behind us.

"She's here," Adi says. "At least, the version of Stella the Bishop sent me."

"I'm so sorry," I tell her. "I didn't know about them until…"

"Rys told me everything," Adi says. "It's okay. He had a plan to get her out of the Moth until all hell broke loose. It was so weird—everything was calm and peaceful, then Rys got here and *wham!* The city turned into a war zone."

Adi guides us to the back of the house and down the stairs to the basement, where we find Cillian and the Stella Replik.

"Ashen!" Cillian says, trying but failing to smile.

"Hi," I reply. "I'm really sorry about what's going on."

"We are, too."

Finn, who has been silent until now, speaks up.

"Is it the Duchess?" he says, finding the courage to ask what I could not.

Adi nods. "She made an announcement—it was projected to all of us. She said she was coming for us, for our homes. That she had amassed an army inside the Behemoth."

"And you've seen them, obviously."

Cillian nods. "Huge numbers. We don't know where they came from. They move like tanks, stopping for nothing. If you're in their way, you'll be trampled, or worse. That's the rule."

"Yeah," I reply. "Unfortunately, I'm familiar with their work."

"We thought maybe we'd be okay when we saw Rys's drones come into the city. It was like a massive black cloud flying overhead—a storm, fighting for our side. There were so many of them that we cheered when we saw them."

"Where are the drones now?"

"He was storing them in an abandoned warehouse on the river. But I'm not sure what became of them when…"

"What happened?" Finn asks, his body tight with tension.

"We were attacked in the park. Many Trodden were shot. Rys tried to protect me, but a few of those…those *soldiers* came for him. They ripped him away from us, almost like they didn't care that we were there. They just wanted him."

I glance over at Finn, who looks like he's trying to figure out why his mother would take such a keen interest in Rys.

"There's something else, Ash," Adi says. "One of those soldiers—he was a man I recognized. Used to live down the block from us. He was a Dreg—a Trodden. I don't know how that woman got to him. How she managed to convert him. He was always kind to us, but when I looked into his eyes he seemed so cold, so unfeeling. It was like she'd ripped his soul away."

"Did he try to hurt you?" I ask, reaching for Finn's hand and holding on tight.

"Yes, but that was the weirdest part," Adi says. "He didn't have a gun. He just...stared at me. But it was intense and painful. I fell to my knees, grabbed my head. I thought it was going to explode. He finally stopped, but only after I'd hit the ground."

Again, I feel Finn tensing next to me, and I know without asking that we're thinking the same thing.

"Rys's message—he wasn't telling us about something that started with an S," I mutter.

"No," Finn replies. "He was saying *Cyphers*."

"What's a Cypher?" Cillian asks.

"A human implanted with nanotech and programmed to obey one master—or mistress. One capable of feats no one should be able to perform. Strong, powerful, superhuman and inhuman at the same time."

"I've seen them take hold of people's minds," I say. "Force others to commit horrendous acts of violence. They're terrifying. The Duchess had a few in the Arc, but the thousands she has in New York—that's a whole new level of bad news."

"Can they be stopped?"

Finn nods. "In theory, yes. The tech implanted to give them their powers and to render them compliant can be disabled, but to do so with thousands of them would be all but impossible. Unless we had an army of our own capable of injecting each and every one of them."

"We can't get close enough to do that," Adi says. "Look—all I've ever wanted was to free Stella—the *real* Stella—from that god-awful place. Rys was going to help me. He was preparing to help us all. I'm not sure how. But we owe it to him to help *him*. I just wish I knew how."

"I have an idea," Finn says. "If our side has one secret weapon against the Duchess, it's me."

Atticus lets out a low hoot of warning, but Finn keeps talking.

"My mother has always had a weakness for me. If she has Rys, I'm willing to bet she would trade him for her oldest son."

"No, Finn," I say, my voice a low warning like the owl's. "Don't you dare. I can't lose you."

"She won't hurt me," he promises, but I'm not at all sure he's right.

"She once sent you into the Arenum to die by my hand," I remind him. "Don't underestimate her cruelty. She's a monster."

I know how harsh I must sound to Adi and Cillian.

But if there's a woman in this world who truly deserves the title *Monster-in-Law*, it's the Duchess.

CONFRONTATION

AFTER ASSURING us that he can find his way into the Behemoth, Atticus leaves to carry a message to the Duchess.

Finn and I are seated in Adi's kitchen, our hands wrapped tensely around two coffee mugs. Our eyes are directed out the window at the array of broken-down rooftops in the distance.

We both know what will happen to the houses we're looking at and to their occupants if the Duchess manages to take full control of the city. She will ruin lives. She'll drive humanity into wretchedness, just as she's done before.

All from a dubious, usurped throne inside a castle of glass and steel.

"Atticus has been instructed to inform my mother I want to meet with her in the remains of Central Park," Finn tells me. "In person. I told her to bring Rys with her—that I would be willing to make a trade."

I struggle to keep myself from crying out in protest.

Finn is offering something noble and good. His life, in return for Rys. But the thought of the Duchess winning yet another battle sickens me to the core. She doesn't deserve the pleasure of hurting me again. She doesn't deserve happiness.

And she sure as hell doesn't deserve her son.

"Finn, no," I muster through unsteady vocal cords. "There has to be a better way. She has his drones—she doesn't need Rys, surely. There's no reason you have to go with her."

He holds me tight when he says, "You know her. You know what she wants—what she's always wanted. Her little family by her side as she rises to power. She will never be content as long as she has a son out in the world who despises everything she stands for. She wants me, and Merit. She wants a dynasty. Heirs to her twisted throne."

With my face pressed to his chest, I say, "I just got you back. Please tell me I don't have to lose you again. Not like this."

Finn pulls back and looks me in the eye. "I will do what I can to fight her. I promise. But my mother is powerful, and she won't hesitate to kill Rys, not if she thinks it will give her the upper hand."

"I can fight too, remember. We can keep that from happening."

"We will." Finn lets out a breath that tells me he's come to terms with what must be done.

I can't imagine how he feels right now, knowing that the only way to make the world a better place is to rid it of one of his parents. Killing Merit's mother.

But it's a world the Duchess has created. She has brought this hell down on her own children.

"I wish Atticus were back with news," I lament, and just as the words leave my mouth, the owl flaps down and lands on the windowsill next to the table where we're sitting.

"What did she say?" Finn asks him.

Instead of replying, Atticus projects a recorded video above the table. The Duchess stands before us, a shrunken version in all her malevolent glory, her eyes narrowed, hair pulled tightly back.

"Finn, my son," she coos. "How lovely to hear from you. I would be delighted to meet with you, and yes—of course I'll bring your friend Rystan. I'd like for you to have words with him, after all. He has something I want. Meet me at the Grand Army Plaza at five p.m."

"Atticus—what time is it now?"

"Three Fifty-Seven," the owl replies.

"How far to the Grand Army Plaza?" I ask, turning to look at Adi, who's standing in the doorway.

"It's not too far, at the south-east corner of the old park," she says. "I'll take you there."

The mood is grim as Finn and I accompany Adi and Cillian, first in a beaten-up jeep borrowed from a fellow Trodden, then on foot across the Brooklyn Bridge, which is now guarded by the Duchess's servants. Atticus flies above us in stealth mode, watching our backs as we march into dangerous territory.

When Finn identifies himself, the guards let us pass, but only after confirming via a wrist communicator that the Duchess does indeed wish to see her son—and that none of us is armed.

We arrive at the plaza with only minutes to spare, positioning ourselves next to a large stone plinth that looks as if it used to be the base for some important statue or other.

As we approach the plaza's center, shadows emerge from the surrounding streets, engulfing us from every side. I press myself to Finn when I register that they aren't shadows at all, but a vast army of Cyphers, closing in around our small group like four impenetrable walls of a fortress.

Reality hits me then.

We will never leave this place, no matter what deal Finn strikes with the Duchess. She didn't summon her entire army to surround us only to let us free at the end of it all. She'll take her son and slaughter the rest of us, unless we find a way to fight back.

As I stare out at the sea of Cyphers whose soulless eyes seem fixed on nothing, a chorus of disparate voices ring in my mind. Menacing whispers coming at me like an overwhelming, sudden madness.

You will die in this place. Give in. She will destroy you—or we will.

No, I think, shaking my head. *We've made it this far. All we need is to get Rys back. That will be enough to set things right.*

We watch and wait in silence as the Duchess descends from the Behemoth in a boxy transport mag-drone—one designed exclusively to come and go from the massive Arcology.

When the craft has landed, the Duchess slips out, wearing a black pant suit and patent leather stiletto heels.

A ridiculous outfit for such an encounter.

But then, the Duchess always did care more about style than substance.

Behind her are her husband, the Duke, and Rys, who is escorted by a large man in military garb. From his blank stare, I can only gather that he, too, is one of the Duchess's Cyphers.

The Duchess offers up a thin smile to Finn, but when she looks at me, her expression instantly turns into an exaggerated sneer.

"I'd hoped the leap from the Behemoth had killed you, Ashen," she says, her tone icy. "Pity."

"The only thing that was about to kill me was you," I retort. "I'm so sorry you didn't get your chance."

"Well—I believe in *second* chances. Don't you?"

"Not where you're concerned, no."

As the guard drags Rys over and positions him next to the Duchess, I examine him with a deepening sense of horror. His face is swollen and red, and marred by several cuts, as if someone has been beating him. But his breathing appears normal, and he's able to stand up straight, at least.

"Are you okay?" I call out.

"I will be," he replies, his voice hoarse. "If I'm lucky."

"Why did you do this?" Finn snaps at his mother. "What reason could you possibly have for kidnapping Rys and assaulting him?"

The Duchess lets out a little laugh—one that sounds like chiming bells but feels like knives in my brain.

"Come now, Finn. When I learned Rystan Decker was coming into the city with thousands of drones, there was no question that I had to claim them for myself. You can hardly blame me for taking advantage of an opportunity."

Does she have the drones?

If that's the case, she's more dangerous than any of us anticipated. Finn and I have seen Rys's deadly birds in action —they're more destructive than an army of Cyphers could ever be.

She answers my question before I've asked it out loud. "The trouble is, Rystan here isn't particularly keen on giving them to me."

Good boy, Rys.

"He has, however, agreed to give me what I need to take control of them, provided I free him."

"Ash," Rys says weakly when he sees the look on my face. "They beat me. I had to agree to it. They were going to kill me."

"I know, Rys," I say with a tight nod. "I'm just glad you're okay."

The truth is, I wish he'd held out. I wish he'd never promised her anything.

Because now, if he breaks that promise, she *will* end him.

"If you give her control, she'll destroy this city and everyone in it," Finn tells Rys. "You know that."

"Yeah," Rys nods, a trickle of blood running down his chin. "I know."

"Let him go, *Mother*," Finn commands. "You have what you want. You have me. You have the drones."

"No," the Duchess says. "I don't yet have the drones. But I will. Rystan, give me the codes."

Clearly, she expects Rys to comply immediately.

But when he still hasn't responded after a few seconds, she turns his way.

Pivoting to face her, he shakes his head. "I…I can't," he says. "Finn is right. You'll destroy this city and everyone in it, and I can't let that happen. If you have to kill me, go ahead and do it."

"I don't think you fully understand what you're saying, boy," the Duchess retorts, stepping toward him. Without a second's hesitation, she grabs hold of his right shoulder, squeezing tight.

I watch in horror as her skin begins to crackle and glow a fierce red-orange. I hold in the scream of warning that wants to explode from my lips.

Rys already knows what's coming, but it does nothing to shield him from the agony as her hand burns into his flesh. He screams in pain, his body contorting as he tries instinctively to evade her grip...but she's too strong.

"The owl is out there somewhere," the Duchess growls. "Tell him to film this. I want him to see this—to see what I'm doing to you. I want him to show the world what happens when you defy the Duchess."

She digs in harder, and again, Rys shrieks with pain.

"No!" I shout, and before Finn can stop me, I'm running full speed toward my enemy.

I can't bear to watch her kill Rys the way she killed Peric. I won't let this happen!

With rage roiling inside me, I leap forward, thrusting my palms out. A blinding flash fills the air as a projectile, blue-white and pulsing with undeniable power, hurtles toward the Duchess.

The Surge crashes against her chest, exploding like a large ball of ice against her frame and knocking her back so that she stumbles several feet before regaining her balance.

With her chin down, she pulls herself together and strides toward me, hands in the air in front of her, cradling and nurturing a ball of fire that's growing larger by the second.

A sphere of flame meant to end me.

The Duchess shoves her hands toward me, hurling the projectile.

Countering her, I summon the Surge once again, sending another explosion of energy to meet the flame head-on. They collide in the air between us, a horrifying shockwave sending a pulse of terror through me as I feel my body and mind drained of strength.

"You can't win, *girl!*" the Duchess shouts derisively as she immediately hurls another fireball, catching me off guard. This one collides with my chest, burning through the fabric of my silver uniform and searing my skin in several places.

I scream in pain as my flesh sizzles and the horrifying reek of roast meat makes its way to my nose and mouth.

One more blow like that and I will die.

And the Duchess knows it.

41

FINAL GIRL

THE NERVES UNDERLYING my singed skin feel like a thousand jabbing knives as I seek out the strength to hurl another blast at the Duchess. But she's quicker than I am, and uninjured, and she summons another searing weapon between her palms, preparing to shoot it at me once again.

But even as she moves to thrust the firebomb my way, Finn throws a hand in the air, conjuring an Aegis wall before me—a near-invisible barrier strong enough to block almost any assault.

The fireball slams against it, exploding in a searing mass that would have ended my life, had it come a second sooner.

"Finn—I can do this," I protest, though I'm not even remotely convinced of it.

"The Surge won't take her down," he says with a shake of his head. "It's forged from energy, and so is her power. The only way to defeat her is old-fashioned weaponry."

"We have to stop her—whatever it takes."

"I know." Finn looks to his father, the Duke, who stands by, his hands behind his back. His eyes are fixed on a spot in the distance, his mind seemingly in utter denial of what his wife is doing.

"Father!" Finn shouts. "How can you allow this? How can you stand by while she threatens the lives of so many people? Are you really this cold?"

The Duchess turns to Finn, laughing. "Since when does your father have any control over me? He has always been a weakling. A pathetic, spineless, submissive man. He is a worm, Finn—and you are, too, if you don't see the importance of what I am about to achieve for the glory of our family."

"You're achieving nothing but cruelty," Finn snaps. "You're torturing our friend. You're going to kill him—and for what?"

"For power," she purrs.

The Duchess spins around, and extends her hands, a white-hot, spinning fireball forming between them.

"Summon them," she snarls at Rys. "Show me my promised trophies, and I will release you."

His shoulder is burnt to blackness, his neck an angry, throbbing red. I know the pain he must be suffering.

"Rys, do as she says!" I shout, tears streaming down my cheeks.

"I'm sorry, Ash," he calls out. "I...I'm so sorry. I never wanted to let you down. Not like this..."

"It's okay," I tell him. "Please...just do it."

Finn reaches out, wrapping a protective arm around me. We watch, eyes locked on Rys's wounds, minds tormented by the pain he must be suffering as he falls to his knees, weakened by agony. He pulls his sleeve up and strokes a finger over the black band on his arm. Almost instantly, the sky above us goes dark as if a grim storm has just blown its way over the city.

I pull my face up to see the largest flock of birds I've ever laid eyes on. Fliers of every size circle the sky above. Hummingbirds. Eagles. Hawks. Vultures.

"We can't let her do this," Finn says under his breath.

"We can't stop her. You said it yourself."

"The Surge can't stop her," he retorts. "But maybe I can."

Finn lets me go and, waving a hand in the air, brings the Aegis wall down just long enough to step away from me. He conjures it again, this time behind him, separating me from his parents and Rys. Adi and Cillian are standing several feet behind me, huddled together as they watch the conflict unfold.

"Each drone is trackable," the Duchess tells him as he approaches. "Each has the potential to be a volatile weapon. Think what we could do, Finn."

"No," Finn shouts, taking another step toward her. "*We* won't be doing anything, Mother."

"Come, Finn. Why are you looking at me like that? You wouldn't hurt your mother, would you?"

"You've done enough," he says. "You've hurt enough people. It's time to stop."

"Never." Her lips gleam a malevolent shade of red against white as she bares her teeth and adds, "I have our family to consider."

The Duke steps forward to stand next to his wife, his head bowed.

"Rystan," the Duchess says. "Give me the arm band. It's time."

Defeated, Rys removes the black band and hands it to her.

As she straps it onto her arm over her suit jacket, she says, "What's the command?"

Rys goes silent for a moment, and the Duchess practically shouts, "What is the command? I will not ask a third time."

Finn halts in his tracks, waiting to see if Rys caves to her demands.

Rys pulls his eyes to mine, and for a split-second, I'm sure I see a smile on his lips.

"A circle," he says. "Quartered by a cross. But...I need to transfer Atticus over to you. He's programmed to control the drones, too. You...you need him if you're going to lead this army."

"Rys, no!" I shout.

The thought of Atticus having to exist under the Duchess's rule is almost too much to bear.

"It's all right, Ash." Rys looks up to the sky, searching for the silver owl. When he spots him, he lets out a low whistle, then says, "Atticus...Initiating Command Protocol D-D-3."

I close my eyes, horrified as the owl swoops down and lands in front of the Duchess. He stares up at her, his eyes glowing red.

"You will do as I ask," the Duchess says to him.

"Yes. I will," Atticus replies.

"Good." The Duchess sweeps the circle and cross over her arm band—the symbol my father used to sign his paintings—before turning to face me. "Have the drones aim and ready themselves to open fire on Ashen Spencer."

Crying out, Finn spins around, sweeping his hands in the air once again to summon a protective dome in the air above me.

Mere seconds later, the army of drones swoops downward as one entity and turns their focus on me, thousands of jagged silver beaks pointing in my direction. Small eyes glow with the same red warning as Atticus's own, and I find myself paralyzed with fear.

"How strong do you think that Aegis of yours is, Finn?" the

Duchess asks. "Strong enough to resist thousands of Rystan's creations? Shall we put it to the test?"

"She's my wife, Mother," Finn snarls. "I love her."

"Your wife?" she sputters, and for the briefest moment, I wonder if she will allow herself an ounce of sympathy. But instead, she laughs. "You may think you love her, just as your father 'loves' me." With that, she hurls another disdainful look toward the Duke. "Trust me, my son—you're far better off without her."

I'm staring at the sky, at the dark wash of birds, each intent on taking me down once they've managed to destroy Finn's Aegis.

To think of all I've been through—all I've survived, and in the end, it will be Rys's incredible flying army that ends me. It's almost comical.

"Finn," I say calmly. "It's okay. Tell Kel I love him. And know that I love you."

"I love you too, Ash—but I'm not losing you. Not today."

"Are you two quite finished?" the Duchess hisses, clearly irritated. "I have things to do."

I level her with an angry glare. "My greatest wish, for a long time, has been that you should die painfully and slowly. But even if I had the right weapon, I've realized I can't kill you myself. You are Finn's mother, and I love him more than anything in the world. I love him too much to hurt him in that way. But clearly, you don't."

Finally, I look at Rys, who's breathing hard and wincing in pain. "You did what you had to. I understand."

He nods again, and once again, I'm convinced I detect the faintest hint of a smile. But I tell myself it's simply another agony-induced wince.

"The owl," the Duchess says impatiently. "Call him to me. I cannot see him."

I look around and realize she's right—Atticus has disappeared. Odd, given that he's supposed to be under the Duchess's control.

Rys lets out a low whistle. "Atticus!" he shouts. "Command Protocol D-290!"

The owl appears in the sky above us, flapping his gleaming wings, red eyes fixed on the Duchess. He swoops at her once, just close enough to blow a few of her hairs out of place.

"What is the beast doing?" she snarls, wildly flicking her finger over the arm band as she tries to gain control.

"You'll see," Rys tells her. "It's nothing to worry about, I assure you."

Atticus banks and shoots upward, letting out a series of rhythmic hoots as he darts in between the drones dotting the sky above us.

All at once, the birds shift their focus away from me, and, breaking up into hundreds of small flocks, begin swooping down toward the street, then back up again. At first, it looks almost like a random dance, a sort of migratory pattern.

But after a few seconds, as my eyes land on the Duchess's Cypher forces, I begin to understand what I'm seeing.

"The Cyphers," I say, watching the soldiers as they duck and cower, trying to avoid the birds' aerial assaults. Some of them have the wherewithal to swat at the birds, and now and then, one manages to clip a fast-moving wing. But after innumerable assaults from above, the Cyphers begin one by one to drop to their knees, falling face-first to the ground.

A few of them rise after a moment, pushing themselves to their feet and looking around like confused, shaky newborn calves.

"What's going on?" I cry, looking for Rys. "What's happening to them?"

"The birds are injecting the Cyphers—they're disabling the nanotech that makes them obey my Mother," Finn tells me through the shield. "Rys, you clever bastard!"

But Rys, it seems, has disappeared.

The Duchess is looking around frantically, desperate to hold him accountable for the madness unfolding before us. The Duke stands calmly to her right, watching with what can only be described as an oddly satisfied grin.

"You've failed," Finn says, striding toward his mother as she slices at the arm band with her fingertip. "You always assume you can buy people's submission—that you can buy entire humans, as if we're commodities to be traded. But you don't own us. You are not entitled to rule—and you are damned well not entitled to an army of drones that never belonged to you, you evil bitch."

The Duchess glares at her son. "How dare you?" she sneers, her skin glowing a fierce, alarming shade of red, a horrifying pattern of orange veins slipping over every inch of her face.

"How dare *you?*" Finn spits. "How can you live with yourself, after all you've done to us? To everyone in the Arc, in the Mire, here in New York? Those people were prisoners—they were taken against their will and kept from their families—and you turned them into a mindless army to serve at your pleasure. You're a monster...*Mother.*"

"Those people were the key to the Davenports' future!" she cries. "Yours and mine—and Merit's! I did it for love of you both!"

I can't help but notice her failure to mention the Duke, who is still standing by her side, his head down. But the Duchess ignores him, and as more Cyphers drop around us, she steps toward Finn, a hand outstretched. It's glowing with a terrifying white heat so profound that I can feel it even behind the Aegis wall.

Finn recoils, but the Duchess continues to advance toward him. "You have a choice. Come with me, Finn. We will live inside the Behemoth, together. Safe from the outside world. Come with me, or..."

"Or die?" Finn shakes his head. "I would rather die a thousand deaths than be with you. Do you hear me? I have a new family now, and you will *never* be a part of it."

She lunges for him, her hand reaching for his silver uniform. He doesn't back away—doesn't flee her touch.

I cry out when I see her hand press into his chest, smoke rising, a scream piercing the air.

She's going to kill him. Even if it's not deliberate, she's going to take his life in front of me.

As Finn struggles to gain the upper hand, the Aegis wall disappears, evaporating around me.

Seeing my chance to take the Duchess down, I leap forward, but a strong set of hands pulls me back.

"Steady, Ash," Rys's voice says into my ear.

"I can't let her kill him," I snarl, my chest heaving with rage. "She needs to die. I'll find a way—I'll make sure she never draws breath again."

"You're right. She does need to die," he whispers. "But if you do this, you have to live with it for the rest of your life—with the knowledge that you killed Finn's and Merit's mother. You said yourself that you love Finn too much to end her. Think about it, please."

Finn has his hands around his mother's neck, but her own hands are still pressing into his chest, smoke rolling in dark waves as he cries out in agony.

"She'll kill him, Rys!" I shout, thrusting my hands toward the Duchess, calling upon the power Finn gave me. *If I can't kill her, at least I can knock her back—I can get her away from him.* "He's going to die! I can't let her take him from me!"

"She won't," Rys says. "It's the last time I'll ever ask you for this, but…trust me."

Trust him? How can he be so calm when the world is going mad around us? When Finn is fighting his mother mere feet from where we stand, and she is winning?

But then, like a miracle conjured by Rys's brilliant mind, it happens.

42

OVER

OF ALL THE scenarios I ever imagined unfolding—of all the ways the Duchess could have met her end—this was the last one I ever anticipated.

Everything moves in slow motion.

Black, toxic smoke wafts from the Duchess's hands as Finn's uniform melts away under her touch. He falls at her feet, weakened by his injuries, crying out in pain and rage as she lunges for him again. This time, she pulls him to his feet by his uniform and reaches a glowing hand toward his face.

I hardly notice when the Duke makes his move, stealthily slipping two objects from inside his suit jacket—silver and glinting in the sunlight. With a wild cry, he leaps toward the Duchess and drives a blade into her back.

She shrieks and lets go of Finn, who stumbles backwards. The Duchess reaches a hand back, trying in vain to remove the knife. Her flesh glows white-hot and terrifying, her clothing burning away as she lets out a series of inhuman wails.

The Duke comes at her again, and this time, he plunges the

second blade into his wife's glowing chest. He cries out as his hand comes into contact with her skin, and once again, the scent of charred meat fills the air around us.

The Duke recoils, thrusting himself backwards, but the Duchess spins around and leaps on him, forcing him to the ground. Her hands are around his neck, his screams of pain filling the air as she burns through muscle and sinew as if his flesh were little more than candle wax. The Duke's once handsome face turns red, his skin melting away even as his cries fade.

The Duchess's glowing skin, too, is fading, the shock of white and red heat dissipating with each second that passes. She steals the last of her husband's life from him as her life leaves her, and then, her flesh fading to an unnatural pallor, she collapses on top of him.

"Finn!" I cry, stumbling forward, finally free of Rys's grip.

On his chest is an angry black hand print. His uniform is singed here and there. But otherwise he looks unhurt.

He looks down at me with tears in his eyes and whispers, "It's over, Ash. It's finally over."

I sit on the ground a few feet from Finn as the Behemoth's medical staff attends to our burns.

I wince as they apply some sort of soothing gel to my charred flesh—a gel that seems to work miracles, because the second it makes contact with my skin, the stabbing, stinging pain vanishes.

When I ask the staff where the gel came from, they tell me it was developed in the Bishop's labs.

"He did exactly one good thing in his life, then," I mutter under my breath.

Finn and Rys also seem to feel instantly better when the gel is applied, and Finn rises to his feet and moves toward me. He slips a hand onto my back, seating himself next to me.

Several feet away, the bodies of the Duke and Duchess lie on the ground, draped in white fabric. Finn's eyes lock on the sight as he says, "I don't know what to tell Merit."

I shake my head, unable to provide him with an answer. What would I have told Kel, if it turned out one of our parents was cruelty personified and the other was forced to kill in order to protect me? There is no happy ending here. No gentle way to let Merit down. His father's brief foray into heroism resulted in his mother's death, and without a doubt, the tale would traumatize the young boy.

"Tell him what you need to," I finally say. "Tell him what seems best for him. Merit is the only one who matters now."

Finn nods, pressing toward me as if seeking support, which I offer gladly.

As we sit in silence, Atticus swoops down to land at my feet, turning his head to look at me.

"Sometimes," I tell him, "I wonder how you see the world."

"Perhaps I'll show you one day," he replies. "Are you all right, Ashen?"

The question surprises me—but more than that, it's the owl's tone, which sounds almost human.

With a smile, I nod. "I'm okay. I'm shaken. I thought...I thought I was going to lose all three of you today. Finn, Rys, you."

Pulling my head around, I scan the area around us where families have begun reuniting with those lost years ago to the Bishop's cruelty.

As I watch, a familiar young woman emerges from the crowd of uniformed strangers to walk toward us. Adi. Her arm is wrapped around another familiar-looking person—a young woman with a smile on her face.

"Is it okay if I go talk to Adi for a minute?" I ask Finn, who nods.

"Yes—go. I'm just going to sit here for the moment."

With a quick kiss to his cheek, I leap to my feet and run over, my sorrow turning briefly to joy.

"It's not—" I stammer as I look at the young woman wearing the Cypher uniform. "It can't be. Can it?"

Adi nods. "This is the real Stella. My sister."

Unable to help myself, I throw my arms around her, yanking her close. "You don't know how happy I am to meet you," I tell her. "I thought I'd failed your sister. I thought—"

"Failed?" Adi laughs as I pull back to look into Stella's eyes. "Ash, you exposed the Bishop for what he was—and God knows, you suffered for it. I'm so sorry, truly. But if it weren't for you, for Rys, for Finn—and all those damned birds..." She laughs again as she pulls her eyes to the sky. "Well, you all managed to rescue us from a fate even worse than the Bishop."

"Not all of you," I say, sorrow deep in my chest. "I'm sorry about the Trodden who were lost. I wish we could have done more."

"Thank you. But what you did was incredible. Thanks to all of you, our lives can return to normal. At least, I *hope* they can." Looking around, her eyes land on Rys. "Is he okay? And Finn?"

"They'll be all right, yeah. It's going to be hard for Finn. He thought he'd already lost his mother, and now, to see her again, then lose her the way he did..."

"His father did something amazing," Stella says quietly. "I watched it. I saw. He saved you and Finn."

"I've never had much affection for the Duke," I confess. "But he did redeem himself a little today. He did what his wife never would have had the strength of character to do—he protected his son."

"To think a simple blade is what took the mighty Duchess down," Adi says. "It seems almost poetic."

"Almost," I concur.

After we've spoken another few minutes, Adi tells me she's going to take Stella home to rest. "We have a lot of catching up to do," she tells me.

I nod, wondering silently about the other Stella—the Replik who still lives with Adi and Cillian. Will they allow her to stay with them, to share their lives?

But I remind myself that their lives are no longer my concern. I have Kel to get home to, and Merit. We have an election to hold in the Arc.

When I've said goodbye to them, I head back to Rys and Finn, seating myself between them. Rys is staring up at the sky where his plethora of birds are still swarming, twisting through the air as if awaiting a command.

With one stroke of his finger over the partly seared arm band he took back after the Duchess's death, he issues an order for them to return to their nesting place, and pulls his eyes to mine.

"What now?" I ask. "Will you come home with us?"

"I will come home," he tells me with a nod. "Soon. I promised the people here I'd oversee things—help those who are recovering, and help rebuild. More than anything, I want to rearrange the inside of the Behemoth."

"Rearrange?" Finn asks, perking up suddenly.

"Well, yeah. It's a grim pit of despair in there," Rys says. "But it doesn't have to be. People want connection. Contact with others. The residences in the Moth are isolated from one another—it's depressing. All those floating living quarters could be connected via tunnels and corridors. The people who live on the inside may as well start enjoying society again. Just because most of them are wealthy doesn't mean they're all jerkwads."

"How benevolent of you," I say with a snicker. "To do something nice for the quasi-jerkwads."

"I'm here to help."

"You know they'd give you a residence, if you wanted it, right? And there are plenty of houses here that I'm sure the Trodden would help you to acquire if you wanted one..."

Rys shakes his head. "Nah. I want to go back to the mountains. They were always my home. My dream was to own a little plot of land looking out at the peaks, and now, I'm finally starting to think it could become a reality."

"Good," Finn replies. "You deserve it, man."

"Thanks...man."

I smirk as I watch their interaction. They've never quite been friends, but there's no question that they admire one another. I have no idea how I got so fortunate as to end up with such an incredible partner and such a fantastic best friend, but I tell myself I will never, ever take it for granted.

"Rys," I say, "there's an election taking place in the Arc soon. I think you should run for office."

"You think?"

I'm surprised he didn't flat out refuse, so I nod. "Absolutely. You'd be amazing in a leadership role. You're good at getting people to trust you, even when you're about to walk them into a potential deadly situation. I'd say you'd make an ideal candidate."

He snickers before replying, "I'll think about it, Ash. Meanwhile, I do have an idea for a new logo in the Arc. Something other than the Consortium logo or that freaking Tree of Life thing, I mean. I think it's time we moved past all the scary dictator stuff."

"Fair enough. What's the logo?"

Rys whistles for Atticus, who flaps over and lands by my feet. "Would you please show them?" Rys asks.

"The banners, you mean?"

"Yep."

Atticus turns to Finn and me and projects an image in the air between us. At first, it's a little hazy and hard to make out. But after a few seconds, I see that it's a long banner like those that used to hang all over the Arc emblazoned with the Directorate's rose.

Only, instead of a rose, it's...a silver owl.

"I fully support this," I say with a laugh, and Finn agrees, taking my hand in his.

I lean my head on his shoulder and let out a long breath.

"Let's go home," Finn finally says.

"Are you sure? Your parents—I mean, won't there be a funeral?"

"My parents died long ago, Ash. I don't intend to mourn them. All I want is to begin a new life with you."

EPILOGUE

Two months after the Duchess's Fall

Finn and I are parents now.

Not literally, of course. It's too soon, and we're too young. Too hung up on enjoying our newfound freedom.

Our family consists of Kel, Merit, Finn, and myself.

We live in a white house with a black roof, on the West Coast—one that Finn purchased with his inheritance. Our bedroom window looks out onto the Pacific Ocean, and each morning I wake up to look out toward the water, wondering if I'm back in a Sensory Deprivation Tank.

Wondering if I'm dreaming once again.

As I watch the waves lap at the shore, the vastness beyond the water's edge is a calming force, reminding me how small our strange, violent world once was. I revel in the lack of jagged edges, in the absence of buildings inhabited by power-hungry killers. All I see is sky and water, and all I feel is peace.

Kel and Merit are the best of friends, and they've managed

to make new friends out here, too, with children whose parents escaped oppressive governments and fled to the coast, away from the cities, hoping to find some calm.

I will never say the name of our quiet strip of land for fear of conjuring demons or summoning ambitious, silver-tongued leaders.

In this place, we have no leaders.

And we're happy.

We don't speak of Finn's and Merit's parents, at least not as the Duke and Duchess. Merit knows of their deaths, but for now, Finn has led him to believe they died fighting in New York during a bloody rebellion. He doesn't know about his mother's cruelty, or his father's heroism.

He may never know.

When Finn and I speak of the past, we limit the subject to our childhoods before the Blight, the time before the Directorate took charge of our lives.

Before the Bishop, and before every single day was a struggle for survival for us both.

When I think of the Duchess in quiet, private moments, I try to picture a woman I never saw. A young mother. A wife who once loved her husband. Not the woman I knew, but the woman I wish I'd known.

The woman I wish she'd remained.

The Arc's elections took place a month ago, just before we moved out west. A President was named—a young man both deserving and hard-working, one who is tasked with overseeing the Arc's affairs as well as those in the Mire. A man with myriad problems to solve...but I have every faith that he, of all people, is fully capable of solving them.

Illian and Kurt, meanwhile, have moved out of the Arc and taken up residence in a pretty brick house in Sector Six.

For the first time in memory, *almost* all is right with our world.

And I will do anything to keep it this way.

One afternoon in late August, I find myself walking along the beach alone, a smile on my lips. I stop to stare out at the ocean, idly playing with my wedding band as a cool breeze caresses my skin.

There have been times when I wasn't sure I deserved the golden ring on my finger. For that matter, I'm still not entirely certain Finn and I were legally married. Our wedding was all for show, a spectacle to please the Arc's masses one last time before the Bishop tried to take over their lives.

As I begin to walk again, I see a figure in the distance, moving toward me at a jog. A neighbor, maybe—someone from one of the cottages down the way.

But as he gets close, I freeze, my heart thudding suddenly in my chest.

I wait, my toes digging into the sand, for his breathless arrival.

"Of all the faces I would expect to see on this beach," I tell him when he's a few feet away, "yours might be the last one."

He laughs, running a hand through his hair. He shifts his weight awkwardly from one foot to the other, then says, "Hi, Ash."

"Hey, Rys. Aren't you supposed to be heading the Arc's government?"

"I am. But a funny thing happened. I remembered something I promised you a while back. Do you remember?"

I cock my head, trying to think what he could possibly mean.

"A small wedding on a beach," he says when I fail to answer. "A real wedding."

"You did say that."

"I was so bummed about not being at your last one—and as it turns out, the President of the Arc is legally allowed to marry you and Finn. I thought I should take advantage of my newfound superhuman status to come through on that promise."

"Well, then. Let's have a wedding."

Without another word, Rys puts his arm around me and we turn to head home. The flapping of silver wings sounds in the air behind us, a beautiful, perfect duet with the steady beat of the ocean's waves.

The cries of pain and sorrow that once throbbed in my head are gone now, left behind like shards of dreams long past...but never quite forgotten.

I don't know if I deserve this happiness.

But I will take every single second I can get.

The End

AFTERWORD: TO MY READERS

Dear Readers,

I've had a few people ask how many books will be in this series.

If you've read this far, you've likely figured out that the answer is this: *Reign is the final novel.* What started out as one book then became three, then five. I always knew an end would come—a time when I had to let Ashen find some happiness. I've tortured her enough...and I'll be honest, I've loved every second of the ride.

Thank you all so much for coming along with me, and, of course, with Ash, Finn, Rys, Atticus, and so many others.

I'm sorry about those who didn't make it to the end.

Even the Duchess.

I know, I know. Some of you sent me notes asking when she would meet her maker. You craved it, just as I did. I fantasized long and hard about ways to end her story arc. In case you jumped to this Afterword before reading, I'm not going to spoil it for you.

(Side note: I'm very sorry, Ash, for all I put you through. I adore you. The truth is that you are me. Not quite strong enough, but constantly trying to find enough strength to do what needs to be done. Not quite trusting enough, but always seeking to trust. You perpetually hope for a better world, one where everyone magically comes to their senses. And frankly, I'm with you on the "Okay, fine. The world will never come to its senses so I'm just gonna move somewhere beautiful and enjoy myself, damn it" attitude. Like I said —you are me.)

In case anyone is wondering, *The Cure* is by no means my last Dystopian series. I have another planned already, though I do not yet have release dates for the books. The covers are absolutely gorgeous and are begging for phenomenal stories —and I have a grand plan for them. But right now, my heart and brain need a brief break from the genre.

In the meantime, two new books are coming your way in the fall: *Apocalypchix* and *A Kingdom Scarred*. The former is a darkly comedic Apocalyptic romp, complete with a Golden Retriever. And yes, I had the idea before my own Golden Retriever, my constant companion and best buddy, went viral on TikTok.

A Kingdom Scarred is High Fantasy (and parents—not for the kids! And to my own parents: Maybe don't read this book if you ever want me to look you in the eye again).

In the next several pages, you'll get a sneak preview of both books.

Once again, thank you to all my wonderful readers near and far for your support, your kind words, and your friendship. Every bit of it is appreciated more than you know.

Cheers, and I'll see you soon!

K. A.

COMING SOON: THRALL

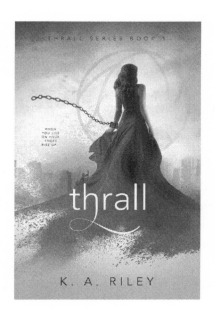

In the realm of Kravan, children of lower-class citizens are raised in a prison-like structure called "The Institution" from birth until adulthood. Known as the Thralled, their powers reveal themselves around the time of their eighteenth birthday.

Every year, the Thralled who are tested and deemed harmless are chosen to leave the Institution and join the outside world as servants to the ruling class. Epics—those who are considered threats for their destructive powers—are sent away. Though none of the Thralled know for sure, they have long suspected that the Epics are killed by the Elite.

Rell has spent her entire life in the Institution, longing for the day she will be chosen to leave. She's always been certain her powers would be minimal just as her mother's were, and that she would be assigned to a life of simply servitude. However, as she nears her eighteenth birthday, she begins to fear the worst. The powers that have begun churning inside her are anything but harmless, and if the truth comes to light, she faces a grim fate at the hands of the ruling class.

When a handsome and wealthy young man visits the Institution and invites her to work in the palace's kitchens, she's ecstatic...but when a mysterious fellow worker offers her an opportunity to attend the annual Elites' Ball and to see their world for what it truly is, she begins to learn an ugly truth about the divisions between the ruling class and the Tethered.

After a life spent in near-isolation, Rell must now learn to distinguish friend from foe, and to decide if her new allies are who they claim to be...

or if they will turn out to be her greatest enemies.

Thrall is based on the fairy tale Cinderella, the first in a new Dystopian Romance series by the author of Recruitment and The Cure.

Pre-order until its release: Thrall

OUT NOW: APOCALYPCHIX

What happens when the first day of school
is the last day of the world?

Summary:

For sixteen-year-old Virtue, navigating 11th grade is hard enough. Throw in the mass carnage of the Purple War, the brain-mangling Lemming Plague, and the overnight, post-apocalyptic breakdown of civilization, and suddenly, arguing with her parents, being picked on by bullies, and tyrannized by her teachers doesn't seem quite so devastating.

Instead, Virtue's new priorities are saving her best friend (and potential boyfriend?), fending off Clique Baiters and Serial Daters, and rescuing Beynac—her golden retriever service dog. Oh, and surviving.

It took sixteen years of torment and insecurity to make Virtue a wallflower. It took a single day of classes (and an academy full of brainwashed, dog-stealing, finger-eating killers) to turn her into the school's most feared and deadly badass.

Prologue

I was in Mrs. Tamasha's first period English class with my dog Beynac curled up at my feet when the world ended.

(Since I'm writing this, you know I probably survived. If you want to know *how* I survived, what that survival cost, what happened to my dog, and if I ever managed to convert Diligence from best friend to boyfriend, you'll have to keep reading.)

So, back then, the Lemming Plague had already been around for over a year, but none of us thought it was real. After all, we didn't know anybody who'd gotten it. Hell, we didn't even know anybody who *knew* anybody who'd gotten it.

The Plague was a myth, a hoax, a bad joke. It was the boogey man who *definitely* didn't exist, but you still checked under your bed every night, anyway…just in case.

The Lemming Plague was all over the news. Forget about sports, weather, and the unclaimed tickets for the weekly Lotto jackpot. All we heard, day and night, was how many more millions of people around the world had lost their minds and bolted into traffic or had taken unexplained headers off of buildings, bridges, rooftops, or treetops.

For us, it didn't get real until cases started popping up in our town. Just a few blocks from my high school, some guy wearing nothing but duct-tape sandals and a red, novelty clown nose charged into a bowling alley and walked lane to lane, blasting away at all the bowling pins with a sawed-off shotgun.

Then he tried to impregnate the pinball machine.

Two days after that, a woman with a pair of bolt-cutters tried to free a peacock from the zoo but got turned around and wound up with her head, torso, all four limbs, and most of her internal organs scattered across the polar bear enclosure.

And just like that, the Lemming plague, for us, went from vague fiction to full-blown, viral reality.

Instead of attacking your entire immune system like most viruses, though, this one reconfigured the cells in the brain's hippocampus and prefrontal cortex. That led to extreme susceptibility to suggestion and compromised decision-making. In non-clinical terms, it turned your brain into a thick sludge of semi-moldable banana pudding. You not only did what you wanted, you also did everything anyone else *told* you you wanted.

Some people compared it to being drunk, except instead of spewing a creamed-corn broth of stomach-ooze or waking up in a stranger's basement with a hangover and an unexplained ass tattoo, you turned into a kind of murderous, brainwashed lunatwerk, who did whatever anyone told you to do.

After a few months of stress, worry, and barricaded doors, our town leaders determined that something had to be done.

Her Honorable Worship Mayor Michelle Janus led a spirited debate at a lively School Board Meeting. Channel Three News covered the entire event, including the reading of the agenda, the reasonable plans of action, the pluses and minuses of various strategic options, the shouting, the fistfights, and all the parents who got arrested after about twenty minutes.

When the dust settled, the Board decided by a five-to-four vote to reopen the schools. That included my high school, Aegis Secondary School, also known as "Ass Academy." So we got to go back to school, but they made us wear protective gear as a precaution. We grumbled and griped about having to wear surgical masks. It turned out that being forced into strapping on disposable, surgical-grade, fabric respirators was only the beginning.

For the first month back, we also had to wear face shields, latex gloves, and baggy, full-body, yellow hazmat suits with elastic drawstrings at the wrists and ankles.

It was like going to school in a giant condom.

Maybe that's why none of the girls in our school got knocked up that year and why the prom looked like an over-crowded Minion convention.

After a few weeks, tensions softened, fears eased, parents made bail, and life and school returned to something along the lines of normal. For me, tenth grade was just tenth grade again. We didn't have to wear any of the protective gear anymore. Before each class, though, we were required to squirt rubbing alcohol on our hands and ram our fingers up our noses to the second knuckle.

Principal Greevy personally plastered warning signs all over the school with the slogan, "There are many minuses to not cleaning your sinuses." The posters featured a close-up of a giant finger and some guy's cavernous, spelunking-worthy nostrils.

And then, after a long, uneventful summer, I turned sixteen and started my junior year. For the first few days, things went along happily and boringly. And then, the second we all dropped our guard, the Lemming Plague resurfaced. Even worse this time around, it swept through our school on the same day the Purple War came to town.

I can't say for sure if one caused the other or which one was deadlier.

What I *can* tell you is that Francine was the first one in our class to die.

* * *

Release Date: September 16, 2022 on Amazon
Preorder here: Apocalypchix

TEASER: A KINGDOM SCARRED

Summary:

In the Blood Trials, only two victors survive.

The others lose their lives. And they also lose everyone they've ever loved.

Every thousand years, each of the Noble Houses in the Valley of the Five sends two Champions—known as the "Gifted"—to prove their worth in the Blood Trials. The two Champions left standing at the end of the competition are bound together as mates, their Gifts passed down from one generation to the next.

Eighteen-year-old Lyrinn has little interest in the Trials, which are the domain of the Nobility. The daughter of a blacksmith, she has spent her life far from those who revel in power and fortune. Lyrinn chooses instead to dwell in the shadows, hooded to conceal the mysterious scars that mar her flesh.

Since she was a child, Lyrinn has heard tales of the Grimpers—the shadowy figures who dwell on the cliffs above her town. Legend has it that a great race of magic-users once lived in a realm high on the clifftop. Centuries ago, the magic-users were corrupted and lost their power—a punishment for breaking the rules at the last Blood Trials.

One night, while fleeing a threatening stranger, Lyrinn finds herself at a towering flight of onyx stairs that appears in the face of a treacherous cliff. She climbs to the top and comes upon a sight she never imagined in her wildest dreams.

From that dark night on, Lyrinn's life is forever altered. The mystery of her origins begins to cast doubt on everything and everyone she's ever known. It is a mystery that will lead her to encounter a man who proves to be both her greatest foe and the object of her deepest, most unquenchable desires.

* * *

Release Date: November 1, 2022
Preorder on Amazon: A Kingdom Scarred

ALSO BY K. A. RILEY

If you're enjoying K. A. Riley's books, please consider leaving a review on Amazon or Goodreads to let your fellow book-lovers know!

DYSTOPIAN BOOKS

THE AMNESTY GAMES

RECRUITMENT | RENDER | REBELLION

THE EMERGENTS TRILOGY

SURVIVAL | SACRIFICE | SYNTHESIS

THE TRANSCENDENT TRILOGY

| TRAVELERS | TRANSFIGURED | TERMINUS |

ACADEMY OF THE APOCALYPSE

THE RAVENMASTER CHRONICLES

Arise | Banished | Crusade

THE CURE CHRONICLES

The Cure | Awaken | Ascend | Fallen | Reign

VIRAL HIGH TRILOGY

APOCALYPCHIX | LOCKDOWN | FINAL EXAM

THE THRALL SERIES

THRALL | BROKEN | QUEEN

ATHENA'S LAW

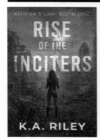 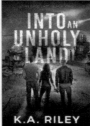 

RISE OF THE INCITERS | INTO AN UNHOLY LAND | NO MAN'S LAND

FANTASY BOOKS

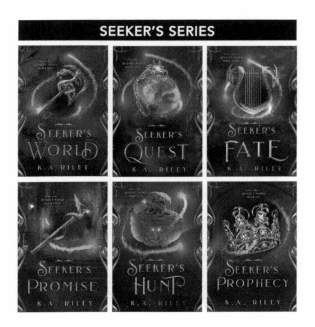

A KINGDOM SCARRED | A CROWN BROKEN | OF FLAME AND FURY

SEEKER'S WORLD | SEEKER'S QUEST | SEEKER'S FATE | SEEKER'S PROMISE | SEEKER'S HUNT | SEEKER'S PROPHECY (Coming soon!)

SOCIAL MEDIA LINKS:

https://karileywrites.org/#subscribe

[K.A. Riley's Bookbub Author Page](#)
[K.A. Riley on Amazon.com](#)
[K.A. Riley on Goodreads.com](#)

Follow K. A. Riley on TikTok: @karileywrites

Made in United States
Troutdale, OR
07/03/2024

20999087R00207